Thryssa,

Thank you for your enthusiasm and support!

Coe

(E. A. Coe)

Full Count

E. A. Coe

Copyright © 2018 by Frank C. Sherrard

All rights reserved. This book or any portion thereof may not be reproduced or used in any manner whatsoever without the express written permission of the publisher except for the use of brief quotations in a book review or scholarly journal.

First Printing: 2018

ISBN 978-1-387-90954-4

Frank C. Sherrard
818 Forest View Road
Edinburg, Virginia, 22824

DEDICATION

To Jean, my wife, partner, and friend in every important endeavor of my life. She is my inspiration for living and still the reason I like to get up in the morning.

CONTENTS

ACKNOWLEDGEMENTS

I thank Sondra Baker Johnson for providing the 'spark' required for me to finally check 'write a book' off my bucket list. Thanks also to my family and the employees of the Woodstock Café who provided the living 'fodder' for the characters of the book. Thank you, Holly, my artist sister, for providing the original artwork for the cover and all the many friends/family/customers and employees who served as voluntary proofreaders. Also thank you, Rich Follett, inspired educator in the Commonwealth of Virginia Public School System, who chose to feature my book in his Creative Writing course. To his students, I say this, "*I waited until I was 69 years old to write my first book, and if I can do it, you can too! Just don't wait as long as me.*"

FOREWORD

Is there a more consistently compelling moment in all of athletics than the one which follows the full count in baseball? By definition, when a baseball pitching count advances to three balls and two strikes, action must happen on the next pitch. The full count is literally and figuratively pregnant with possibilities and ripe with potential. The next pitch will usually determine the outcome of an at-bat and, often, the outcome of an inning. In extreme circumstances, the pitch can determine the outcome of a game, or even a season!

How often do we face the same full count scenarios in life? Some matter little, while others can impact life greatly. As in baseball, no matter the outcome, there is no replay; no do-over. The play becomes history, and we must plan life around the history made. Dreaming of what 'might have been' or 'could have happened' had the outcome been different ... is wasted energy. The game goes on, and competitive players know they may only impact the next play, not the last one.

Rounding Third

I've driven too fast, and drunk too much beer
And danced when I should have slept
I've earned a good bit in the course of my run
But have spent a lot more than I've kept

I've played some good hands and folded a few
But always enjoyed a good game
I've won my fair share but when I did lose
Made sure no one heard me complain

I'm comin' 'round third now, headed for home
But purposely not running fast
I've still got some things that I want to do
And I just want this great game to last

E. A. Coe

Full Count

The renegade thought passed through his mind so quickly that he couldn't catch it. Not like a bolt of lightning but more like a shadow, the notion slipped into the recesses of his brain where he could no longer find it, try as he might. It was a beautiful late summer day in eastern Indiana and Coach Blevins was on the way to his office at the gymnasium. The campus was alive with activity on this first day of the fall semester at Lefton College and Blevins had communicated to the baseball players on his team to meet at the gym at 4:00 PM.

The coach was excited about the prospects for the team this year and he wanted to ensure that his players were on board with their off-season workout routines. The baseball season was still six months away, but the coach knew that successful execution began with deliberate preparation. During the previous season the Lefton Monarchs surprised everyone in the Heartland Collegiate Athletic Conference (HCAC) by winning their division and earning a berth in the Mid-East Regional Championships. After winning their first game in the tournament, they lost in the quarterfinals and didn't have enough quality pitching to fight their way back through the losers' brackets. Things might be different this year.

Only two players graduated from the previous year's talented squad, and Blevins had unexpectedly landed a prized pitching prospect for the college over the summer. Shane Reynolds, a hard-throwing left-handed pitcher, had made a late commitment to Lefton just a month prior. After taking his high school team to back-to-back state championships as a junior and a senior, most believed he would be playing for Indiana University in the fall. The University had recruited him from the time he had been a sophomore, and Shane had apparently not even considered other schools that had expressed interest in him. It seemed a foregone conclusion that he would remain in the state and play for the state's largest University.

Something happened though. Indiana's baseball coaching legend, Clarence Holmgren, met with Shane and his family after the state championships and suggested that Shane attend Indiana Central Junior College the following year. ICJC was a Junior College baseball powerhouse and a consistent pipeline of players to Holmgren's University squad. Holmgren explained to Shane that two years there would allow him to put on some weight, strengthen his arm, and further develop his craft. After finishing at ICJC, Shane could transfer to IU for his junior and senior years.

At 5' 9" and 175 pounds, Shane wasn't large, but he was strong. He was also smart … meaning "academic book-smart." He was a straight-A student and the salutatorian of his graduating class. While baseball was his athletic love, it wasn't his life. Shane just didn't want to start his all-important college education at a Junior College if he didn't have to. His parents supported his decision and his dad, an alumnus ballplayer of Lefton College, made a call to his old coach. Blevins took it from there and, within days, Shane had a full academic scholarship offer to attend tiny Lefton College, where he'd get a first-class education … and also be able to play baseball.

Blevins was still marveling at his extraordinary good fortune, and the regional newspapers were having a field day with Coach Holmgren's apparent misjudgment. The byline in the Indianapolis Star had playfully announced, "Holmgren Strikes Out - Reynolds Walks." Blevins understood Shane's decision but had been somewhat surprised by his dad's call. Case had been an outstanding catcher on Blevins' college team over 20 years prior, but the coach had not heard from him since the young man had graduated. He thought that Case's decision to send his son to a Division III school unusual, and found the timing, at best, 'interesting.' For now, no matter the circumstances, Shane Reynolds would be playing for the Lefton College Monarchs.

Coach Blevins had been the Monarchs' baseball coach for almost 30 years. He had been awarded the job when the team's previous coach had violated some obscure NCAA rule relating to the maximum innings Division III pitchers could pitch within any seven-day period. Under current NCAA regulations, the rules that the former coach violated no longer existed. Pitcher's rest and the number of innings a pitcher could pitch within any period of time were entirely at the discretion of the player and the coach. Good or bad, the relaxed regulations presumed that coaches would exercise sound judgment in the care of their players, and the difficult task of league oversight was eliminated. The former coach had almost immediately obtained another coaching job at the Division I level and had successfully retired a few years back.

After playing baseball at Indiana University, Blevins graduated with a degree in Education. He accepted a job teaching Biology at Indianapolis Central High School and volunteered as an assistant baseball coach. When the head baseball coach at Central retired two years later, Blevins assumed the vacated position. He took the high school's baseball team to the state championships four out of the next five years he coached there, which caught the attention of Lefton College's Dean of Athletics at the time. His evident and enthusiastic love for the game of baseball had earned Blevins the opportunity to coach at the college level, but it had probably cost him a marriage. His wife during his high school coaching days had tired of his year-

11

round obsession with baseball and did not join him in his move to Lefton. Since that time, he had only been married to Baseball, and he seemed perfectly content with the relationship.

As Blevins continued down the sidewalk contemplating the upcoming team meeting scheduled for that afternoon, the elusive and errant thought that had occurred earlier in his walk flicked through his mind again. Like earlier, the revelation escaped too quickly for him to identify it. The mystery bothered him and, while Blevins was not the least bit superstitious, he found himself avoiding the cracks in the sidewalk all the way to the gym.

Charlie Hamilton turned the corner from student check-in and almost ran into Shane. Shane appeared to be coming from the bookstore and was loaded down with new textbooks. One fell off the stack in the near collision, and Charlie retrieved it, placing it back in Shane's arms.

"Sorry," said Charlie. "Guess I need to watch where I'm going."

"No problem," Shane replied. "I'm the one with a pile of books in my face and hardly able to see in front of me."

"Do you need some help? My name is Charlie Hamilton."

"I know who you are," said Shane. "Since committing to Lefton in August, I've been checking online to see what I could find out about your baseball team. Your picture comes up quite a bit," he said, smiling.

"Thanks, Shane, but the truth is ... I know who you are too. Everyone on our team does. Your picture has been in a lot more newspapers than mine has over the past two years. Welcome to Lefton!"

"Glad to be here," replied Shane. "I think there's a baseball team meeting today at 4:00, right?" asked Shane.

"Right," said Charlie. "At the gym. Are you going to be there?"

"Absolutely," replied Shane. "I'll see you there."

As they parted, Charlie thought: *So, there's our new pitching ace. Nice kid.*

Charlie was the Monarchs' catcher and had been for the past two years. He had tried out for the team as a non-recruited freshman and impressed Coach Blevins enough to be added to the varsity roster. He had insisted to Coach Blevins that he was a catcher, but Blevins told him he wasn't big enough to be a college catcher and that he'd be better suited at a corner outfield position. On the first day of spring practice, Blevins had been a bit irritated with Charlie when the young player joined the other outfielders for fungo fly balls ... still wearing a catcher's mitt. The coach had called him back and asked him to put on a fielder's glove. Charlie politely told the coach that he didn't own one of those and that he'd be fine in the outfield with a catcher's mitt. The coach informed him that he could practice out there that day, but he would have to purchase the right kind of glove before the next practice. Charlie did that and, a day later, was again fielding fungo flies with the other outfielders. The coach noticed right away, though, that Charlie didn't catch as well with the outfielder's glove as he had fielded with a catcher's mitt the day before. When the boys came in from the field, Blevins took Charlie aside.

"Listen, Son," Blevins had said. "If you're trying to make a point with me, you can stop!"

"What do you mean, Coach?" answered the genuinely confused Charlie.

"The glove, Son ... the glove!" continued Blevins. "Yesterday you caught everything hit to you with the catcher's mitt; today you're fielding like you've got a frying pan on your hand instead of a glove."

"Oh, sorry, Coach, I'll try to do better. It's just that I've never fielded with this kind of glove before."

"Never?"

"Nope ... never. I found an old catcher's mitt in my grandfather's closet when I was about four years old, and it's the only kind of glove I've ever worn since. And honestly, Coach, it's the only kind of glove I ever really wanted to wear. But I'll keep practicing, and I'll get better. You'll see!"

Blevins gazed at the young player for a moment, then told him to get the rest of his catching equipment and join the pitchers and catchers at the other end of the field.

"Really? Oh, thanks, Coach," said Charlie. "I'm a way better catcher than an outfielder!" Then he sprinted back to the bench to retrieve his catching gear.

Blevins resigned himself, reluctantly, to work Charlie as a catcher. Placing him in the outfield was equivalent to putting a square peg in a round hole, and while the boy was undersized, he might have the skills to be a backup. Blevins was also reminded of a quote he had once read relating to the fact that the genuinely exceptional athletes weren't only great because of their size, skills, or technique ... but also because of their passion. This kid definitely had the passion for catching.

In the years since that critical decision, Charlie had rewarded Blevins for taking the chance. As the backup catcher during his freshman year, Charlie provided a solid performance and proved that his size was not a liability. Charlie won the starting job as a sophomore and had missed few innings since. Almost nothing got by him, and he owned a cannon for a right arm that was seldom tested

14

anymore by the league's knowledgeable base runners. These same base runners had also become wary of close-play collisions at home plate, comparing Charlie's presence on the baseline in front of the plate to that of an immovable fire hydrant. In these situations, informed runners knew that their chances to score were better if they slid around Charlie rather than to try to run through him.

Charlie had figured large in the team's success, and especially in the magical past season. In addition to providing all-conference level catching, Charlie had posted a .352 batting average, with a fair number of home runs and a lot of RBIs. With his well-trained catcher's eye, he had also led the conference in base on balls. The stat that Charlie, himself, may have been most proud of, though, was leading the HCAC in being Hit by Pitch. Charlie's batting stance always found him as close to the plate as was legally possible, and he never backed off from a thrown baseball. Any baseball traveling even slightly to the inside of the strike zone had a fair chance of hitting him. The rules of baseball require that hitters cannot make an intentional effort to be hit by a pitch, and most hitters accept this responsibility willingly, more from a sense of self-preservation than a reverence for the game's rules. Not Charlie, though.

Charlie's granddad had caught for the Lefton Township Titans two generations before Charlie, and Claude Hamilton had been Charlie's role model and mentor since his birth. Charlie's mother was Jennifer Drake, Lefton College's Controller. She had also graduated from Lefton College, in 1992, but at the time of Charlie's birth, she had been unwed. On his birth certificate, which Charlie only saw after looking it up online as a teenager, where the father's name would typically appear, the inscription just stated, 'Unnamed'. Where the father's address should have been on the birth certificate, was the inscription, 'Unknown.'

15

The facts surrounding his existence had never troubled him. From the time of his birth, he had been surrounded by his mother and his grandparents and, until he was five and started pre-school, he had no idea that other families typically had another male figure in the household. Shortly after he started school, his mother had seemed to fix this inconsistency by getting married to Tim Drake.

It wasn't until his sophomore year in high school that he became familiar with the term, 'bastard.' His English class was studying Shakespeare, and one of Charlie's favorite characters in the play, King John, was Philip the Bastard. It didn't take long for Charlie to realize that he, himself, was one of those. As it turned out in the play, Philip the Bastard was fathered by one of England's great heroes, Richard the Lionhearted. This made Charlie wonder who his own father might have been.

When he had questioned his mother in the past about his birth, she made a vague reference to the young man being a soldier and going off to war. The fact that the man had not returned seemed to indicate to Charlie that the soldier had probably been killed. It was apparent to Charlie that these memories pained his mother, and, out of respect, he never pressed the matter. As an older youth, he realized there were no significant military installations anywhere near Lefton Township, and he sometimes wondered how his mother had chanced to meet a soldier.

Charlie's paternal heritage neither defined him nor bothered him. It also didn't make him think less of his mother. As a toddler, Charlie had been fascinated with his grandfather's old catching equipment, and the old mask and catcher's mitt were his favorite toys. This delighted his grandfather and, when Charlie started playing organized baseball, his position was catcher. Throughout his Little League and senior youth league baseball years, he never played any place else on the field, and he'd become his high school's catcher as a freshman. In college, there had been that brief attempt to switch Charlie into the outfield, which had failed.

If athletics profoundly influenced Charlie's life, they didn't dominate it. He was consistently an honor roll student and, as a teenager, was socially active while remaining dependably responsible. Charlie's decision to attend Lefton College had been an easy one. His mother was employed there, and the school had an extremely attractive financial arrangement for immediate family members. As an undersized catcher who had played on a relatively mediocre team through his high school years, Charlie had not been recruited by any other colleges or universities for athletics. Since Charlie had no real aspirations to become a Major League ballplayer, he had been content to enjoy four more years of baseball at the Division III college level.

As Shane progressed up the sidewalk to his new home in the dorm, he thought about the chance encounter with who would soon be his baseball battery mate. Charlie seemed like a good guy, but Shane had been surprised that he wasn't a bit bigger. Catchers, as a group, tended to be short and beefy and, while Charlie wasn't much taller than Shane himself, he also wasn't beefy. He looked solid, but Shane guessed that Charlie probably didn't weigh much more than he did.

"Good," thought Shane, "we smaller guys play with a chip on our shoulder!"

Shane remembered the awkward conversations that had occurred with Coach Holmgren of Indiana University during the final stages of the recruiting process. These discussions had also seemed to revolve around size. Shane had his heart set on attending Indiana University since his early days of high school, and there had been many visits by Holmgren between Shane's sophomore and senior years. Shane was hurt, and a little astounded, by Holmgren's suggestion that he attend Junior College. Shane thought he had put up the right numbers and exhibited the talent to earn a place on the large University's ballclub. Certainly, Holmgren was probably thinking about Shane's and the University's best baseball interests in suggesting the Junior College for Shane. It just didn't fit into Shane's life plan.

Holmgren had been shocked when Shane told him that he didn't want to go to a Junior College, and the coach had appealed to Shane's father for support. Case and Julia Reynolds had stuck by their son, however, and allowed Shane to make his own decision.

"Men," said Coach Blevins at a few minutes after 4 PM on the gymnasium clock, "We had a great season last year. We went further than anyone around here thought we would and came darn close to getting to the championship game at the Mid-East Regionals. That's history now, and we have to start all over to get ready for next year. We're going to have an even better team than we did last year ... I think, but we're not going to sneak up on anyone next year. Every team we play will be starting their ace against us and starting their best lineups. That's okay because we're going to have some surprises for them as well. So far, we have three new players joining us this year and we could also pick up some walk-ons this spring. How we do, and how far we go, though, is completely up to you, not me. The season starts right now. Lefton College doesn't allow any official practices or mandatory individual workouts until February 1st. Players can only work out on their own, with no coach supervision. The primary mission of this college is to provide students a good education, not prepare them for an athletic career. That's why I say that how we do next year is mostly up to you. As a coach, I'm allowed to recommend offseason workout routines for players, but I'm not allowed to monitor them or supervise them. At your request, I will assist each of you in creating an exercise and skills development schedule. Whether you do the exercises or follow up on the workout routines, is entirely up to you. Any questions?"

Junie Moore, the team's fleet-footed shortstop, raised his hand, "Coach, will the batting cages be open like last year, and are we allowed to use them?"

"Yes," replied Blevins, "The cages are available and team members can use them anytime. For that purpose, I have made 23 keys that I will issue to any player who wants one. Remember, though, the cages are only for players ... not your girlfriends, your fraternity brothers, or other random friends on campus. The punishment for violating this rule is expulsion from the team. Does everyone understand that?"

All players nodded in the affirmative, and Danny Colovito's hand went up. "Coach, will it be possible to get inside the gym to work out?"

Blevins replied, "Absolutely! This gym is open to students 24 hours per day and seven days per week. You are only limited by the needs of the men's and women's basketball teams, and the wrestling team during the winter. Obviously, any of the winter sports teams have priority over individual workouts."

Charlie Hamilton's hand was up, and the coach acknowledged him. "I see that Mr. Hamilton has a question, but before I give him the floor, let me introduce the rest of the team to this year's Team Captain, Charlie Hamilton. He has played for this team the last three years and has earned the respect of both players and coaches. Charlie was a walk-on player as a freshman and earned his playing time through hard work and sheer determination. I'm extremely proud of him and believe that he is one of the reasons this team will be even better than last year's. Now, Charlie, what is it you wanted to say?"

Charlie seemed stunned for a second and gazed around at his teammates, many of whom were still applauding the coach's announcement. "Thank you, Coach," said Charlie. "I don't ... I just don't even know what to say, except ...thank you. Thank you very much!"

"You're welcome," replied the coach, who then prodded him lightly, "... but was that what you had your hand up for?"

"Oh yeah, I mean, no ... sorry ... I almost forgot," stammered Charlie. "For any pitchers who want to work out in the offseason, I'm available Tuesday and Thursday afternoons after 2 PM. Just call or text me on my cell phone at 320-726-1328. When possible, I'd rather set up regular schedules versus just sporadically here and there. But, either way, just text me."

"That is a very generous offer, Charlie, but not one that surprises me," said Blevins. "Certainly, any pitchers who want to get better, take Charlie up on the offer. He's a master!" Blevins continued, "Before we all break up, I'd also like to introduce the three new players who are joining the team. From Oshkosh, Hayden Piper, an outfielder and in high school an extremely dangerous hitter. From Muncey, via Riordan Junior College, Jack Ryan, a right-handed pitcher who won 17 games over the past two years for RJC. And from Indianapolis, Shane Reynolds, a left-handed pitcher who took Indianapolis Central High School to consecutive state championships. His high school record was 37 and 6, and he didn't lose a game in his last two years."

All the new players stood, and their teammates applauded them. When the meeting concluded, the new players were surrounded by the rest of the team and making friendly introductions. Coach Blevins smiled and walked over to Charlie, who was talking to Shane.

"Shane, you're going to like working with Charlie," said Blevins. "He has a way of making pitchers look good. He sort of reminds me of your dad, who played the same position for me a long time ago."

Charlie responded to the coach before Shane could, saying "Thanks for the compliment, Coach, but I don't think I'm going to have to make Shane look good. He's the one who is going to make the rest of us look good!"

"Maybe," said Blevins. "We'll see soon enough. Just don't overwork the arm over the winter, Shane. Work mechanics, keep the arm loose, and not much more ... remind me, how many quality pitches do you have?"

"Honestly?" said Shane. "One ... my fastball. My curve is a big one, but not totally reliable in the strike zone ... and my change-up sucks!"

"A very honest and humble self-evaluation," said Blevins. "Thank you. One pitch, even if it's the best fastball at the college level, isn't enough for a starting pitcher. A short inning relief pitcher might survive with that, but not a starter. Charlie," continued Blevins, "...concentrate on getting control of the curve and developing the change-up. I don't want Shane throwing a full speed fastball until sometime in February!"

"Got it, Coach," replied Charlie, returning to his conversation with Shane.

As Blevins left the building, he felt good about the meeting and about his choice for a Team Captain. Charlie Hamilton was the hardest working player on the club and had exhibited leadership qualities that were unusual for a man of his young age. Charlie's grandfather was one of Coach Blevins' closest friends and Blevins also had a great deal of respect for Charlie's mother, Jennifer, who was the college's Controller. It was apparent that Charlie had good genes working for him ... and then ... it happened again. That quick moving shadow of a thought which had toyed with him that morning during his walk to the gym made another dash across Blevins' brain. This time the coach caught it ... and held it captive in his mind to analyze for a few moments. When his initial analysis was completed, he put the thought in a safe place where he could find it again, and was glad that he hadn't stepped on any cracks in the sidewalk that morning.

When Charlie returned home after the team meeting, he was greeted by both his mom and his granddad. Since Charlie was from the town of Lefton Township, he didn't live on campus, but rather a few blocks away in a small house with his mother and her husband, Timmon or, as he was known in the family, Tim. Tim had joined the family when Charlie was five years old. While Tim had performed all the duties of a first-class dad for the past 15 years, he insisted that Charlie call him Tim, as everyone else did. If other kids had better dads than Tim, Charlie would be amazed. Tim was also Charlie's friend.

Claude was nearly as responsible for Charlie's upbringing as his mother and Tim. Claude was the town's veterinarian, and he lived about two blocks away in one of the town's larger homes. He now lived there alone, since his wife, Florinda, had succumbed to breast cancer about ten years earlier. Grandma Floe had been Charlie's primary caretaker the first ten years of his life. His mother dropped Charlie off at his grandparents' house five days per week until Charlie entered kindergarten. As a single mother with a full-time job at the college, Jennifer couldn't afford other forms of daycare, and Claude and Floe were more than happy to help. Charlie was ten when Grandma Floe died, and the loss had been as hard on Charlie as it had been on Claude and his mom.

"How did the meeting go?" shouted Claude, before Charlie's mother could even greet him.

"Dad," chided Jennifer, "Maybe we should be a little more interested in what classes Charlie was able to get than how an off-season baseball meeting went."

Charlie rescued his granddad by hugging his mom and telling her, "I got everything I requested this semester, and now the only course I need next year to graduate is Business Tax Accounting."

Then, Charlie rewarded his granddad by telling him, "The meeting was great, Granddad, and guess what? I'm the Team Captain this year!"

"Outstanding!" exclaimed Claude, while Jennifer gave Charlie another warm hug.

"Congratulations, Charlie," she said. "Nobody is more deserving ... and nobody could do a better job!"

"Thanks, Mom," said Charlie.

Claude, still more interested in baseball than academics, asked, "What do the new guys look like?"

"Pretty good, Granddad," Charlie replied. "Looks like we got a good hitting outfielder, a big, beefy Junior College pitcher ... righty .... and a fireballing lefty who took his high school team to back-to-back state championships."

"That's the kid from Indianapolis Central, right?" said Claude. "He was the one who was in all the papers this summer. Supposed to go to IU, but didn't?"

"Yep," replied Charlie. "That's him. Don't know what happened, but he's definitely playing for us this year."

"Am I the only one who doesn't follow everything that happened in Indiana High School Baseball last year?" complained Jennifer. "Seems like we had enough baseball news of our own this past season, Dad. How do you know so much about this new kid?"

"Aw, Honey, I don't know," replied the cheerful Claude. "Could be because I read everything on the sports pages, not just the articles that mention your son."

"Okay, okay, Dad," said Jennifer. "...but you're just as proud of Charlie as I am!"

"We can agree on that, I think," said Claude.

"So, who is this kid? Where did he play? And how did Lefton manage to land him?" asked Jennifer.

Charlie answered, "His name is Shane Reynolds, he played at Indianapolis Central in Indianapolis, and I don't know."

"Don't know what?" asked Jennifer

"Don't know how Coach Blevins landed him at Lefton," said Charlie. "Just glad he did. If the Junior College transfer is even half good, we'll have a solid starting rotation next year, including a marquee left-hander!"

"Did you say, 'Reynolds'?" asked Jennifer.

"Yeah, Shane Reynolds," answered Charlie. "Seems like a good kid. I talked to him quite a bit today."

"Great," said Jennifer, as she returned to the kitchen.

Charlie and Claude stayed in the living room discussing Charlie's off-season workout schedule. When Claude left his daughter's house a little later, Tim Drake was coming home from the drugstore he owned. They exchanged pleasantries, and Claude walked the two blocks to his home. As he entered, he was engulfed by the loneliness of the place that had existed since Floe died ten years earlier. Claude missed his wife dearly and, though he loathed the emptiness of the large house since she had passed, it had far too many memories within its walls for him to ever consider selling it. He was glad that he could spend as much time as he did at his veterinary practice and at his daughter's house.

Claude was a product of the Lefton Township community, and certainly one of the town's favorite sons. After high school, where he had been an all-conference catcher ... and a relatively poor student, he joined the Navy.

25

Trained as a medical corpsman, he was assigned to a United States Marine Corps fighting unit in Vietnam. What he saw there nobody, including Floe, ever knew. He refused to talk about it. All that was known was that he left the service after his tour in Vietnam, receiving a host of military medals including a Purple Heart. He recovered from the shrapnel wound he had received and used his GI Bill to enroll at Virginia Tech. He turned the significant medical experience obtained courtesy of the tour in Vietnam into a Veterinarian degree from Virginia Tech. He returned to Lefton Township with both the degree and a wife. Florinda had also attended Virginia Tech, where she earned a degree in Biological Sciences. She was from nearby Roanoke, where her family owned a small Mexican restaurant. Her father, Luis, was a legendary cook in the area. Her mother could trace family roots in America back to the Jamestown Colony. Floe grew up bilingual, which accounted for how Charlie knew the alphabet and all his numbers in both Spanish and English when he started kindergarten.

Floe was Claude's primary assistant at Hamilton's Veterinary for the first five years of the practice, until their daughter, Jennifer, was born. After that, Floe became the primary caregiver for the baby and Claude hired a new nurse for the veterinary practice. The business was both popular and successful, and the Hamiltons purchased a more substantial house when Jennifer was two years old.

If Claude was disappointed when his baby turned out to be a girl, he never showed it. If anything, it was the opposite. Girl or not, Jennifer still learned how to hunt and fish. She was also on just about every athletic team any of her schools ever had for girls. Her parents were in the audience at every school event and for all her athletic activities. Despite her tomboy habits and athletic aggressiveness, she was relatively shy at school, with only a small number of very close friends. Among these, there were few boys. Though attractive and very intelligent, she dated sporadically in high school, spending most of her energy on class work and athletics. When it was time to go to college, she didn't want to go away and chose to stay in Lefton Township to attend the small college there.

Over Jennifer's objections, Claude and Floe insisted that their prized daughter live on campus among the other students rather than at home. She did this but still spent many nights in her own room at home, often with friends from the college. Jennifer had dates with other Lefton students for big events like Homecoming and the annual Spring Fling, but she never dated any one guy for very long.

Claude and Floe didn't know whether to be concerned about this or glad. Jennifer was an almost straight-A Accounting student and seemed both perfectly adjusted and well anchored. If she wasn't as socially active as many of the other students on campus, she at least was using her college time wisely to obtain a good and useful degree. Other parents of Lefton students with whom Claude and Floe talked often, were apparently not so fortunate. Many of these parents openly expressed a hint of jealousy that the Hamiltons had been blessed with such a responsible and motivated child.

Until Jennifer became pregnant after her junior year.

"I'm sorry," said her dad. "What did you say?"

Jennifer solemnly repeated the words, "I'm pregnant."

Floe, sitting next to Claude, clasped her hand to her mouth. Claude stared at Jennifer, somewhat in disbelief and waiting for his daughter to say something more.

Jennifer, with her eyes now streaming tears, broke the silence. "I'm sorry, Mom and Dad. So sorry! I wish I didn't have to tell you this ... and I'm so ashamed. I just... I don't... I mean...," and her voice trailed off as she buried her head in her hands.

"Jennifer, this isn't news we necessarily wanted to hear, but are you okay?" asked Claude.

"Yes, Dad," Jennifer replied. "I'm fine, and I guess everything in my body is working just like it's supposed to. When my period was two weeks late, I went to see Dr. Wells, and he confirmed what I didn't want to know. He says 'Hi', by the way, and he wanted to know if he should come with me when I told you."

"Why would he ask that?" said Claude. "Was he afraid we were going to beat you or something?"

"No, Dad, not at all," answered Jennifer. "He was just offering some moral support and thought he might be able to help you and mom handle the news as well. I told him that I could handle this on my own."

"Thank you, Jennifer," said Floe, speaking for the first time. "We are all in this together, and our first concern is for you. Can you tell us more? Do we know the father? Will you be getting married?"

Jennifer cried softly again and hesitated before answering. "Thank you, Mom. I want to share everything with you and dad, but there are reasons that I can't right now." She continued, "I only confirmed my condition today, and I have a lot to do, and to think about before I can make any definite plans." Jennifer's voice choked as she spoke these last words, and the next ones were even tougher for her. "I <u>do know</u> that I won't be doing anything to harm this baby or terminate the pregnancy. According to Dr. Wells, I'll be delivering in about mid-March."

"Wow!" exclaimed Claude. "We've got some planning to do. That isn't far away."

"What do you mean, Dad?" asked Jennifer

"Well," he replied, "Unless you're going to be living someplace else, we're going to have to make a nursery in one of the bedrooms ...and we're going to have to figure out about school next year...at least the second semester of it." If Claude was upset with his daughter, he was hiding it by jumping into the planning that would need to be done by the family for the new arrival. Jennifer appreciated his sensitivity but, in some ways, it just made her feel worse for her irresponsibility.

"Dad, I'm so sorry to disappoint you," Jennifer said through her tears.

"Jenny, you've never disappointed me in your entire life, and you're not going to start now," said Claude. "None of us are perfect, and we all make mistakes. We all have lapses in judgment occasionally, too. When these things happen, we can't go back to fix them. We can only go forward, and it appears to me you're already doing that. Like your mom says, we're in this together, and I'm certain you're going to let us help when we can. You've got a full count, girl, and you just need to get ready for the next pitch."

Jennifer gazed at her dad with red eyes for just an instant before crossing the space between them to hug him. Floe joined the hug immediately and, at that moment, Jennifer knew everything would be alright. No words were spoken for several moments as the three embraced. Jennifer finally murmured, "I love you both so much. Thank you for trying to understand."

"Welcome to life, Jenny," said Claude. "We've got this!"

Claude fingered the small picture frame holding the image of Jennifer and Charlie taken just days after Charlie had been born. It was a happy day in March over 20 years ago. The pregnancy had gone well, and Charlie came right on time with no more than the usual stressful effort in the delivery room. Floe had stayed in the delivery room with her daughter, with an anxious Claude in the waiting room.

During the nine months of the pregnancy, very little of the mystery surrounding it was resolved. There was no father anywhere near the delivery room when Charlie was born, and Jennifer had not provided a single hint as to who that person might even be. Claude had, at least, confirmed that the pregnancy had not been the result of a rape and that the sex involved had been entirely consensual. As he and Floe racked their brains to think of any possible men their daughter might have been seeing towards the end of her junior year, they couldn't come up with a single name. They didn't press their daughter for answers, and Jennifer handled the gossiping, the whispers, and the stares stoically. She completed her first semester of senior year and did not take her second semester. Claude and Floe watched the baby in the fall while Jennifer completed the final courses required to receive a degree. She sat for the state CPA certification within months of graduating and passed on her first try. By the following September, she had been hired by the college as their Assistant Controller.

Claude set the picture down, smiling, and thinking how life would have been different if Jennifer had taken a more traditional approach to having a family. The way things had happened, the circumstances of her pregnancy had caused both his daughter and his grandson to live with him, or near him, for their entire lives. As much as he loved his daughter, his relationship with his grandson was just as special. He was given the opportunity to interact with his grandson in ways usually reserved only for fathers. Claude had been the most significant male figure in Charlie's life until Jennifer had married Tim, and Claude had not an ounce of jealousy for Tim. In fact, Claude was delighted that Jennifer had found such a loving and caring person to help take care of both her and Charlie. Tim and Claude shared their time with Charlie frequently and gladly.

Claude knew that he was responsible for much of Charlie's enthusiasm for the game of baseball. As a toddler, Charlie was fascinated with the chest in his grandparent's room that held Claude's aged catching equipment. Claude and Floe opened the chest regularly when they watched Charlie and laughed as they watched him play with the old equipment. One of Claude's fondest memories was of the day Charlie's T- Ball coach, Tim Drake, had invited Claude to help him with the team. Claude had a way of infecting the youngsters with his own excitement for the game. One of Claude's signature coaching enhancements was the 'team yell' that started every game. While most teams had a team huddle before the start of a game which concluded with some sort of shout, such as, 'Fight!' ... or 'Go, Team!' ... or 'Win!', Tim and Claude's team shouted in unison, 'It's A Great Day for Baseball!' The truth was, for Claude, every day was a great day for baseball, whether it was sunny, cloudy, cold or hot. In fact, for Claude, the worse a day might be for anything else ... the better it was for the alternative ... baseball ... whether he was playing it, coaching it, or just watching it. It usually didn't take long for any young player lucky enough to be on a team coached by Claude to feel the same way. On Claude's teams, mistakes and errors were just part of the game, and the coaching was gentle. His approach seemed to make mediocre players good, good players great, and all players motivated.

Again, glancing at the framed photo he had just put back on the shelf, his mind wandered to the conversations held earlier in the evening at his daughter's house. He walked into his den and over to the shelves to the side of the fireplace, which were filled with volumes of old books. In one section of the shelves, all of Jennifer's old high school and college yearbooks were neatly lined up together, still in the chronological order of her attendance. He pulled one of the volumes down and retreated to his easy chair to look at it.

Jennifer cleaned up the dishes after dinner and left Charlie and Tim talking in the den. Like Claude, Tim was proud of Charlie's promotion to captain of the baseball team, but he also had many questions about the academic load for the next semester. Once the two discussed the high points of the baseball meeting, they continued to talk about the many things that make a senior year in college both important and exciting.

Tim Drake had arrived in Lefton, from Illinois, as the town's pharmacist almost 20 years ago. By historical coincidence, the town's pharmacy was named Drake's Pharmacy. Tim wasn't related to any of the original Drakes who started the business almost 100 years earlier, but the coincidence worked in his favor. After working as the pharmacist for seven years, he was able to purchase the company from Nelly Posten, Elijah Drake's great-granddaughter. While most long-term residents knew the real history of the drug store, newcomers and visitors assumed that Tim was running a business that had been in his family for decades.

Before coming to Lefton, Tim had endured a brief marriage to a young lady who had left him for a professional wrestler. That episode in his life had made him a little bitter and generally wary of females. Coming to Lefton had represented a sort of fresh start for him, and his affable nature allowed him to matriculate into the community effortlessly. To fill out his relatively vacant social schedule, he volunteered for a variety of things in town, including coaching in the local Little League. As an avid baseball fan who had played the game through high school, he had plenty of enthusiasm to offer beginning players. The fact that he had no children of his own on the teams he coached was a plus for most parents. Tim was

Charlie's first T-ball coach and became immediately popular in the Hamilton family when he asked Claude to help him with the team.

It was an eventful summer, as the regular T-ball games forced two of the town's most eligible single people to share time together on a weekly basis. Jennifer's 'dates' always included granddad, Floe, Charlie and Tim, and usually a pizza and soft drinks. Tim's gentle nature was an attraction for Jennifer, and it was apparent to Tim that Jennifer was unlike any woman he had ever known before. None were happier than granddad and Charlie when Jennifer presented them the possibility of a marriage between her and Tim. The marriage took place a year later in a small ceremony attended by only Charlie, Claude, Floe and Tim's parents, Eleanor and Frank Drake.

Tim almost immediately broached the subject of officially adopting Charlie, whom he loved dearly. Jennifer initially liked the idea, but then backed away from it. Upon examining the procedures for adoption, she found that both biological parents must agree to an official adoption. At that time, she neither knew how to find Charlie's biological father nor wanted to open a door that she had already closed so many years before. Charlie's last name was Hamilton, just like his grandparents, who were more responsible than anyone else for helping Charlie and Jennifer through a difficult passage in life. While having a last name which was the same as his mother's and stepfather's could prevent questions down the line from other kids, it seemed a bit manufactured to Jennifer. Charlie seemed fine with his current name, and that name had a real meaning in Charlie's life. It was another full-count decision, as her dad liked to say, and she decided that Charlie should keep his original name. Tim was completely understanding.

"You seemed sort of distracted at dinner," said Tim, as he joined Jennifer at the sink. "You okay?"

"I'm fine, Tim. Thanks. It's just Charlie gave us a lot to think about with his news today, didn't he?"

"You mean about the Team Captain? Was that really a surprise to you?"

"No," she replied. "I guess not."

"So, what then? Jen, I know you well, and you weren't just thinking about Charlie being the Team Captain of his baseball team during dinner. What's going on?"

Jennifer dipped her head, turned to Tim, and put her arms around his neck. "Have you decided to be a psychiatrist now, besides a pharmacist, or are you thinking of maybe becoming a mind reader?" she said, nervously laughing.

"Neither. I'm happy with my current occupation, and after 14 years of marriage to you I don't need to be a mind-reader to know something is going on up here," Tim said, tapping her forehead.

Jennifer dropped her head to Tim's chest and said, "No fooling you, is there? Sorry. Is Charlie still in the den?"

"No, he went up to his room. He was going to look through his new textbooks."

"Okay. Good. Can we talk in the den?"

"Sure," said Tim.

They made their way to the den, and Jen situated herself on the easy chair facing the couch, versus sitting in her usual seat next to Tim on the couch. Tim sat on the couch. "This looks serious," said Tim.

"Don't get worried, Dear. It's probably nothing, but I would like to talk to somebody. Thank you for noticing my distraction and for being concerned."

"I love you, Jen! When you have a problem, I have a problem."

"I know. It's just that this problem goes way back ... before I even knew you. I have never talked to anybody about it. I made some mistakes when I was younger, and I'm afraid that some of those mistakes might someday come back and cause harm to the people I love most in life."

"Is this something about Charlie?" asked Tim.

Jennifer looked at Tim, tears brimming in her eyes. "Yes, Tim, it is."

"Well," said Tim, "If you're about to tell me that any of your past mistakes had anything to do with Charlie, I'm going to tell you that it was the best mistake you ever made!"

Jennifer's eyes could no longer hold back the tears, and she said, "Thank you, Tim. No, Charlie wasn't a mistake. He was and is a blessing. I just didn't handle the circumstances of my pregnancy as well as I probably should have. I thought I could take care of everything on my own, and I didn't ask for any help, and I ... I ..." she stopped talking and cried softly for a few moments.

Tim asked, "What did you handle wrong? What happened tonight which made you think about it?"

Jennifer waited a moment, composed herself, then said, "Tim, I need to check on something when I go to work tomorrow. You and dad are my most trusted advisers, and I want you to know everything. I need you to know everything so that you can help me but let me do a little research. Charlie has a school mixer tomorrow evening, so he won't be home until late. We'll have most of the evening to talk."

36

"Okay," said Tim. "Deal! Are you going to be okay tonight?"

"Yes. I'll be fine. I just need to think a little bit."

The couple retired to their bedroom, where Jennifer slept fitfully. She got up before the alarm sounded, dressed, and went to the College.

As Controller for the small College, Jennifer had her own key to all the buildings, and full access to any records she might want to see. She had been hired as the Assistant Controller for the school right after she graduated from Lefton. When Helen Grimes retired five years ago, Jennifer had been promoted to the Controller position. Nobody could remember Jennifer ever missing a day of work, and the school's accounting records were routinely spotless. The school had dispensed with annual audits from an independent CPA firm, and now only performed these reviews every other year. The reports after these examinations remained consistently excellent with "no issues and no discrepancies."

Jennifer flipped through the incoming students' information sheets, her heart beating fast, and her breath a little short. When she came to Shane Reynolds' page, she stopped. Glancing down the page, she quickly read the relevant information:

Shane Reynolds

Born: February 24, 1994

Parents: Case and Julia Reynolds

125 Whitepost Lane

Indianapolis, IN 47521

There it was: Case Reynolds. The chances that there were two Case Reynolds was remote. Jennifer was sure that if she did a little more research, she would find that Case Reynolds had graduated from Lefton College in 1990; that he had been a catcher on the college baseball team; and that he'd been the Regimental Commander of the school's ROTC unit. Jennifer didn't have to research this, because, as a junior when Case was a senior, she had been there. She had also been there when Case created a son ... that he still didn't know about.

Jennifer put the admissions records back in the filing cabinet and went up the stairs to her office. It was still early, and nobody else had yet arrived at the college's administrative building. Jennifer walked behind her desk and put her head on it. Most of the personal energy involved in making this climactic discovery had already dissipated for Jennifer between the moment when Charlie first mentioned the name, Shane Reynolds, and this morning. The name 'Reynolds' was common enough that Jennifer knew there was a much better chance Shane would have had no relationship to Case, than the possibilities that he would. Still, when Jennifer heard the name, something inside her said that a circle was about to be completed. What to do now? The answer eluded her, but she knew that doing nothing was no longer an option.

When Jennifer returned home, she waited patiently for Tim. Charlie was not back, and wouldn't be until late. She had stopped at the veterinary clinic on her way home to warn her dad that she and Tim had some plans for the evening. She knew that she had most of the evening to talk with Timmons. The crying and worrying were over for the time being. She knew that, now, she just had to think clearly and plan.

When Tim arrived home, Jennifer was waiting for him in the den. She had prepared sandwiches and a salad for a quick dinner that they'd eat in the den. Tim hugged Jennifer and asked if she was okay.

"Yes, I am," she replied. "I need you to help me think some things through, though. I have made some terrible mistakes in life, and I need to correct them in ways that won't destroy lives or families."

"That sounds a little dramatic," said Tim. "You aren't the type of person who is capable of hurting anyone ... or destroying lives."

"Thank you, but maybe you should reserve judgment until you've heard everything. I'm going to tell you things that nobody in this world knows, except me. That includes Charlie and my dad."

"Okay. I can handle it. I don't think there is anything you could tell me now that would make me love you less or make me think less of you."

"Thank you, Tim. I hope you are right. You have been so patient with me all these years and have never pried into any of the circumstances surrounding my pregnancy with Charlie. I'm certain you must have been curious but, knowing that this was so extremely personal to me, you have been a saint. You'll never know how much I have appreciated that ... but now I need you to know everything, so that you can help me. Here goes...

I got pregnant with Charlie in June, 1990. Classes were over, and there was a big party at Henson's downtown, sponsored by the Senior Class. I went with a girlfriend to listen to the band. The music was great, and everyone was dancing. People were drinking, but nobody was drunk. It was just a fun party! I was talking to my girlfriend when the star of the baseball team, Case Reynolds, came by and said hello to me. I didn't even know he knew my name, but he said, 'Hi, Jennifer,' like we were old friends, and asked me to dance. Tim, I was the biggest nerd in the Junior Class, and Case was probably the most popular man at the College. I couldn't believe he was asking me to dance and, I guess when I looked a little confused, he said he'd seen me dancing with one of my girlfriends. Grandma Floe had

40

taught me how to Shag, and it wasn't a dance that was necessarily popular at our school. Case said that his big sister had taught him and, in his four years at Lefton, he had not met anyone who could do it ... until he saw me with my girlfriend.

We danced the rest of the night, and both of us had a blast! He told me he wished he'd found me sooner, and not two days after he graduated. He was the Regimental Commander of the school's ROTC Division, and he automatically became a second lieutenant in the Army as soon as he graduated. He was due to report to Fort Benning for Airborne Training in two weeks. He had finished Basic Combat Training and Advanced Individual Training during the summers after his sophomore and junior years of college. Anyway, the magical evening for me continued after the dance and somehow ended at my parents' house that evening. Mom and dad were at a veterinarian's conference in Chicago, and I had the house to myself. ... Are you sure you want to hear the next part, Tim?" she asked.

"Jennifer, this is ancient history, and I'm not overly concerned with romances you might have had 20 years ago," said Tim.

"Okay. It was my suggestion to go to my house, not his. I'd had a few drinks, but I can't use that as an excuse. The fact is, the most coveted man on campus seemed interested in me, and I was enjoying the attention. I didn't want it to end! At my house, we fumbled through the initial stages of foreplay, and it was apparent that neither of us had had much practice. When the big moment arrived, Case was gentleman enough to tell me that he had not come prepared. He didn't have a condom. We had already gone too far for me, and I wasn't thinking clearly anyway. I told him just to be careful and pull out when he needed to. He couldn't have been inside me for more than a few seconds before he was pulling out. I was begging him not

41

to, but he did. That quickly ... it was over. After lying together for a few minutes, he apologized for not being able to last a little longer. I told him it was all right but asked him if he was sure he had gotten out in time. He said that he thought so ... not exactly the level of confidence that I hoped to hear but, even in a worst-case scenario, I thought, what were the odds of getting pregnant the very first time you ever had real sex? Case lived in Indianapolis, but he came back to Lefton Township to see me a couple more times before he left for Fort Benning. On these visits, there was never another opportunity for anything more than a quick pizza. When he left two weeks later, he gave me an address to write him. His course only lasted three weeks, though, so he wasn't going to be there long. I thought about writing, but didn't, ... because I literally didn't know what to say. I had only known this boy for a total of about two weeks!

After Airborne Training, his unit went to Saudi Arabia. According to the Indianapolis newspaper, which is the only way I found out what happened to him, he had been in Saudi Arabia for a couple of weeks when he was thrown from a HUMVEE during a war exercise. He suffered severe injuries, including head trauma, and was flown to a hospital in El Paso, Texas. Most of this happened before I even knew I was pregnant. Case got sent back from Saudi Arabia in late July, and Dr. Wells gave me the news about Charlie in the first part of that month. I knew that I had to get word to him somehow but, at first, I didn't have a clue as to how to reach him. Eventually, I found his parents' telephone number in Indianapolis, and I called them. I told them I was just a friend trying to catch up with him, and they told me the bad news about his accident. They told me that the details were in a past edition of the Indianapolis Star, and they gave me the number of the military hospital in Texas. I went to our College Library and found the old issue of the *Star* in the archives and read the article about the accident in Saudi Arabia.

When I called the hospital asking for Lieutenant Reynolds, I was told that, unless I were family, I would not be able to speak to him. I wondered what his prognosis was, and the lady told me they were not allowed to provide that information. I waited two weeks and called the hospital again. This time, I was able to get up to the Nurses Ward, where a young woman took my call. After telling her that I was just an old friend checking in on him, she shut me down. She said to me that Lieutenant Reynolds' condition was still severe and that he was not yet able to communicate clearly. Only family could see him, or talk to him, at that time.

I waited another month to call the hospital. It was September by then, and I was starting to show. I hadn't told anyone, not even my parents, who the father of the baby was because I didn't think it was fair for anyone else to know until the father knew. I wasn't expecting anything from the father, either romantically or financially. I just thought he should know. This time, the hospital reported that Case was transferred from the hospital to a residential address. They gave me a forwarding address at the Fort Bliss Army Base in Texas. I did a reverse directory search for a telephone number and was successful in finding one.

When I rang the number, a female answered on the second or third ring. I asked if this was Lieutenant Case Reynolds' telephone number, and the woman asked me who was calling. I was nervous, and I didn't give her my name. I just told her that I was a friend of Case's. After a long pause, the girl said to me that Case wasn't available to talk. She explained that he was recovering from a terrible accident and that he was undergoing daily mental and physical therapy. She also told me that Case was, in fact, living with her at her home. She said that she would arrange a time for me to talk to him if the message was family related or very urgent. I thanked her and told her that I understood. Then I hung up.

For me, that was strike three. I had tried three times to contact Case, and each time had been unsuccessful. On the latest attempt, I had found that, while he was still recovering from a terrible accident, he also had a significant relationship going on with a woman. In my mind, I rationalized that I had no right to further complicate either Case's recovery or his relationship. Case had no knowledge of what he had managed to accomplish in his short time with me, and I had no reason to punish him for it ... or jeopardize either his health or his personal relationships. I felt fully capable of handling the pregnancy with no other help beyond what my parents offered, and I was committed to providing my baby with a good life, with no other financial assistance beyond what I would be able to provide for myself. When I hung up the phone, I was relieved.

My parents continued to hint at wanting to know more about who the father might be, but I stonewalled everyone. Again, if the child's own father didn't know, it didn't seem fair for anyone else to know. Eventually, friends and family quit prodding. When Charlie was old enough to start asking questions, I simply told him that his father had gone off to a war and had not returned home."

Tim spoke for the first time since Jennifer had started the later part of her narrative. "I think I've heard Charlie relate that part of his history once or twice."

Jennifer replied, "Tim, you can't imagine how guilty that makes me feel! I never want to lie to Charlie. In my heart, I rationalize that what I've told him is true. His dad did actually go off to war, and he didn't return ... home ... meaning our home."

Tim sat with Jennifer for a minute, thinking, then asked, "So now that Case will be coming to the college on a frequent basis to watch his son pitch, you think you need to tell him about his other son?"

"I don't know, Tim. That's why I'm so conflicted. Case and his wife seem to have a wonderful life going on, with a great son who is a pitching superstar. We ... meaning you, me, Charlie and dad ... also have a great life going on. Why should I do anything to upset any of that?"

Tim replied, "Is this a trick question? I'm not sure why you would want to do anything."

"It's complicated," said Jennifer. "If I thought we could get through the next year with everything exactly like it is, I'm pretty sure I wouldn't risk doing anything. And that's because I think that I'm really just a weak person!"

"OK," said Tim, "I'm getting a little lost. Give me some more."

"Maybe I'm overthinking this," said Jennifer, "... but, Case will, at some point, notice me in the stands, and even though my last name is now Drake, he'll eventually make the connection that I was Jennifer Hamilton. If Shane and Charlie get to be close friends, which seems like a good possibility based on last evening's conversation, Case is going to start doing the math. I haven't seen Shane yet, but Charlie looks exactly like Case did in 1990. Case was no dummy in school ... and he knows that I wasn't sleeping with everyone who came along. I think he is going to eventually wonder. And if he wonders correctly, I don't have it in me to lie!"

"Ahh," said Tim. "Now I'm caught up. You've done a lot of thinking!"

"I have," said Jennifer. "Am I crazy?"

"No," said Tim. "But tell me the downside of having a family meeting and telling everyone everything."

"For starters, Case's wife ... I think her name is Julia ... could have a serious problem with finding out her husband has a child she didn't know about. Case could have a serious problem with the same thing ... not knowing of a son that he had conceived. Charlie could have some problems with his mother for not telling him that his dad was actually alive someplace ... and who knows what the news might do to Shane, who thought all this time he was an only child!"

"Got it," said Tim. "This is complicated! Before we go any further this evening, though, let me tell you this. I understand your thinking in all the decisions you've made, and I don't think I'd have done anything differently. You made decisions that were completely unselfish, and totally in the interest of others. I agree that some of those decisions might not have been correct, but you (and we) can't do anything about them now. All we can do is deal with the realities of the present. I don't know what the right answers are right now, but I'd like to think about what they might be with you over the next few weeks. Can we do that?"

"Thank you, Tim!" replied Jennifer. "Yes, we can!"

The late afternoon party was at Frocks, one of two private banquet facilities in the small town. Both Frocks and the other facility, Hensen Hall, survived economically on the weekly social functions of the various fraternities, sororities, and social organizations of the Lefton College campus. Both buildings were large and cavernous and offered secure parking. The owners of the businesses also left the supervision of the functions held at their premises to the organizations that were sponsoring the events. Professor advisors or college administrative personnel were always discreetly in attendance for all college-related functions.

If local police enforcement of underage drinking seemed lax relative to the functions held at Frocks and Hensen Hall, history at least seemed to indicate that more strict enforcement wasn't necessary. Lefton College was an important economic generator for the small township, and an unwritten treaty seemed to exist between the township's leadership and the college's leadership. If the school did its job to manage the behavior of its students, then the town would do its job to continue to provide a healthy business environment for the college.

The GIGIF (Gee, I'm Glad It's Friday) parties were held almost every week at Frocks, starting at around 4 PM and ending at 7 PM on Fridays. The events were sponsored by the college's Student Activities Association (SAA), and they were, for the most part, self-supporting. Admittance to Frocks was a nominal $5 per student, and only Lefton College students with valid college IDs were allowed. Light snacks were available for additional charge. Also available were soft drinks for $1 and draft beer for $2. At these functions, only one kind of draft beer was offered, and when the two kegs allocated for the functions ran out, no more was available. Usually, a local DJ provided music, but occasionally a live band performed. On this afternoon, the music was provided by a DJ named Bill Ober.

Shane walked in with two other first-year students from his dorm, and Charlie saw him from across the room. "Shane!" he yelled over the music. "Over here!" Shane looked around the crowded room and saw Charlie with several of the other baseball players he'd met at the baseball meeting earlier in the week. He worked his way through the crush of students to join Charlie's group.

"Junie, Pudge, Danny," Charlie said, "... you remember Shane from the baseball meeting, right?"

They all exchanged fist bumps and handshakes, and Danny asked, "How did you get here, Shane? You're a little late."

"I walked with a couple of other guys who knew the way," replied Shane. "One of the guys had a class until 4 PM, so we got a bit of a late start. Did you guys walk, too?"

Pudge laughed and said, "No. This afternoon it's my turn to be the designated driver, so everyone came in my car. Next time, give one of us a call, and you can pile in with us."

"Thanks, Dave," said Shane. "I'll be able to return the favor next year when I'm allowed to have a car on campus."

Lefton College did not allow freshmen to have cars parked on campus. No one knew if that was because of the scarcity of parking on campus, or if it was just an archaic rule left over from another generation. Whatever the reason, Shane would either have to walk to downtown events or depend on upperclassmen for rides for at least another year. Pudge replied, "Shane, most people call me Pudge ... you can too ... and you won't be paying _me_ back next year because I'll be long gone. I graduate in June ... but you won't owe anybody here anything anyway because you're now part of our team!"

"Okay, thanks ... Pudge. I really appreciate that."

Danny, who was holding an empty plastic container that had once had beer in it asked Shane, "Can I get you a draft, Shane? I'm going to get in line for a refill."

"Thanks, Danny," said Shane, "...but I'm only 19."

The other boys laughed, and Charlie told Shane, "Pudge, Danny and I are all 21, but most of the other students here aren't. Drinking rules are a little lax in this town, at least at functions held at Frocks and Henson Hall. You don't have to have a beer if you don't want to, but you won't get in any trouble if you do."

"Oh ... well, I guess I'd like a beer then," said Shane. "What kinds do they have?"

"Only one kind," said Danny. "Cold!"

The others laughed, and Shane said, "What a coincidence! That's the only kind I like!"

Danny came back, handed Shane the beer, and refused to take the cash Shane tried to give him. "On me, Shane," he said. Welcome to Lefton College and to the baseball team! I'd like to stay and chat, but I just saw Jud's sister over there, and I think she still owes me a dance!"

"Good luck, Danny," Charlie said. "Usually, the line to dance with Jill is longer than the line for beer." Again, the group of friends laughed and watched Danny disappear into the crowd on the dance floor.

"Jillian Long is Jud Long's little sister," Charlie told Shane. "You met Jud at the meeting ... he's one of our outfielders. Anyway, his sister started school here last year, and she's already one of the most popular girls on campus. She was the freshman attendant on the Homecoming Court

49

last year, and most of us think she'll be the sophomore attendant this year. She <u>loves</u> her brother, Jud ... and she <u>loves</u> baseball, so just about all of us on the team are good friends with her. She's also a great dancer!"

Shane tried to track Danny through the crowd he had disappeared into, but he had become lost among a mass of dancing students. One of the students in particular created more of a sight block than others because of his sheer size. When the giant dancer turned, Shane realized he had also been introduced to this student earlier in the week. He couldn't remember his name from the baseball meeting, but he was one of two black players on the team, and Shane knew that he was also a pitcher. Charlie noticed who Shane was watching, and said, "You remember Ten Ton, don't you? He's one of our pitchers."

"Right!" said Shane. "I couldn't remember his name. What did you say it was?"

"Oh ... well, his real name is Denton Jones, but we call him Ten Ton," said Charlie.

"I can see why," said Shane. "Does he pitch as well as he dances?"

"No! In fact, I'm not sure anyone can pitch as well as Ten Ton dances," laughed Charlie.

"Look at that big man move!" said Shane. "How many girls is he dancing with anyway?"

"Who knows?" said Charlie. "They all like dancing with him ... but few of 'em can keep up with him."

As the song ended, Denton was laughing with the crowd around him, when Denton saw another couple approaching. He gave the guy a high-five and the girl a gentle hug. Shane realized that the guy was Danny Colovito and wondered if the attractive girl was Jud's sister. When the music started again, the two teammates slapped hands, and the girl stayed on the floor next to Denton.

The song was a popular rap song, with a melodic and repetitive background. Denton and the girl next to him had obviously danced to the song before. They had a syncopated dance routine to the lyrics, which nearly everyone around them was now watching. The routine included stern-looking facial expressions that made Denton look downright scary ... and the girl look downright adorable. The dance started with the couple facing each other making a series of identical arm and leg movements but, as the dance progressed, each was making a slow 360 degree turn away from each other. Despite not even being able to see each other, the arm and leg movements remained identical, and exactly in rhythm to the beat of the song. The crowd had now joined in, with some kind of chant every time the dancers made a particular arm motion. It was fun to watch, and all in the room were enjoying it, but Shane could not take his eyes off the girl. When the dance ended, everyone in the room applauded the performance, and the dancers gave each other a friendly hug.

Charlie yelled to Denton and the big man, seeing him, began edging through the crowd in their direction. "Ten Ton, you are too much!" said Charlie. "If you could hit half as well as you dance, you'd be a first-round draft choice next year when you graduate!"

Denton laughed, and said, "Charlie, that would be nice, but I've got to keep my priorities straight. Someday, you' gonna find out yourself that learnin' to dance is way more important than learnin' to hit!"

"And, remind me why that is?" said Charlie, taking Denton's bait.

"Charlie, my man," said Denton. "You ever had any girls come up to you after you been hittin' and say, 'Wow,

Charlie, you can really hit! Can I come hit with you sometime?"

Charlie laughed, and said "No, Ten Ton. I don't recollect that ever happening."

"See?" said Denton. "You notice how many babes I got around me out there on the dance floor?"

Charlie, Pudge, and Shane all laughed, and Charlie said, "Okay, Ten Ton, you've made a good case there, but how'd you know that? Who taught you that?"

"Ha ha," laughed Denton. "My mama did. Ya' see ... I didn't have no daddy, and when I was about seven years old and struggling in the Little League, I went to my mama and told her I needed her to teach me to bat better. She told me she couldn't do that, but that she could darn sure teach me to dance better." He continued, "Well, Mama, I said, I don't need to learn to dance better right now. I need to learn to bat better." Denton then looked at Charlie very seriously, and said, "Charlie, my mama, she looked me right in the eye, and said, 'Fool, if you learn to bat well, you might get a few boys on your team to like you a little better ... for a short time. If you learn to dance well, you'll have a whole lotta' women who'll want to love you ... for a long time!'"

The whole group erupted in laughter, including Denton. "Ten Ton," said Pudge, "Sounds like you had a pretty smart mom!"

"Shore did, Pudge. Shorely did," he replied

Danny had joined the group, and right behind him was the cute girl that Shane had seen dancing with Ten Ton. "What's so funny?" asked Danny.

Charlie answered, "Ten Ton, here, was just reviewing the facts of life with us ... and his version is a little funny ... but seems to have some validity and merit." He then looked at the girl next to Danny, and said, "Hey, Jill! You looked almost as good as Ten Ton out there!"

She laughed, and said, "Now *that* is quite a compliment. Thanks!"

Danny said, "Jill, have you met Shane Reynolds? He's one of the new guys on the team this year. Shane, this is Jillian Long … she's Jud's sister."

Jillian extended her hand to Shane, saying, "Nice to meet you, Shane. Welcome to Lefton. My brother told me about you, and I think the whole team is excited about their prospects next year."

"Nice to meet you too, Jillian, and thank you. I think I'm going to like it here," he said, holding his eyes on Jillian for just a beat too long.

"Where's Jud?" asked Denton.

She said, laughing, "Oh, he's over there trying to put the moves on a freshman. She doesn't seem to be buying what he's trying to sell, though. I don't think I have to worry about carting any extra bodies back to the campus. I'm the designated driver today," she explained. Jud and Jillian shared a small, old, Renault on campus. Both had keys for it, and they coordinated their respective needs for the vehicle. The little car seated two uncomfortably, and a maximum of four in an extreme emergency if two of the four weren't the size of Jud. Jillian glanced at Shane as the DJ started the next song, and asked, "Do you dance, Shane?"

Shane, initially shocked by the question, recovered in time to say, "Not in the same league as Ten Ton, but I'm not dangerous."

She laughed, grabbed his hand, and led him to the dance floor. As his teammates watched him with their favorite little sister, they collectively agreed that their new teammate was a man of some dimension. While his legendary pitching reputation had preceded him to campus, his skills in a social setting ... and on a dance floor ... were now also apparent. As he watched Shane dance, Ten Ton said, "I like that kid!"

Danny, with an exaggerated sigh, said, "Looks like you're not the only one!"

Shane and Jill danced for most of the remaining hour of the GIGIF with very few interruptions for conversation. Even after Shane's legs began to tire, he was not about to take a chance on losing his spot on the dance floor with this girl. As the DJ announced the last song, Jill began looking around the room. "I need to find my brother, Shane," she said. "Do you need a ride back to the dorm?"

Shane, still not believing his good fortune, said, "Thanks, Jillian. I walked. If Jud has found a friend, it sounds like your car might be crowded. I think I can find my way back to the college, walking."

"Unless he's found a friend the size of Ten Ton, that won't be a problem," she said. "The car is small, but we've got less than two miles to go."

Shane did not want to appear too forward, but the thought of sitting in the relatively confined space of a small automobile with this girl had much appeal. "In that case, thanks!" said Shane.

When Jud and Shane arrived at the Renault with Jillian, Shane began to get into the tiny back seat. Jud stopped him, and said, "Get in the front, Shane. I'll get in the back. There is more room in the back when there is only one sitting there than there is in the front."

"Thank you, Jud!" thought Shane.

"That's true," agreed Jill. "Sometimes when we go shopping or something, he sits back there while I drive. People think he has a personal chauffeur!"

"I doubt," Jud said, "... that too many think that ... when we're driving a 2004 Renault!"

Jud climbed into the back, and Shane took the passenger seat. During the short trip back, Jud asked his sister from the back seat, "Where was Chuck today?"

Jill gave her brother a quick, hard, stare in the rearview mirror and replied, "How would I know that? I think he still had to finish his summer reading for Contemporary Literature."

"Oh ... sorry, Sis," said Jud. "I thought you and Chuck were dating."

Jill glanced at Shane quickly, and said to her brother, "You guys are all alike! You think two consecutive dates constitutes a relationship. Chuck is a nice guy, but I wouldn't say we were dating."

By this time, the packed little car had arrived at the principal men's dormitory. The trip had taken longer than the uncomfortably seated Jud wanted ... and much shorter than the infatuated Shane wanted. All piled out of the car and Jud said goodbye to his sister. Jillian waited patiently at the driver's side of the vehicle while Shane struggled mentally to think of something he could say ... or do ... that would preclude an end to this first encounter with Jillian. He failed to come up with anything and finally said, "Thanks for the ride, Jillian, and the dance. I had a really good time."

She replied, "Only my dad calls me Jillian, Shane. Why don't you call me Jill? I had a good time, too."

As she opened the door to get into her car, Shane nervously asked, "Do you have any plans for next weekend?"

Jill remained standing by the car, with the driver side door open, and said, "I guess that depends. Why?"

Shane was now out on the cliff, but he knew that he had to plunge ahead. "Well," he began, "I know you probably have another boyfriend ... and that I'm just a freshman and all ... but I was hoping maybe I could do something with you again ... sometime."

Jill let Shane finish and then shut the car door. She leaned over the roof of the small car, looking at Shane for a moment before she spoke. "First off, Shane, I don't have another boyfriend ... at least, not yet. Second, I couldn't care less that you're a freshman. I'm guessing that, since I started college a year ahead of most students, I'm close to the same age as you ... not that that would make any difference to me either. And third, I'd love to do something with you ... but why do we have to wait until next weekend? It's only 7:30 on a Friday night. We don't have classes tomorrow, and I'm starving! Would you like to walk to the Campus Grille with me and get something to eat?"

Shane was somewhat stunned, and inwardly elated, by both the directness <u>and</u> the content of her reply. "That's exactly what I'd like to do," he said. "Thanks for taking me off the hook!"

As they dined on burgers and fries, Jill told Shane the circumstances relative to her early admission to Lefton College. When she was in the 8th grade and her brother was in the 11th grade, Jud began looking at colleges. It was then that she realized that she and her beloved big brother wouldn't be living in the same house forever. The thought devastated her, and she set out on a path to get to the same college as him for at least a couple of years together. She took all the AP courses available in high school and attended summer sessions at the nearby Junior College to complete her high school requirements a year early. As she had predicted to Shane, she was also 19 years old, like Shane, born just three months ahead of him, in November.

"So, tell me, Jill," asked Shane over dinner, "... how long did it take you and Ten Ton to work up that amazing dance routine?"

"Not as long as you'd think," she laughed. "We started working on it toward the end of the baseball season last year. Denton is such a sweet guy ... sort of a gentle giant ... and he saw me trying to imitate his moves with one of my girlfriends at a party last spring. It only took him about 15 minutes to show me the basic moves, and then a couple of practice sessions to perfect it. The dance is called *The Judge* and apparently is popular at the R&B clubs in Cincinnati, where Denton is from. It really only consists of eight different steps or moves, and then there is an order that you just vary a bit to make it look more complicated."

"Do you think you could teach me?" asked Shane.

"Of course I can, Shane. You're a good dancer, and you'd pick it up quickly! That would be hilarious to Denton if you could learn it before the next GIGIF."

Shane said, "Coach Blevins says the gym stays open for students all the time. I'm guessing that on a Friday night after 8:00 PM, few, if any, will be using it. We could probably practice over there."

To herself, Jill thought, "Good move, Shane!" but to Shane, she said, "What are we waiting for?"

The Lefton College Gymnasium remained opened for student use every day, around the clock, and when they arrived there, it was deserted, as Shane had predicted it might be. Jill tapped in a few commands on her iPhone, and the track for *Here Comes The Judge* started playing. She paused it, and told Shane, "I've got about sixty percent on my iPhone battery. That should give us about a half an hour."

Shane checked his phone and was disappointed to see that it was already showing a red bar, with less than ten percent left. He hadn't charged it the night before. "Mine's about gone, but 30 minutes will give us a good start," he said.

After about 20 minutes, Shane understood the basic steps and hand motions. They both laughed as he tried to imitate the fierce facial expressions that Denton had displayed during the dance at the GIGIF, and Shane particularly enjoyed the moments when Jill put her hands on his shoulders to adjust his 'Gangsta' stances for the dance.

By the third time she had to do this, she smiled at him, and said, "Are you just playing with me? You've learned every part of this dance quickly ... except for this part."

Shane smiled back and said "Busted! Sorry ... I have to admit that I like when you hold my shoulders."

Not even blinking at the compliment, she asked, "So what do I have to do to make you hold *my* shoulders?"

Her question was direct and charged with exciting possibilities. Much raced through Shane's mind before he answered, but he settled on, "Change the music."

Smiling, she retrieved her iPhone, entered a command, and the song *Faithfully* by Journey started playing. Shane put his arms around her waist in a waltzing position and the two moved slowly around the gymnasium floor to the beautiful love song. When Jill's battery gave out and the music stopped, the young couple continued to dance. Finally, Jill lifted her head to Shane and moved her body out of his arms. "Thanks for that dance. I think we've practiced long enough tonight, don't you?"

Shane smiled at her and said, "You're probably right, but I'd like to work on that waltz again sometime."

"I'm pretty sure you're going to get that opportunity," she said.

As they walked back to Jill's car, Shane said, "I don't know this town well yet, but is there a movie or something we could go to next weekend?"

"Yes," she replied. "There is a small theater downtown, not far from the campus. Jud has the car next weekend, so if you want to go, we'd have to walk."

"Sounds great!" said Shane. "Do you know what's playing?"

"No," said Jill. Then she asked coyly, "Do you care?"

"Not a bit," said Shane.

They had arrived at Jill's car, and Shane's mind was racing as to how he should say goodbye for the evening. Would it be too forward to kiss her? Should he just give her a small hug? What to do ... what to do. Jill made it simple, by giving him a quick hug and jumping into the car. Rolling down her window, she smiled at Shane, and said, "I had a great time today, Shane. Thank you."

"I did too," he replied. "I'm sure I'll see you around campus this week, but I'll plan on walking over to your dorm at about 6:30 PM next Saturday."

"Good deal!" she said, and then pulled away in her car.

Jill put her car in the parking lot and skipped up the steps to her room on the third floor. This had been a memorable day and, as she reviewed it in her mind, she found little that she would have done differently. As a popular and pretty high school student, there had always been an endless supply of willing suitors. Boys, however, were mostly the same, always trying to push the sensual parts of dating too quickly. As a healthy young woman, she often felt the same sorts of raging desires as they did but was proud of the fact that her mind had always won the battle for control in these situations. While she had, at times, gone 'a long way' on dates, she had yet to go 'all the way.'

At the GIGIF, she had noticed the new boy watching her dance with Denton. He had been standing among some other members of Jud's baseball team, and she suspected who he was based on her brother's description of the new players several days earlier. After the dance with Denton, she had followed Danny Colovito over to the small gathering of ballplayers, where she had been introduced to Shane. She had actually surprised herself by asking Shane to dance. His response had been quick, humble, and witty, and they had spent the remainder of the GIGIF on the dance floor.

While Shane had almost let her get away after she dropped him off at his dormitory, he had recovered and given her a natural opening. She knew that she had taken the lead when she suggested they eat together at the grill. She had been surprised, however, when Shane had taken the lead in proposing dance lessons at the gym. She had half-expected some awkward advances by Shane in the empty gym but was relieved when these didn't occur.

She had resumed the lead when she asked Shane the very provocative question pertaining to her shoulders. By this time, she knew the boy had won her, and she wanted him to hold her. That moment had many possibilities, but Shane had simply told her to 'change the music.' *Wow!* she thought. *Good response, Kid!* She had opened an opportunity for him to be aggressive, but he had responded in a rather noble way. The slow dance had been sweet and tame. Other boys in the same situation would have started moving their hands around her body, but he hadn't. He had left them quietly around her waist, although she could tell that her chest next to his was having an effect. When the music stopped, he had kept dancing. *More points, Shane. Good move!* she thought.

When the dance had ended, he didn't try to press his advantage. When she was getting into her car, he had made no blatant attempt to try to kiss her. Shane Reynolds was apparently a great athlete, had proven to be a good dancer, and he had now shown remarkable restraint on his first date with her. She could not wait for the next date.

The phone rang several times before Julia answered, "Hello. Reynolds residence."

"Hi Mom," said Shane

"Hey, Shane," said Julia. "How are you? How was the first week at Lefton? We miss you so much around here!"

"I miss you and dad, too," said Shane, "... but everything is fine here. Biology is going to be a bear, and English Lit puts me to sleep but, other than that, I like my courses."

"Well, four out of six isn't bad. What about the ball team?" she queried. "When dad and I dropped you off last week, I remember hearing that the baseball coach had called a team meeting for that afternoon."

Shane replied, "The meeting was fine, and all the boys seem friendly. Other than that, it's too early to know much else. I really liked my catcher, and we've scheduled a regular workout routine for the off-season."

"Okay, okay," said Julia. "Stop right there. Let me get your dad and put you on speaker. You know he's going to want to hear all about this."

"Okay, Mom," said Shane. "But honestly, there isn't that much to tell."

"I know, but just hold on."

A few minutes later, the big voice of Case Reynolds boomed through Shane's cell phone, "Hey, Son! Mom says you like your catcher and that you have a workout schedule for the off-season! What else?"

Shane smiled at his dad's rather predictable greeting, and said, "There wasn't anything else relating to baseball,

Dad. I mentioned to her about my classes. Did she tell you that?"

"Mmm, yeah. I think she did. Something about biology is hard and English Lit sucks!"

"Those weren't my exact words, but it's a fair summary," said Shane.

"Well, we miss you, Shane," said Case. "Did your mom tell you that Coach Holmgren has called us twice this week?"

"No, we hadn't gotten too far into the conversation when she went to get you."

"What did Holmgren want?" said Shane

"Well, on the first call, he just beat around the bush, asking if we were all satisfied with your decision," said Case. "On the call yesterday, he indicated that he had met with the other coaches and the school's administration and had found a place for you on their roster. He said that a scholarship was in the works and that starting the school semester a few weeks late wouldn't be a problem."

"What did you tell him?" asked Shane

"I told him that I'd let him know after I had talked to you," said Case.

"What do you think?" asked Shane.

Julia replied first, "Shane, your dad and I haven't even discussed this much, but my vote is, you decide ... not us!"

Case followed up, "Totally agree, Julia! Shane, you have the athletic talent to play on a bigger stage than the one at Lefton if you want to, but you're also in a perfectly fine place where you are. We'll support any decision you make!"

"Thanks, Mom and Dad. I'm staying here. I've already started classes, and I like Coach Blevins and my catcher. Holmgren's at-bat finished two months ago for me."

"That's what I thought you'd say," said Case," ... but I wanted to make sure before calling Holmgren back. As you probably know, the local sports writers are skewering him in the papers for his decision about you."

"Not my problem," said Shane.

"Mine either," agreed Case. "What's your catcher's name?"

"Charlie Hamilton. He's a senior who walked on as a freshman, and he's the Team Captain this year. Everybody likes him, and if you look up his stats from last year, he's quite a player."

"Big guy?" asked Case.

"No, not at all," replied Shane. "He's about the same size as me, but that doesn't seem to hold him back any. He's rock solid and tough as nails. Get this ... he led the conference in hit-by-pitch last year!" Shane ended, laughing.

"My kind of guy," said Case. "Sounds like you've got a winner. How many days per week are you going to throw over the off-season?"

"Just two, and we're not going to be throwing hard," said Shane. "Just enough to stay loose. We're going to work mostly on technique, and maybe try to improve my change up."

"What change up?" said Case, laughing into the phone. "You aren't referring to that awkward pitch you threw sometimes, that was only about two miles per hour slower than your fastball, and usually called a ball, are you?"

"Very funny, Dad," replied Shane. "Yep, that's the one. Coach Blevins says a starting pitcher can't survive in college on just one quality pitch."

"Blevins is right," replied Case. "Fact is, most <u>high school</u> starting pitchers can't either, but you managed somehow."

"Well, I think it will be different next spring, Dad."

"Great! Can't wait for the first game!"

"And I can't wait for the first grades," said Julia, still on the second line.

"Don't worry, Mom. I'm only working two hours per week in the gym on baseball. All the rest of my time will be for my courses."

"Ummm, no parties? No girls?" asked Julia.

"Okay, maybe just *most* of the rest of my time on my courses." Shane laughed through the phone, then admitted, "I already met a girl that I like at one of the first college mixers."

"That didn't take long," said Julia.

"Mom, I did take 'Long'," Shane joked to his mother.

"You think a week at school is a long time?" Julia asked.

"No, Mom," he said. "That's the girl's name ... Long ... Jillian Long. She's a sophomore at Lefton, and her older brother plays outfield on the team."

"Wow!" said Case. "It only took you a week, and you've already managed an older woman!"

"Not really, Dad," said Shane. "Jillian is my age. She started college a year early."

"Oh, good!" said Julia. "Her picture will be in the Lefton College Yearbook, then. They told us at the parent orientation that the yearbook is available in a PDF format online."

Shane answered, "Sure, if you want to do that, but that picture will be at least a year old. I'm seeing her again on Saturday. I'll just take a picture and send it to you. Of course, you might find out some other things about her from the yearbook ... like that she was the freshman attendant on the Homecoming Court last year."

"Wow!" said Case. "How did you manage that? We'll be up before Thanksgiving to bring you home. Maybe we'll meet her then."

"Well, maybe," said Shane. "That's a long time from now. She may dump me before then."

"I'm glad you're enjoying the school, Shane," said Julia. "Keep us posted on everything."

"Yes, keep us posted," added Case.

"Will do. I gotta go. It's beautiful here today, and Charlie and I are going to toss the baseball outside for a bit. Love you both!"

Case met Julia coming down the stairs from the bedroom extension phone. "Sounded good, didn't he?" said Case.

"Yes, he did," agreed Julia. "He seems to like his environment at Lefton. Did his decision about Indiana University surprise you?"

"No," said Case. "It didn't."

"But did it disappoint you?" asked Julia.

Case winked at his wife and thought for a moment before answering. Finally, he said, "As a proud dad, I'd be lying if I said that I wouldn't enjoy seeing my son play for one of the top University programs in the nation. There is a side of me, though, that is just as proud of his decision to play at a small college."

"And why is that?" questioned Julia.

"Well, here's a kid who has displayed the talent, and gotten the press, to play anywhere he wants to. Though the possibilities might be a little remote, he might even be good enough to play in the pros someday ... and yet none of that has ever gone to his head. He has always played baseball because he liked the game, not because of where it might get him. Who wouldn't be proud of raising that kind of a son?"

"Certainly not me," agreed Julia. "He's the most grounded 19-year-old I've ever met, and I'm proud that he just happens to be my boy!"

Case hugged Julia, and after a few moments said, "I still can't wait for the baseball season to start! We're going to be burning up the highway between here and Lefton next spring."

"I hear you," replied Julia. "Who's going to run the business while you're taking all that time off?"

"I've got almost four months to figure that out," he replied, smiling at his wife.

After graduating with a degree in finance from Lefton College, Case had spent one of the shortest careers ever in the military. He had been in Lefton's ROTC program for four years and was commissioned a Second Lieutenant in the Army upon graduation. He attended three weeks of Airborne training at Fort Benning, Georgia, before his unit, the 82nd Airborne, was sent to Eskan Village Air Base in Saudi Arabia. In the build-up to what would soon be called the Gulf War, President Bush had ordered about 10,000 troops to Saudi Arabia. Iraq had invaded Kuwait, and the rest of the Middle East was awaiting Saddam Hussein's next move. Once the 82nd had landed in Saudi, the unit immediately began participation in a series of war exercises designed to prepare them for any impending conflict. Ten days after Lt Reynolds claimed his bunk at the Eskan Base, he was thrown violently out of an army Humvee participating in one of the exercises. He suffered multiple broken bones, severe head trauma, and was air evacuated to the William Beaumont Army Medical Center in El Paso, Texas. After several operations and treatment for his injuries there, and after a lengthy period of rehabilitation, he had been medically discharged from the Army. Not counting his college time as an army reservist, he had served on active duty for a grand total of nine months.

When Case was discharged from the hospital, he took up residence with his new girlfriend, fellow Lieutenant, Julia Montgomery, at her quarters at Fort Bliss. Lt. Montgomery was an Army nurse, and she had been the primary medical liaison during his recovery period at Beaumont. When she suggested to Case that she continue taking care of him at her residence when he was released from the hospital, he readily accepted. Julia was good at many things, and they were married at the Army chapel at Fort Bliss on Valentine's Day, 1992.

While living at Fort Bliss, Case got a part-time job at an energy farm near El Paso. The concept of garnishing usable and economical energy from natural resources, such as the wind and the sun, was still relatively novel in the early '90s. Low oil prices made fossil fuel energy much less expensive than any of the alternatives, but many in the country foresaw a time in the future when that might not be the case. One such entrepreneur was Shipley Beck. Shipley owned a sheep ranch west of El Paso, and he had been using several windmills on his property for years to draw water from the ground for his flocks. The wind always seemed to be blowing in West Texas, and Shipley noticed he was never out of water for his sheep, despite the barren nature of the land in that area of the country. Over the years, he had expanded his windmills, connecting many to large, rechargeable batteries. He was eventually able to operate his large ranch without any purchased electricity. He envisioned a day when he might be able to provide enough energy to satisfy several of the smaller communities west of the city.

Case saw Shipley loading his pickup one day with several large turbine fan fins that the local machine shop had fabricated for him. The fins were big, awkward to handle, and fairly heavy. Case offered to help Shipley, who gladly accepted. Once the fins had been secured on the truck, Shipley told Case he would pay him an additional $50 to help him unload the fins at his ranch outside of town. Case was still receiving a regular military check, as part of his medical leave severance. All medical expenses relating to his military incurred injuries would be covered for life by the government. While he was still required to complete a physical therapy regimen five mornings per week, he had nothing else to do in the afternoons. He had nearly recovered from his injuries and was now only strengthening muscles that had been dormant for several months. He accepted Shipley's afternoon job, which quickly turned into an 'every afternoon' job.

Case was amazed at Shipley's ranch and had many questions about the windmills. One evening, after working at the ranch, he decided to do some of his own research on wind farming. He came across an article published by a wind farmer in California, and the article referred to environmental grants that the Californian had used to expand the energy infrastructure for his ranching operations. The following day, after his physical therapy workout, Case started calling state and federal government agencies. After spending hours of time and getting nowhere, Case finally hit the jackpot. A friendly bureaucrat at the Federal Government's Department of Energy had suggested that Case contact that department's Wind Energy Technologies Office (WETO). When he did, doors started opening, and fireworks started going off in Case's brain.

By the time Shipley picked Case up that afternoon to go to the ranch, Case had a list of things that he and Shipley had to complete before next week's visit by a Federal Department of Energy scientist. Shipley seemed stunned, and happy ... until Case showed him the long list of things that had to be completed in less than a week. He told Case that they could never get all those things done ... but they did.

An exhausted pair of amateur wind farmers picked up the Department of Energy scientist from the El Paso Airport the following week, as scheduled, and brought him to Shipley's ranch. The scientist quietly surveyed the ranch, taking many pictures, and even more notes. He asked a few questions, but mostly just observed and wrote for the three-hour duration of the tour. At the end of the visit, he asked Shipley what his request was from WETO. Shipley had been unprepared for this question ... or for that matter, any question. Case jumped in, filling the awkward silence with an outline of what the grand plan for Shipley's wind farm was and a short list of what equipment they would need to reach their goal.

When the scientist asked if the two wind farmers had an estimate of what this might cost, Case again answered immediately. Referring to his notebook (which was actually blank) he told the scientist that, without complete detailing of the project, he thought they would need around $300,000. When Case said this number, Shipley looked like he might faint. The bespectacled scientist, however, exhibited no noticeable reaction. He merely recorded the number Case had given him in his notebook and headed to the boarding area for his flight.

When the scientist was well out of sight, Shipley turned to Case, exclaiming, "Are you out of your mind? You gave that guy the version of my plan that ... in my dreams ... might be ten years down the road! And how did you ever come up with that number?"

"Same place I came up with most of the rest of the things I told him," Case replied, holding up the blank notebook. "What have we got to lose? I think he liked your ranch."

"Case," laughed Shipley, "You have got some balls, but I like you. That scientist is probably going to laugh all the way back to Washington!"

"You think? Well, we'll see," said Case. "What happens when we get a $300,000 check?"

"What happens then is ... I'll eat that dirty, scroungy old cowboy hat you're wearing!" replied Shipley

The large government package had been delivered to Case and Julia's quarters at Fort Bliss about three weeks after the meeting with the Department of Energy scientist. Case tore into it, finding a volume of forms and a lot of government documents with very fine print. Near the bottom of the pile was an official-looking letter clipped to a three-page list of equipment, supplies, and the names of several contractors. Case quickly read the letter:

March 3, 1991

Dear Mr. Beck and Mr. Reynolds,

Dr. Ned Stancliff, DOE, D.SC., was most impressed with your small wind farming endeavor. The Department of Energy, through its Wind Energy Technologies Office, is inclined to consider your organization's request for funding, contingent on your organization's ability to meet all the requirements listed in the enclosed documents. A Federal grant may only be awarded after the completion of the enclosed application and after review of the application by the WETO Funding Advisory Committee. You may find the attached list of equipment, supplies, and contractors to be useful to you in completing the required documentation and the application.

During his visit to your operation in El Paso, Dr. Stancliff made many notes relating to your current activities. While you are to be congratulated on your efforts to advance the utilization of alternative forms of energy, Dr. Stancliff noted that many of your current methods do not represent the latest advances in technological development in this field. Also, much of your existing equipment is similarly outdated.

In the attachment to this letter, we have taken the liberty of suggesting materials and equipment that you might consider for your expansion effort. We have also provided the names of several credible contracting firms who have already been approved by this Department, that might assist in the next phase of your growth. If you choose to use the resources we have suggested, we believe that the total funding required for your project might be a little less than what you estimated. Pending the aforementioned accurate completion of documentation provided, and pending approval by the Funding Advisory Committee, we have preliminarily allocated $250,000 of potential Federal grant funds for use on your project. Again, I emphasize that this letter represents neither approval of your project nor a commitment to funding. It simply provides you an indication of our sincere interest in your plans, as well as the approximate funding which could be provided.

Thank you for your interest and your efforts to help this Department mitigate the earth's energy crisis.

Signed,

Nelson Landau
Director of Wind Energy Technologies Office
Department of Energy

"We got it!" Case yelled to nobody. Julia was at the hospital, and there was nobody but Case at the house. "We got it!" he yelled again anyway, before getting on the phone.

"Shipley," Case said into the phone. "How do you like old cowboy hats served? Rare or medium rare?"

"What are you talking about, Case?" asked Shipley.

"You said you'd eat my hat if we got the DOE grant," said Case. "and I'm holding a letter from them saying we'll get it ... as long as I fill out about three pounds of forms that came with it!"

"You're kidding!" exclaimed Shipley.

"No, not kidding, and it gets even better. They think our current operations are a little inefficient, and they've given us a list of materials and equipment which they say will save us some money!"

"Am I just dumb, Case?" asked Shipley.

"For what, Shipley? You're a born entrepreneur, and without any help from anyone, you've constructed a credible enough wind farm operation to make the government want to help you expand it. That doesn't seem so dumb to me," said Case.

"So why haven't I ever thought about even trying to find some kind of government program to help me build it or expand it?" asked Shipley.

"Probably because you're just a typical, independent, West Texas cowboy who wants as little interference from the State and Federal governments as possible. Don't blame you a bit but, despite its flaws, our government does try to do its best to take care of its people. If the government has programs to help us, we should take advantage of 'em," said Case.

Shipley waited to answer for a long moment, then said, "Considering what you've been through serving your government over the past year, I'm sort of surprised by your defense of it."

"Shipley, the government paid for part of my college education through the ROTC program. I volunteered for the military ... nobody forced me. I knew what I was getting into when I graduated, and I didn't fault President Bush for trying to help stop a ruthless dictator from trying to take over the whole Middle East. I got hurt in a training exercise, and if it hadn't been that, I might have gotten killed in what is going on over there right now. Most who serve in the military, and their families, realize that bad personal consequences are always a possibility. I was lucky. I'm still here, and the government is going to take care of most of my medical expenses for the rest of my life. The government also facilitated my introduction to Julia ... and now, I have a feeling they are going to try to help fund my next career. I've got no beef with the government, now. We've got a lot of work to do, though!"

"Got it," replied Shipley. "Thank you, man ... for everything. I'll be over in a few minutes to pick you up."

They *did* have a lot of work to do, but before Case could do another thing, Shipley had forced him to sign a document making Case a full partner in his wind farming operation. The only contingency in the offer was that Case sell Shipley his cowboy hat for a dollar. When Case asked why, Shipley told him, "I'm a man of my word, Case. I told you I'd eat your hat if we got that grant. It ain't your hat anymore if I've officially bought it, and I'm just not fond of the taste of dirty cowboy hats."

"Deal!" said Case, and the two became partners.

Shipley and Case worked in earnest, and that summer had been awarded the government grant. With the help of some of the contractors suggested by D.O.E., the whole project had been completed in a matter of months. The expansion garnered a fair amount of local publicity, and Shipley was surprised when he received a call from the El Paso Electric Company.

"You're not going to believe this," said Shipley. "El Paso Electric has an interest in purchasing any extra energy that we might produce through the windmills!"

"Wow!" said Case. "That's a new development. You've always said that EPE was eventually going to be your enemy relative to your wind energy project."

"Well, that's what I thought," answer Shipley. "Maybe not, though. They don't seem overly concerned by our little microscopic operation, but they *do* have interest in tracking the alternative energy technologies. They don't currently have any resources in that field. They also told me that the Federal Energy Regulatory Commission has some weird rules about how much they're allowed to charge customers for electricity. Apparently, there is some sort of average rate that all customers in a class of usage get charged. This rate can't be arbitrarily changed by their company, even if this rate isn't totally profitable for individual, remote, or hard-to-service customers. It seems really complicated but, in a nutshell, they would be willing to pay us some nominal rate for any excess energy we produce, as long as we collaborate with them on our technology."

"Ah," said Case. "So, if our technology ever becomes really efficient, they can steal it!"

"Maybe," replied Shipley. "But you know what? How difficult would any of that technology really be to steal, with us or without us? We got most of it for free from the DOE. I'm sure they could find the same things we have, with a little effort."

"You're probably right," answered Case. "What do they mean by nominal rate anyway?"

"Their calculation for what we're producing right now, with no expansion, is almost $2,000 a month. They would increase that as our expansion produced more," said Shipley.

"That's not a whole lot," answered Case. "But it keeps them as our friend and out of competition with us for the time being. It also solves the infrastructure problem we'd have trying to connect everything west of El Paso with electric wire to our batteries," Case answered, smiling. "It gives me another idea, too. I might give our friend Dr. Stancliff a call and see if he has any ideas about other small utility companies who might be interested in our services."

That idea of Case's sent the company he and Shipley had started, Beck Reynolds Energy Technologies (BRET), in an entirely new direction. Without even trying, Case was receiving invitations from utility companies all over the country to visit. Since these companies were paying for his transportation and expenses, he accepted many of the invitations. After several months of rather exhaustive traveling, he felt like he had learned way more from the companies he visited than what he had been able to provide them. Dr. Stancliff, the nerdy DOE scientist, had been an invaluable resource, and several of Case's visits had also generated requests for Shipley to provide some construction services. By the end of the year, it was evident that Case and Shipley actually owned two companies. One was an operationally oriented one, and the other one was a consulting company. They named the consulting company Beck Reynolds Infrastructure Consulting (BRIC) and decided that the ownership of the two separate, but related, divisions should reflect more fairly the time and effort spent by each partner in each of the respective divisions. Shipley assumed seventy percent ownership in BRET, with Case and Julia retaining thirty percent. Case and Julia would own seventy percent of BRIC, with Shipley having a thirty percent stake in that division.

Shipley sold his sheep at the end of the year and added some engineers to his payroll to help tackle the backlog of contracting business Case had generated through BRIC. Case and Julia added Dr. Stancliff to the staff of BRIC after a short negotiation with the scientist in D.C. Stancliff's salary was $20K more than he had received at DOE and represented twice the income that BRIC was earning at the time through consulting contracts.

Case had seen a window of opportunity however and felt confident that the plan would work. Julia's active duty commitment ended that summer, but she had 60 days of unpaid leave to collect before her military checks ceased. Case had spent almost none of the military pay he had received during the time he had been hospitalized, so he also had some savings. BRET, the operations company, was earning a little bit of income, and Case felt confident that he could increase his consulting fees.

Case and Julia had gotten married on the base in February. It had been a small ceremony, attended only by his parents, John and Elizabeth, his older sister and her husband, Linda and Fred Stallings, and Julia's parents, James and Emily Montgomery. Case had grown up in Indianapolis, where his parents still lived. Julia's parents were from Cincinnati and had met Case's parents on the plane from Cincinnati to El Paso.

After Julia's active-duty commitment ended, she and Case moved to a double-wide trailer on Shipley's Ranch. Shipley had offered a very favorable rate for Case and Julia for the trailer, $1 per month, which Case refused to accept. The $200 per month checks that were mailed by Case to Shipley were left uncashed.

Julia became both Case's and Shipley's full-time unpaid Administrative Assistant during that summer. She was so busy that she didn't even notice when she missed her period for almost two months. She was already three months pregnant with Shane when an old doctor friend of hers from the base confirmed it. This didn't slow either Julia or her husband down. If anything, it made them each redouble their efforts to make their young business successful.

In the early years, there never seemed to be much money in the bank, but there was always enough to cover the rather Spartan lifestyle that Case and Julia lived. Case's consulting company couldn't keep up with the demand for his services, and many of BRIC's consulting visits resulted in additional contract work for BRET, Shipley's contracting business. When Shane was two, Julia and Case decided that the double-wide might be getting too small for their family. Before looking for another house, Case approached Shipley with a different idea.

Almost all of Case's time was spent traveling to different cities located all over the country. El Paso was not the most accessible city to travel to or from, and the El Paso Airport boasted few direct flights to the places Case generally had to go. He asked Shipley if the partner would have a problem with Case relocating BRIC somewhere in the Midwest. Dr. Stancliff was working from his home in Alexandria, Va., with no problem, and if Case had a computer and a telephone connection to Shipley, not being in El Paso wouldn't seem to pose a problem for Shipley either.

"Other than the fact that I'll miss the daily contact with you and Julia and Shane, there's no problem at all," answered Shipley. "I couldn't ask for a better partner, and I've never known a better man! You and Julia both have family in the Midwest, and that could make it a whole lot easier for you to raise Shane the way you'd like to."

"Thanks, Ship," replied Case. "Shane is the reason I was thinking of the move. He's fine now, here, but if our business keeps growing, and I'm as busy as I have been, I'd like Julia to at least have access to some additional family who might be able to help her."

"Get going, Case!" replied Shipley. "Let me know where you land."

Case and Julia settled in Indianapolis, several miles from Case's parents' home, and only about an hour north of Julia's parents. Both his company and Shipley's had grown, with each division now employing over twenty people. While the businesses each provided generous incomes for their respective owners, all of Case's and Julia's wealth was tied up in BRIC and BRET. What the two enterprises were worth, individually or combined, was anybody's guess. Neither partner had any desire to sell or a reason to have any kind of an appraisal done.

Shane had bumped into Jill at the Campus Grille during the week and confirmed his date for Saturday. During the conversation, he asked if she'd be at the GIGIF on Friday. She told him she wouldn't be able to go this week because all the nominees for the Homecoming court had been invited to a 'Tea' at Ms. Guernica's home on Friday afternoon. Ms. Guernica, the college's vivacious Spanish professor, was the faculty advisor for the Homecoming event and it was a tradition for all the girls nominated to enjoy an afternoon together before student voting. Jill had attended last year and, while the event wasn't her first choice, she felt she should go again this year. Shane understood and told her he'd see her on Saturday around 6:30 PM.

When he arrived at her dormitory, she was already waiting for him in the lobby. They walked from the campus entrance toward the downtown area for about ½ mile before Shane saw the old theater marquee jutting from a building just ahead. "Oh great," he said, "One I've been hoping to see," as he read the title of the movie under the NOW PLAYING sign. *The Alien Professor*, read the title.

"You like science fiction?" asked Jill, innocently.

"I was being a little sarcastic," he admitted. "It looks like the only choice today, though," he said.

Shane bought the tickets and the couple easily found seats in the mostly deserted theater. The movie began, and Shane quickly realized that the only good thing about the movie was his seat ... and the girl sitting beside him. He couldn't tell if Jill was enjoying the picture because she had said nothing since it had started. He checked to ensure that her eyes were open. They were. Very quietly, he whispered, "What do you think of this show so far?"

81

"It sucks," she said, "... but I'm willing to sit it out if you are enjoying it."

"I'd rather spend the next two hours talking to you than wasting it in here. Is there someplace else we can go?"

"Head to the exit ... I'm right behind you."

When they reached the daylight again outside of the theater, Jill laughed and said, "Thank you for saving us from that. I wasn't sure how much longer I was going to be able to last. We passed the duck pond on the way here. It's not huge, but it has some benches and a nice lighted pavilion they use for band concerts sometimes."

They headed back up the hill, taking a left on a small footpath that Shane hadn't noticed on the way into town from the campus. The walkway opened into a more significant trail that encircled a small pond. Benches were in place at different locations on the path, and Shane saw the small pavilion up ahead and to the right.

It was a beautiful September evening and, at only 7:30 PM, the sun could still be seen slipping into the west. It was warm, and several walkers were using the path around the pond. Jill headed toward a bench near the pond's edge and sat down. The pond's geographical location allowed for the image of the setting sun to be duplicated on its gently rippling surface. Ducks floating serenely over the top of the image completed the tapestry. It was beautiful, and the young couple watched the scene evolve in silence.

After the sun had finally disappeared and its image was no longer displayed on the pond's surface, Shane said, "That was a way better show than the one playing at the theater! I'm sorry we only got here for the ending!"

At that point, Jill couldn't stop herself from reaching for Shane's hand. She squeezed it tightly ... hoping... and it took an instant too long, but Shane finally gave her a light squeeze back. "I'm just glad you got us out of that ridiculous movie in time to see the end."

They continued to gaze at the pond for a few moments before Shane asked, "How was your tea on Friday?"

Jill answered, "Oh... it was okay. The usual stuff and Ms. Guernica is so sweet to sponsor it. She tries to make all the contestants feel like winners no matter the final ballots, and the girls all put on fake smiles and give each other fake compliments. For most of the girls participating, this is the most stressful two weeks of their school year. It's a little sad."

"It isn't stressful for you?" Shane asked.

"No! Not a bit!" she exclaimed. "I could care less if I am named our class's attendant or not. I wouldn't even participate if I wasn't afraid of hurting the feelings of the folks who nominated me." Shane laughed, and Jill asked, "What's funny?"

"Nothing... really," said Shane. "It's just ... that's the way life is sometimes, isn't it? I mean ... you don't even care about the Homecoming Court, and you're the one who's going to get elected. The ones who think this is so important and are going to worry about it for the next two weeks lose out on several levels."

"Well, hold on there, Shane," said Jill. "I'm flattered to have been chosen to participate by my friends, but just because I was elected last year, doesn't mean that will happen again this year. I think my brother did a lot of politicking with his baseball buddies last year that influenced some of the Freshmen voting."

Shane replied, smiling, "That may be, but according to everyone I talk to, there isn't even a contest for the Sophomore attendant. You might as well go buy the gown."

Jill blushed and, in a sincere effort to remove the focus of the conversation from herself, said, "If that's the case, I hope you've got a tuxedo in your closet. If you don't, you're going to have to rent one. The whole Homecoming court and their escorts have to be in formal attire for the Homecoming party."

Shane listened quietly, not entirely sure of the information Jill had just relayed to him. To clarify it, he innocently asked, "Jill, are you speaking hypothetically, or are you saying that you expect that I'll be escorting you for Homecoming ... if you win?"

Jill blushed immediately, pulling her hand from Shane's, and putting it to her mouth. Finally, she said, "Shane, I am so sorry ..., I don't even know what I was thinking. We aren't halfway through our second date, and here I am trying to set your social calendar for the next month! I'm embarrassed ... and I'm sorry. I guess... I guess ..."

Shane stopped her from stuttering, saying, "Jill ... Jill, don't be embarrassed! I probably didn't ask my question the right way. I just wanted to make sure I wasn't reading more into your comments than I should have been. If you're telling me that you want me to escort you next month for Homecoming, I'm taking the job before you change your mind. In fact, I'll walk downtown tomorrow to rent the tuxedo."

Jill looked like she might cry, but instead put her arms lightly around Shane's neck. "Shane, I honestly don't know what got into me to be so presumptuous. Thanks for making me feel better."

Shane smiled, then told her, "Excuse the baseball metaphor, Jill, but since we danced last week at the GIGIF I feel like I've been trying to prolong my at-bat with you with a two-strike count against me. I've been chipping away and

84

fouling off pitches … and doing whatever I could to keep the at-bat alive. I think you just gave me a walk, though … and maybe a couple of innings to relax! If I'm not mistaken, Homecoming is still three weeks away, right?"

Jill now laughed at the typical jockstrap analogy, and said, "That isn't the most romantic description of the dating ritual I've ever heard, but I like it. And yes, if you're willing … and if I win … I'd be honored to have you as my escort for all of the Homecoming festivities."

"Hold on there, Jill," said Shane. "If I may make one minor negotiation to this arrangement. I'd like to agree that this deal is only good if I get to escort you to all Homecoming festivities … whether you win or lose."

She pulled Shane's head closer to hers, lightly bumping foreheads. "You're a good negotiator," she laughed. "Deal!"

She'd have kissed him then, long and deeply. Shane didn't press for this, though. Instead, he kept his forehead against hers, until she finally asked, "You didn't mention the GIGIF yesterday. Was it fun?"

"Didn't go," he said.

"Why not?" asked Jill.

You set a pretty high benchmark for GIGIF's, Jill, on my very first one," said Shane. "There wasn't much attraction for me if you weren't going to be there. I caught up on my English Literature reading."

Jill's body control meter was now registering in uncharted territory, and she told her mind to get back in the game. This freshman was either really good, or this was what her parents had always told her about. The Real Thing. She caught herself, remembering that she'd known this boy for only a little over a week, and said, "I can't say that I'm sorry you didn't go to the GIGIF because of me, but that would also indicate that you haven't worked on The Judge anymore either. There's a lighted pavilion over there; my iPhone is fully charged, and I'll be at the GIGIF next week. We need to get this dance down before we show Ten Ton."

Shane laughed, looked at his own phone, and said, "I'm charged up this week as well. We've probably got an hour to work tonight. Do you care that there are still a lot of folks in the park?"

"Do you?" she asked.

"Nope," said Shane, and they made their way to the pavilion.

Shane and Jill worked for almost a half hour with the help of the relatively weak sound from the cell phone before a young couple started watching them near the bandstand. Not too long after, several others were watching, including two families with young children. Finally, a young black teenager and his girlfriend joined the group. The young man was carrying a boom box and, when he heard the song playing from Jill's iPhone, he jumped up onto the band shell with Jill and Shane.

"Hey, Man," he said to Shane. "I've got that song in my mix. Hold on."

Within seconds, the boom box was playing *Here Comes The Judge*, much louder than Jill's iPhone had been. The crowd that had gathered, including old, young, Hispanic, Black and Caucasian, were clapping to the beat as Jill and Shane practiced. The owner of the boom box knew the song well and had taught the crowd the chants to use when the two dancers made the appropriate arm motions. Shane and Jill also taught the younger children some of the dance moves and, somewhere in the evening, Shane had added his own unique move to the dance. Just after one of the repetitive turns, Shane would now disappear toward the bandstand's deck in some sort of leg split, then bounce straight back up, never missing a beat of the music. The scene created a modern day, Norman Rockwell-esque picture that represented what America looked like today. There, on a lighted bandshell next to a small pond at a public park in a little town in Indiana, a freckle-faced strawberry blonde performed with her sandy-haired partner a dance routine to a song by a hip-hop artist named Po Daddy. Their audience, representing a broad range of ethnic backgrounds and age groups, was enthusiastic. Music had somehow created a common denominator for this eclectic group, and all were having fun ... until the boom box batteries finally died.

There was a groan from the audience, but then loud applause for Shane and Jill. The boom box's owner brought a hat up to Jill and handed it to her. It was full of paper money of various denominations. She smiled at the teenager and started to decline the hat, when he stopped her, politely saying, "Ma'am, you and your man here just gave this crowd some of the best entertainment they've seen in months. You probably don't need this ... and I know you didn't expect it ... but if you don't take it, you'll be sending the wrong message. You'll be tellin' these folks that you think you're better than them ..., and that your dance was just your form of charity. It will hurt their feelin's."

Both Shane and Jill listened intently to the well-spoken young man and learned an extremely important lesson about life in the process. Jill took the contents from the hat, gave the teenager a warm hug, and thanked all within earshot. Shane gave the boy his boom box and a fist bump, saying, "Thank you so much for letting us use this."

It was now past 10:00 PM and, this time, when Shane and Jill walked back up the hill toward campus, Shane was holding Jill's hand. Halfway to the college's arched entrance, Jill had transferred her hand to the inside of Shane's arm. They passed Jill's dormitory on their way to the Campus Grille, which would only be open for another 30 minutes. Their second meal together was like their first one a week earlier.

Between bites, Jill, who had paid for dinner out of the funds collected at the park, said, "We still have over fifty dollars left from our tips. What do you want to do with that money, partner?"

"Save it for whatever we do next weekend," said Shane.

"And what will that be?" she asked.

"Jill," he said. "Nothing that I planned the last two weeks really worked ... and everything I didn't plan, did! I'm okay with just sayin' we'll get together next weekend and do something ... if you're okay with that."

She replied, "I'm fine with that ... as long as it's a promise. I've got the car next weekend, so if we want to do something off-campus, we can. Also, remember we've got a performance at the GIGIF on Friday."

"Right," said Shane. "If the weather stays nice, Charlie and I work out on Saturday afternoons. Other than that, my weekend is free ... except I have some serious studying I need to do sometime during the two days."

"Me too," said Jill. "We could study together at the library on Sunday if you want to."

Smiling, Shane said, "That sounds good ... in theory... but it wouldn't work for me. If you happen to be anywhere close, I'm afraid I'd have a hard time keeping my mind on studying."

Jill laughed. "Good. I'm glad to hear that. I'm not sure I'd be much better, so that probably isn't a good idea."

The couple left the grill for Jill's dormitory and, again, were hand in hand. When they arrived near the front of the building, Shane stopped and took Jill's other hand, now facing her. "Thanks for another nice evening, Jill."

"Thank you, Shane. I'm enjoying getting to know you, and I'm having fun too."

"I remember what you said to your brother in the car last week ... about boys getting the wrong idea about what two consecutive dates means. Next week will be number three for us," said Shane. "Does that have any significance?"

Jill smiled and said, "I think we're dating, Shane. Do you have a problem with that?"

"No," he smiled. "I just wanted to make sure we were on the same page." He then bent his head to hers and kissed her on the lips. The kiss was soft, and Jill parted her own lips slightly after it started. Shane kept the kiss warm and moist but didn't allow it to become carnal. He also pulled his head back from the kiss before Jill wanted him to. "Goodnight, Jill. Thanks again."

As she climbed the steps toward her room, Jill's young mind was racing nearly as fast as her heart. She realized that, at some time in the past week, Shane had moved into control of this relationship, and he was going slowly and deliberately. While this was leaving her slightly unfulfilled and wanting more, it also left her looking forward to the next date. "Not a bad thing," she thought.

Charlie and Shane had completed several light workouts during the first several weeks of school, and Charlie continued to be impressed with both Shane's skills and his persona. Shane seemed to be able to throw a baseball to any area that Charlie held his glove and, while his curveball wasn't as accurate, it was still effective. Shane was right about the change-up: he didn't seem to have one, but there was still plenty of time before the season.

Jillian had joined Shane and Charlie for a couple of their sessions. She was a baseball fanatic herself, and she was good company during the workouts. She never interfered and was never impatient for the sessions to end. The couple was equally popular at the Friday GIGIFs, where they had even captured the high praise of Ten Ton for their dancing abilities. At the third or fourth GIGIF of the year, they had surprised Ten Ton, and everyone else, by their own rendition of Denton's dance, The Judge. Shane's attempts to duplicate Ten Ton's facial expressions during the dance had been hilarious, but the couple's coordinated dance moves were Broadway quality. Halfway through the dance, Ten Ton had joined them on the floor, and the three friends had delivered quite a show.

Recruited for his ability to play baseball, Shane had proven to all that there was much more to him than athletics. He had quickly assumed a starring role in campus social life and had become one of Charlie's closest friends. Shane's sweet relationship with Jill didn't get in the way of that friendship and, in some ways, might have enhanced it.

Charlie was, by nature, a relatively private person off the playing field, and living off campus further exaggerated this privacy. When Jill found out from Shane that Charlie did not plan on attending the Homecoming party in October, she told Shane that she didn't think that should be an option. Shane had learned early in their relationship that getting in the way of Jill's opinion was usually not worth the effort. When she told Shane her plan, all he could do was wish her good luck.

Later that week Charlie got a call from his old friend, Doug Jennings. Doug had graduated a year earlier and had been the Monarchs' right fielder. He had been accepted at the prestigious Notre Dame Law School, where he was now attending. "Hey Charlie," said Jennings. "How's it going down there?"

"Great, Doug!" he replied. "I think we've got a heckuva team this year. How's Notre Dame Law?"

"Hard, Charlie …. really, really hard!" said Doug. "That's partly why I'm calling. Linda is the senior attendant for Homecoming this year, and there's no way I can come down there for that weekend. She completely understands, but I don't want her to have to be the only unescorted gal on the Homecoming court, and I also don't want her to miss her last college Homecoming party." Linda Hawkins was Doug's fiancé. They had dated for the last two years and had plans to get married once Doug finished law school. Doug continued, "Someone told me that you didn't plan to attend and, if that's the case, I was wondering if you'd stand in for me with Linda on that weekend?"

"Hold on there, Doug," said Charlie. "You know I'd do just about anything to help you out, but I'm not sure about this. Have you asked Linda about this plan?"

"She's the one who told me about it, Charlie. I think one of her friends on the Homecoming court gave her the idea. Anyway, she'd never call you and be that forward, so I told her I'd call you," said Doug. "You two are friends from all the baseball parties, and I think both of you would have a blast!"

Charlie figured that Jill must be behind all this, but he had one more question for Doug. "You sure you want people calling you up after Homecoming telling you that your fiancé is running around with another ballplayer down here?"

"Ha!" laughed Jennings. "I hope they do! I'd trust you with my life, Charlie, which means I'd also trust you with my wife! You'd be doing me a big favor."

"OK," said Charlie. "I'll give Linda a call and make sure this is all right with her. I've still got a tux from last year when I escorted Paula Cross. It was cheaper to buy a second-hand tux than renting one, and tuxedos don't change much from year to year."

"Thanks, Charlie," ended Jennings.

The fall semester was going well for Charlie. He was on track to graduate with a 3.5 average in his major, Accounting. If he took two more courses in Physics during his final semester, he would also qualify for a minor in that subject. He was still debating that. Physics was a difficult major, usually reserved for Lefton College students who wanted to pursue master's degrees in engineering after they finished at Lefton. Charlie took the various science courses because he enjoyed them. Naturally inquisitive and mechanically adept, he always wanted to know 'how things worked.' He wanted to enjoy his last semester at Lefton without being too tied down to difficult courses and he had no plans to pursue a graduate degree, so whether he burdened himself with two difficult physics courses was still undecided. Charlie was confident that he would be able to find a job after college as an accountant, as his mom had.

The baseball workouts had been fun, so far. Shane was a regular, as were the Junior College transfer, Jack Ryan, and Sam Casey. The team's other starters, Jake Grimsley and Josh Stine, had classes on Tuesdays and Thursdays, but Charlie knew they had also been throwing regularly with Roger Ball, the Monarchs' other catcher. Roger was a sophomore and would probably be the team's regular catcher after Charlie graduated.

Shane was still Charlie's favorite. Besides being naturally talented, he was just a downright nice kid, with no apparent ego. While Charlie had him throw very few full speed fastballs, the ones he had seen needed no work. They were blazing BB's and could be delivered to just about any four-inch area where Charlie placed his glove. Shane's curveball wasn't as reliable in the strike zone but, it, too, was an effective pitch. Charlie was confident that he and

Shane would have a handle on the control issue of the curveball by spring. The change-up was another story. Shane just didn't have one. He knew how to throw it and how to grip the baseball correctly, but something just didn't connect. Shane and Charlie tried different grips with no success and Charlie, at this point, had no answer. Both laughed about this minor flaw, knowing that they still had some months to figure it out.

The two boys became friends outside of the weekly workout schedule, often joining each other for lunch at the Campus Grille. Each had their own set of friends from their respective classes, and Shane had quickly found a girlfriend when he started at Lefton. Jill Long, the sister of one of Charlie's baseball buddies, was also a good friend of Charlie's and had orchestrated an unusual date for him so that Charlie would attend all the recent Homecoming activities with her and Shane. The weekend had been fun and further cemented his friendship with Shane. The three often got together socially on weekends and saw each other enough that Shane's name came up frequently at the Drake dinner table.

"Okay," Jennifer said to Tim one evening. "It has been over a month since I gave you the rest of my life story, including my current terrible dilemma. You were supposed to give me some advice."

"I know," said Tim. "I have thought about it a lot and tried to put myself in each person's shoes who might be affected by knowing the entire history. I still don't have a clear opinion on what you should do. My first instinct would be to go with straight-up honesty, but I understand your concern about the potential that might have to cause problems in Case's current life. You don't know how Julia might react and, if it would be poorly, Case doesn't deserve that. On the other hand, none of these folks deserve to find any of this out by accident either!"

"Right," said Jennifer. "Thanks for not making my decision any easier."

"Sorry," said Tim. "What does your gut say right now?"

"Well, right now, my gut says … 'don't do anything.' I know that makes me seem weak, and I'm not proud of that, but at this moment all those people … you … me … Case … Julia … Shane… Charlie … and my father … are happy. What right do I have to bring any of them news that could make any of them unhappy, just because of mistakes I made years ago?"

"Don't be so hard on yourself," volunteered Tim. "Case was as much a part of the situation as you were!"

"No! No, he wasn't!" said Jennifer, her voice rising a bit. "Sorry, Tim, I didn't mean to raise my voice…but he wasn't. Case didn't do anything wrong. He made no mistakes. He had consensual sex with a young girl and was never told that she had become pregnant. We don't know what he might have done if he had been told, but he wasn't even given the opportunity to do the wrong thing, much less the right thing, whatever the right thing was back then."

"Sorry," said Tim. "I see your point."

"Case has a right to know he fathered another child. He has a right to know the kind of great son he has in Charlie. Charlie has a right to know who his father is. Shane probably has the right to know that his new friend at college, who he worships, is his half-brother! I just don't know that I have the right to potentially upset any of those lives.

"When will you know?" asked Tim.

"I'm not sure, and maybe I'm just stalling," said Jennifer. "But I think I'll know this spring after I've seen Case and his wife. I think that something will give me a signal."

"I don't think anything will change before then," agreed Tim. "I just worry for you that this is going to cause a lot of stress for the next three months."

"Tim, I've handled this stress for about 20 years," said Jennifer. "I can hold on for another three months, I think."

"I'm sort of disappointed," said Shane, "... that you don't want to come to Michigan with my family and ski."

"Shane," said Jill, "... I can't think of anything I'd rather do during the holidays, but number one, I can't ski. Number two, I'm a little afraid to do the 'meet the parents' thing quite yet... especially when the commitment is a whole week... with no escape."

"Okay," said Shane, "... but, number one, I can teach you to ski and, number two, what scares you about my parents?"

Jill smiled, and said, "Nothing scares me about your parents, Shane. I enjoyed meeting them when they picked you up for Thanksgiving. It's just... well... I guess it's just... that you are so important to me right now... that I don't want to take a chance on anything bad happening. You have told me that you held back with 'stuff' from me for the same reason... that you didn't want our moving too fast to ruin anything. That may have been the most romantic thing I ever heard! And, I get it! I feel the same way! Being with your family for a week would probably be fantastic... but I don't want to take any chance right now... that it wouldn't be."

"I understand," said Shane. "I do. I know I'm still young, but I've never experienced a relationship quite like the one I have with you. The term 'love' seems to be so overused that I'm a little confused at what it really entails. I'm not sure I'm even knowledgeable enough to legitimately use the term, but I know my feelings for you are pretty strong."

"I know exactly what you mean, Shane," Jill responded, laughing. "I don't know how many times I've heard girlfriends of mine say they were 'in love' when they were in high school ... and I just thought it was a term they used to justify sex. I'm pretty sure they were in 'lust' ... not necessarily 'love.'"

"Right," agreed Shane. "I think the word is supposed to mean more than that, don't you?"

"I do, Shane," she replied. "I believe the human physical attraction is important, but that real love requires a mental attraction as well."

"Yes!" agreed Shane. "When I first saw you dancing with Ten Ton, I couldn't take my eyes off you. I thought you were so cute ... and that was the purely physical attraction. It wasn't until after we spent most of that evening talking that I realized I really *liked* you as well."

Jill smiled, and said, "I remember seeing you watching me during that dance. I wanted to take a good look at you, myself ... but I couldn't, because every time I looked your way, I caught you looking at me!"

"Sorry," said Shane. "I didn't know it was that obvious!"

"Don't be sorry," she replied. "If it hadn't been that obvious, I'd have never followed Danny over to your group to check you out. When that night was over, I was glad I had made the extra effort. I enjoyed talking to *you* that evening as well."

"I'm still developing my own theories about 'love,'" said Shane, "... but I'm starting to think that there is no one, specific, correct definition. I think that each case is sort of custom-designed, unique, and made up of a lot of different things."

"I've never heard it described that way," said Jill, "but I think your theory has some merit. My mom thinks that 'love' is just the most extreme form of 'like.' She makes me laugh when she says it but, in her words, 'love will provide the sparks at night, but it's the like that gets you through the day!'"

Shane laughed and said, "That is funny! I'm going to write it down! Your mom may also be right, though. As much as I enjoy moments like this when I can be close to you, I also look forward to the times when we can just hang out. I like doing everyday things with you ... and talking to you."

"Yeah," Jill answered. "Me too ... but right now I think you said you wanted to work on our slow dancing technique ... right? By my watch, we only have a couple of hours."

The young couple was having a very philosophical dialogue about the mysteries of love while they lay next to each other, fully clothed, on a queen-sized bed at the Hampton Inn in downtown Indianapolis. Jill had checked into the room a little after 4:00 PM while Shane waited in her car. The room was being expensed to Lefton College as a part of Jill's internship requirement at the Indianapolis Psychiatric Hospital. Her observation shift at the hospital began the following morning at 5:00 AM and the College's Psychology Department preferred that their intern students arrive the evening before.

It was Jill who floated the idea of driving Shane to his home in Indianapolis that weekend, perhaps with a stop at her hotel on the way. Her suggestion was bold, direct, and left no question as to her intentions. She had further advised him that if he agreed to the plan, he should come prepared. By way of an explanation, Jill told Shane that she was not interested in having intimate moments behind a vacant building, in a small car, or in a dormitory room. That was just not her style. She explained to Shane that, in her opinion, their relationship had reached a point where, as a couple, each was feeling strong desires that would eventually have to be satisfied, one way or another. She hoped that they might address these needs as thinking adults rather than as irresponsible, lovesick teenagers.

Shane was surprised by her suggestion, but he had gotten used to Jill's forthright, no-nonsense, style. He had no good reasons to decline the invitation ... and many to accept it ... which he did. Typical of their relationship to date, they had spent the first 30 minutes of their limited time in the hotel room in intelligent conversation. During the next hour and a half, they practiced many things.

As they prepared to leave the room and head to Shane's home, Shane stopped Jill at the door. "Jill," he said, "We talked a little bit about this earlier, but I need you to know something. I love you. I don't think I have a complete understanding of the concept yet, but whatever I don't understand, I'd like to continue to learn with you ... not somebody else."

Jill was visibly touched and put her arms around Shane's neck. "I don't want to abuse the term either, Shane, but I've been sure that I loved you since our second date. I think you're probably right about having much to learn, but you're the only one I want to go to school with."

"Okay," said Shane. "...for the last several months we've been 'dating.' What is it called that we're doing now?"

"I think we're 'going together' now," said Jill, smiling. "In fact, I think I'm your girlfriend now."

"Good," said Shane, "... then that's what I'm going to tell my parents."

"Hmm," said Jill, "... what else are you going to tell them?"

Shane said, "That we had a very nice drive from Lefton."

Both laughed, and when she dropped Shane off at his house, Jill told him she'd pick him up around five o'clock the following day to return to campus. Shane warned her that having dinner with his parents before they started back to the college would be expected. She agreed that would be fine.

When Jill arrived in the little Renault to pick Shane up, she was invited inside for dinner, as Shane had warned she would be. She put the car in the driveway and accompanied Shane into the house. "Mr. and Mrs. Reynolds," she said as she entered the house, "Thank you so much for inviting me to dinner! It sure beats my plan to stop on the outskirts of town at the nearest McDonald's."

"Jill," said Julia, "we're just glad you can join us ... and thank you for bringing Shane home this weekend!"

"Believe me," said Jill, "that was my pleasure. I hate driving alone, and Shane is great company."

"Tell us about what you're doing at the Psychiatric Hospital," said Case. "Shane was a bit vague with details."

Jill laughed easily and said, "Well, that's probably because we don't talk much about our courses. I doubt that Shane would have any idea of what I do when I come out here to the hospital. I'm taking my second year of Psychology this year, and one of my assignments is a thesis on some aspects of modern day treatment of Alzheimer's. One of our professors at Lefton has a relationship with Indianapolis Psychiatric Hospital, and the hospital has been kind enough to allow Lefton students to do some limited research at the hospital."

"Wow," said Case. "I'm impressed. Are you a Psych major?"

"Yes, sir," replied Jill. "I'm hoping to go to medical school after Lefton College."

"I see," said Case. "What does your research at the hospital involve?"

"I come out about once per month to have monitored dialogues with certain types of patients at the hospital," replied Jill. "My thesis is on a phenomenon called 'Post Selective Memory Disorder,' and the hospital has several physicians performing clinical studies on the condition. They allow me to follow the progress of several select patients who are being treated for this disorder here in Indianapolis."

"Good for Lefton College," said Julia. "I had no idea that a small college could create such unusual opportunities for its students."

"Yes," agreed Jill. "It is pretty amazing. I have friends who attend IU who don't seem to be able to get this kind of access inside a real-time research hospital."

Julia said, "I'd like to hear more about your thesis, Jill. Let's sit down at the table, and you can tell us over dinner."

After everyone was at the table, Jill told them a little more, before refocusing the conversation on Case's business. Case gave her the short version, before volleying the conversation back her way. "Shane tells us," said Case, "that you also have a brother at Lefton College."

"Yes sir, I do," answered Jill. "Jud is a senior, and he's also on the baseball team with Shane."

"Is that a good thing or a bad thing, having an older brother at school?" asked Julia.

Jill smiled and said, "Definitely a good thing! I'm going to miss him next year after he graduates. Thanks to Jud, though, I have a lot of other 'big brothers' on campus.

Most of the guys on the baseball team are like brothers to me."

"Sounds like he's taken good care of you, Jill," said Case. "We're looking forward to meeting all the guys in the spring. Shane has already told us a lot about the catcher, Charlie Hamilton. I guess you know him as well?"

"Know him?" said Jill. "I'm almost as close to Charlie as I am Jud! Shane has probably already told you what a great guy Charlie is."

"We have gotten that impression," laughed Case. "It sounds like Charlie may have also adopted Shane as a little brother."

"Well, that would be Charlie, for sure," said Jill. "... and, if that's the case, Shane is a lucky man. You couldn't have a better big brother than Charlie!"

Shane laughed at this comment, adding, "I agree with Jill, Dad. Charlie is every bit as awesome as Jill describes, and I feel lucky to have made such good friends as both Jill and him this semester."

Julia smiled and said, "That makes us, as parents, feel pretty lucky too, Shane. I've got a pie in the kitchen if anybody has room for dessert."

"My goodness ... no!" said Jill. "I have eaten like a pig. Everything was so good Mrs. Reynolds, but I couldn't eat another bite. Let me help you clean the table, though."

"Not a chance, Jill!" said Julia. "You've got a two-hour drive back to Lefton. Case and I can clean the dishes... you two get on the road. I'll pack the pie to take with you. Also, by the way, why don't you call me Julia ... and that's Case," she said, pointing to her husband.

Jill blushed lightly, and said, "Thank you ... Julia ... and Case. Dinner was wonderful."

After the young couple had gotten out of the driveway, Case met Julia in the den. Case asked first, "What do you think?"

Julia answered, "Only one word comes to mind. Wow!"

"That's the same word I was thinking," said Case.

"Case, I have to admit to you that I was looking for reasons not to like Jill. I wasn't sure that I liked the idea of Shane meeting a girl in his first week of school and immediately starting a relationship. I thought he should probably be dating around a bit. Now, though, after meeting Jill, I find it hard to imagine that there is a more grounded, mature, young lady than Jill on the Lefton College campus."

"You left out 'pretty,' Julia," said Case.

Julia laughed and said, "Beauty is in the eye of the beholder, Case... but, no ... her looks weren't lost on me. Are we missing something?"

"I don't think so," said Case. "I thoroughly enjoyed her company this evening and can find no fault in Shane's judgment."

"I liked what she said about Charlie, too," said Julia. "Did Shane mention to you that he might ask Charlie to go with us to Michigan in January?"

"He did," said Case. "He asked if it would be okay with me yesterday while we were watching the ballgame. I told him I'd love to have Charlie join us but would also check with you. I forgot to do that today, dear."

"It's okay," said Julia. "He asked me what I thought this morning and I told him the same thing you did. It will be great to have Charlie join us. After hearing Jill talk about him, I can't wait to get to know him. Were all the students at this school like these two when you went there, Case?"

Case laughed and said, "I can't remember, dear. It was too long ago."

In December, before the holidays, Charlie was home and having dinner with his mom and Tim. When dinner was over, Charlie asked, "Are we doing anything special over the January break this year?"

Jennifer looked at Tim, and answered, "Well, Tim and I were going to ask you the same thing ... sort of. Tim won a trip from one of the drug companies and, if we want to, we can go to Cancun for four days during the January break. We were going to check to make sure that wouldn't interfere with any of your plans, Charlie."

"No, not at all, Mom!" said Charlie. "That sounds like fun. You should go. Shane's family is going skiing in Michigan in January, and Shane asked if I'd like to go with them."

Jennifer's face colored noticeably, and she answered, "Oh, well ... oh, ... how nice of him. Is his family okay with that?"

"Yes, they're fine with it. They have a four-bedroom cabin rented, and skis and equipment are already provided. Lift tickets are also included, and Shane said they'd love for him to have a friend join them. I thought he might want to take Jill, his girlfriend, but he says she's not ready yet for parent prime time."

"Wow ... well ... I guess that will be fine," Jennifer stuttered. "Is Coach Blevins okay with two of his stars skiing just before spring practice starts?"

"Mom! This is Division III! Of course, he doesn't care. He just said to be careful. You're acting like you don't want me to go."

"Oh, no, Charlie," she replied. "It's not that. It's just ... well, it's just ..."

Tim interrupted, "It's just that she's your mom, and she feels that it's necessary to worry about everything! Sounds like a great opportunity. Have fun!"

"Yes," recovered Jennifer. "Absolutely! Have fun!"

After Charlie went to his room, Jennifer sat down next to Tim in the den. "Now what?" she asked.

"What do you mean, 'now what?'" he replied. "Nothing has changed. Charlie is going to Michigan to ski, not for DNA testing!"

"But when Case sees Charlie and the resemblance, he's bound to start asking Charlie about his family," said Jennifer.

"Number one," replied Tim, "it's a stretch to think Case is going to be looking for a family resemblance from one of Shane's friends from college. Number two, even if he does, what's he going to do?"

"Well, if Charlie happens to tell him that his mother was Jennifer Hamilton, and then Case happens to start doing the math backward from Charlie's age, he could become curious," said Jennifer.

"Yes, he could ... but that's a lot of 'ifs.' And if he does become curious, you may get a call from him sometime after the ski trip. That will be the signal you've been waiting for," said Tim.

"Okay, thanks," said Jennifer. "I think you're right. He certainly wouldn't say anything to Charlie or his wife before having a conversation with me."

"If he *ever* has a conversation with you," said Tim.

"Right!" answered Jennifer.

Jennifer retired to her bedroom, unable to get that blasted baseball metaphor that her dad always used out of her mind. *Full Count.* The pitches seemed to be mounting up, and she felt sure that an action pitch was imminent. She had another restless night of sleep.

Shane and Charlie were waiting in front of their dorm when Case and Julia pulled up to the curb in the big Suburban. The boys were each standing in front of one small suitcase, and each had a backpack strapped to his shoulder.

"Wow," said Case, as he got out of the car. "You guys are efficient packers! Just throw the suitcases in the back." As he opened the back hatch, he reached his right hand out to Charlie saying, "Charlie, I'm Case Reynolds."

Charlie responded with a firm handshake, "It's nice to meet you, Mr. Reynolds. Thank you for inviting me."

"We are glad to have you, Charlie. Shane has told us a lot about you. By the way, just call me Case."

"Thank you, sir," replied Charlie. Glancing at the roof of the car, Charlie saw three sets of skis on racks, and said, "I don't have skis, sir. Shane said that your lodge was already equipped with some gear, and if none of that fits, I can rent some skis and boots on the mountain."

"Shane was correct." replied Case. "Supposedly, the cabin has quite a bit of gear in a special locker or closet there, but we'll take care of renting some gear for you if what they have doesn't work."

"Thank you, sir," said Charlie, "but you don't have to do that. I brought some money for food and anything else I might need."

Case looked at Shane, then back at Charlie. "Perhaps my son wasn't clear in his invitation to you,

Charlie, but you are our guest this week. There will be no arguments about who foots the bill for your expenses."

"Well, thank you, sir, but I fully expected to pay my share of any extra expenses," said Charlie.

"I'm sure you were," replied Case, "and I'm appreciative of your offer, but this is one way that I can ensure that I always have company on the mountain. Shane has learned over the years that hanging close to me around lunchtime at the ski resorts pays some dividends." He was smiling at both Charlie and his son.

"Okay. If you insist ... but thank you very much."

"You're welcome, now let's get going. My GPS says we can be on the mountain in three and a half hours, and there is more snow on the way for up there later this evening."

When the boys got into the car, Shane introduced Charlie to his mother, Julia, who was in the front seat. "Charlie, we are so glad that you could come with us on this trip. Are you an avid skier?"

"Thank you, ma'am," said Charlie. "I would call myself an enthusiastic skier. My form isn't beautiful, but I can get down most hills."

"Well, the Michigan hills aren't too overwhelming," replied Julia, "... which, by the way, suits me just fine. Charlie, is there a drugstore nearby we could visit before getting on the highway? I didn't pack any lip balm and, according to the weather forecast, I'm going to need some."

"Sure, Mrs. Reynolds," said Charlie. "Drake's Pharmacy is just around the corner. Tim Drake owns it. He's sort of my stepdad."

"Great!" replied Julia, not sure how to address Charlie's description of Tim. "Will he be there this afternoon? And, by the way, you can call me Julia."

"No," replied Charlie. "He and my mom left this morning for Cancun for a few days. I know everyone at the store, though. I can run in and get the lip balm."

"You don't have to do that, Charlie," replied Julia. "I want to use the restroom before we get on the Interstate, anyway." Looking at her husband and smiling, she continued, "Shane's dad doesn't like stopping much once he gets underway."

Julia got out of the car at the drugstore and returned in a matter of minutes with four tubes of Chapstick. "What a nice little drug store!" she said. "Case, it has the cutest retail area and a soda counter and the friendliest employees!" To Charlie, she said, "Your dad runs a great looking business, Charlie."

"Thanks, Mrs. Reynolds ... I mean, Julia," replied Charlie. "But Tim isn't my dad. He married my mom when I was about five, and he's done everything a dad should do and more, but since I'm not officially 'adopted,' I'm not sure I can call him my stepdad. He's my friend, I know that!"

"Well, he sounds like a great guy," replied Julia.

"He is that!" answered Charlie.

As the Suburban rumbled onto the interstate, the car became quiet. Charlie and Shane both had earbuds connected to their phones and were listening to music. Shane appeared to be nodding off already. In a voice that nobody in the backseat could hear, Case said to Julia, "Wonder what happened to his biological father. Divorce? Died?"

Julia answered, "Don't know, Case, but we shouldn't pry. It may be a sensitive situation."

"Right," said Case. "He couldn't have made a better first impression on me. Polite; respectful; no problems communicating with adults. I can see why Shane is so fond of him. Do we know his mother's name yet?"

"I don't think so," replied Julia. "He hasn't mentioned her name today, and I don't believe I have heard Shane mention it on any of our phone calls. Why do you ask?"

"No reason," replied Case. "I'm sure we'll know all there is to know about Charlie's family by the end of the week. One thing seems clear, and that is, whoever has raised him seems to have done a good job."

"Yes," agreed Julia. "Shane has always had a knack for gravitating to a good class of friends. Looks like he's done it again."

As the car continued up the mostly deserted Interstate, all the occupants, except the driver, were soon asleep. When Case announced that they were making the last exit for the ski village, bodies began to stir again. As the car pulled up the lane toward the cabin, Case asked Julia if the rental company had mailed her a key. "No," she replied. "I'm supposed to find a key under a flowerpot near the door."

"Well, I see a door," said Case. "And sure enough, there's a flower pot too!"

Julia found the key and opened the door as the rest of the car's occupants started gathering suitcases. When they entered the cabin, all were impressed with the size of the den and were surprised that a fire already blazed in the fireplace. Julia soon found a note from the property manager indicating he had started the fire about an hour before in anticipation of their arrival. He provided his personal contact information, as well as instructions on how to use the TV remotes. His last sentence indicated that the Reynolds were welcome to any food or beverage left by the previous occupants. He explained that the rental company's policy did not require renters to remove unopened food or beverages at the end of their stay. On the mountain, local protocol suggested that new renters enjoy what was left for them by previous renters and then leave something behind for the next renters.

"I like that policy," said Shane, surveying the selection of fruits and cheeses left in the refrigerator.

"Me too," yelled Charlie, as he opened one of the kitchen cabinets. "Look at all these cereals!"

"Wow," said Case as he glanced over Shane's shoulder into the ample refrigerator, "Look at all that beer!"

Shane and Charlie glanced at each other, as Julia came over to the refrigerator. "Hmmm," she said coyly, looking at her husband," Not sure you and I can finish that much beer in a week, Case!"

Charlie offered, somewhat shyly, "Actually, I turned 21 last March, so I might be able to help a little."

"Great," said Case, glancing at his son. "Shane, I don't suppose you've been introduced to beer at the college yet, have you?"

"Oh, Dad," sighed Shane. "You're joking with me, right? I'm not going to lie to you. There has been a little beer at a few of the parties at Lefton."

"Yes, Shane," said Case, "I'm playing with you, son! When your mom and I cleaned out the basement this summer, it appears that there may have been a little beer at some of your parties downstairs during high school as well, judging by the empty beer cans we found under the couches." Case was smiling, and Julia was giving her husband a hard stare.

"Oops," said Shane.

"Shane," said Julia. "We're not idiots, and we're not naïve, either. We know what goes on in high school and at college. We trusted you to be responsible in high school, and we're certain that you are still using good judgment at Lefton."

"Absolutely, son," said Case. "There was a reason we preferred that your senior year parties be held in our basement, versus someone else's. And when some of your friends decided to spend the night at our place versus driving home after a couple of those events, we gave them personal points for good judgment. Relax, son! You're an adult now. We can't monitor everything you do anymore, but we trust that you'll continue to use the good judgment you displayed when you lived in our home. Drinking beer, or any other kind of alcohol, before you're 21 ... isn't immoral ... it's just illegal. Be smart about when and where you do it."

Shane said, "Thanks, Dad," and then, without missing a beat from his dad's speech, asked," Do you think that this cabin is fairly safe?"

Case, Julia, and Charlie all laughed, and Case answered, "Help yourself!"

Julia, still laughing, said, "I thought we'd have to go out for dinner this evening, but I think there is enough food in this refrigerator to eat here instead. Would anybody be opposed to settling in here and having soup and sandwiches a little later, versus going out?"

"Not me," said Case. "Especially if that means that I can have one of those beers now."

"I'd rather stay here, Mom," chimed in Shane.

"Sounds great to me, too," said Charlie, adding, "I'm not a great cook, but I can handle soup and sandwiches. Let me help you with dinner."

"No way, Charlie!" said Julia. "You and Shane go pick rooms upstairs, then I think you need to check the equipment locker in the garage. If you can't find boots that fit or skis that will work, we may still have to go down to the village this evening to rent some equipment. I can handle the soup and sandwiches as long as nobody puts a stopwatch on me!"

Charlie and Shane retreated with their suitcases upstairs, where they had a choice of three bedrooms to choose from. One of the rooms had bunk beds; another had a king-sized bed, and the third had two queen-sized beds. All the upstairs rooms shared a single large bathroom. Charlie, sensing that Shane, as a good host, would offer him the bigger room with a king-sized bed, immediately picked the slightly smaller room with the queens.

The boys then went downstairs and out to the garage, where there was a long rack of skis against the far wall. Boots of varying sizes were arranged on a bench neatly in front of the skis. Case followed them to this area, with a cold bottle of beer in his hand.

"Wow," said Charlie. "This place really does come outfitted!"

"What size boot do you wear?" called Shane, looking at the assortment available on the bench.

"Usually a ten," said Charlie, "...but I can go a little larger if I need to."

"That's my size, too," said Shane. "Looks like your choices are a nine and a half or a ten and a half in the men's boots that are here."

When Charlie tried on the 10 ½, he proclaimed that they would work just fine with an extra pair of socks. He picked a pair of new-looking performance skis from the rack that were only slightly longer than he was tall.

"These are a little longer than I usually use," Charlie said, "but I think they'll work just fine."

"Great," said Case. "I think we're ready, then. I've got the UCLA/Oregon basketball game on upstairs, and that beer in the refrigerator is cold. I'll warn you in advance, though. I don't think there are two of any one kind of beer in the whole selection. It's a pretty eclectic mix."

"We aren't exactly beer connoisseurs yet, Dad. I don't think that will matter much," laughed Shane.

The little vacation had gotten off to a great start, and the dinner conversation was easy and animated. Charlie fit into the group as if he had been a part of it for years. There was much laughter, some funny stories, and not a single awkward moment. When the talk finally turned to baseball, it was Shane who told Charlie that his dad had also once been a catcher for Lefton College.

"I think I've heard Coach Blevins mention that," said Charlie. "Is that why you chose Lefton College, Shane?"

"Well," answered Case for his son. "That was partly it, but there were some other dynamics involved. Stu Blevins was only in his second year of coaching when I got to Lefton, but he was a great guy back then, and it seems like he is still a great coach now."

"He is," replied Charlie. "I didn't know that he had coached that long at Lefton. When did you play for him?"

"1986 through 1990," said Case. "I was only the starting catcher in '89 and '90, though. Blevins thought I was too small to be a catcher, and it took me two years to prove that he was wrong," said Case, laughing.

"I had the same problem as a freshman," related Charlie. "... but It only took me one practice to prove him wrong."

"How'd you pull that off?" asked Case.

"I showed him that I couldn't begin to catch a ball with anything but a catcher's mitt!" All at the table were laughing at Charlie's story, when Charlie asked, "If you were at Lefton between 1986 and 1990, you might have known my mom. She started there in 1987 and graduated in 1992, I think."

"Sounds like our years there certainly overlapped," said Case. "What was your mom's name back then?"

"Jennifer Hamilton. She was an accounting major, and she still works at the college as the Controller."

Case put his beer down and put one hand under his chin. Sparks were flicking in his brain, and he didn't know quite why. "Jennifer Hamilton ...," he repeated. "I <u>do</u> remember her, Charlie. She was a junior when I was a senior, and I seem to remember that she was a really good dancer."

"Really?" asked Charlie. "I don't think I've ever seen her dance. Do you mean like a ballet dancer or just regular dancing?"

"I wouldn't call it just regular dancing," said Case. "If your mom is the same one I'm remembering, she could do a dance called the Shag better than any other girl at the school."

"Wow," said Charlie. "Doesn't really sound like my mom, but I'll have to ask her about that when I get home."

"Yes," said Case. "Do that. I am looking forward to meeting both her and Tim when the baseball season starts this spring."

Julia watched the interchange with interest. After nearly 20 years of marriage to Case, she could almost read his mind, and she could tell that something was going on in it right now. After the boys had gone to their rooms, she sat down with Case in front of the dying fire in the den. "Great night," she said.

"Yes, it was," said Case. "Those boys are terrific company! I'd hire that Charlie for our company, Julia, if he were available!"

"I agree," she replied. "He's quite a young man. Were you surprised that you knew his mother from college?"

"Yes," said Case. "I was. That has been bothering me for some reason, and I can't quite put my finger on why. I'm not even sure I remember Charlie's mom much as a student. I remember a party after graduation where she and I danced a lot. I saw her shagging with one of her girlfriends and, since I knew how to shag, I asked her to dance. It was fun, but I reported to Airborne Training at Benning about two weeks after that dance. I never heard from her after I went to Fort Benning."

"Why is it bothering you, then?" asked Julia

"I don't know. I honestly don't know. She's the Controller for the college. Don't you think she knows that Shane is the son of someone she knew from school? Yet, the fact that I was at Lefton during some of the same years as his mother was news to Charlie this evening."

"Well, Dear," said Julia, "...maybe you didn't make as big an impression on her as you hoped," jabbed the smiling Julia.

Case smiled at his wife, and said, "Guess not. We'll be seeing Jennifer and her husband in a couple of months. Maybe she'll recognize me then."

"She certainly should," answered Julia, "... since when Charlie gets home from this trip, he'll be asking his mom what she was doing dancing with Shane's dad 20 years ago. I'm betting it won't take Charlie long to follow up with his mom about tonight's dinner conversation."

Case laughed, "Probably right." Then contemplatively, still turning the conundrum going on in his head around again, he asked Julia, "Why does Charlie still use Jennifer's last name? That wouldn't indicate that there had been a divorce."

"Don't know," said Julia, "but let's go to bed before your fragile ego becomes further shattered."

"You're funny," replied Case. They retired to their suite on the first level, but Case couldn't make his mind stop working.

The rest of the vacation was nearly perfect, with lots of skiing, good food, and many laughs. Toward the end of the trip, Case and Charlie had spent quite a bit of time talking about Case's business, and Case had openly inquired about Charlie's plans after graduation. When Charlie got back to Lefton, his mind was spinning with life possibilities. He had fun with Shane's family and was looking forward to the coming baseball season more than ever. He had also decided to add the two physics courses to his load for the final semester. And finally, he needed to talk to his mom about a long-ago dance!

When Jennifer came through the door, Charlie was waiting anxiously for her. He hugged her, and Jennifer asked him, "How was the trip, Charlie? Did you have fun?"

"It was great, Mom. Shane's family is nice, and the skiing was great! How was Cancun?"

"Frankly, a bit of a tourist trap, but Tim and I enjoyed the beach. It was a nice little break ... and the price was right!" related Jennifer.

"Guess what, Mom? You know Shane's dad."

"What?" questioned Jennifer hesitantly, "What do you mean?"

"He went to school at Lefton at the same time you did ... well, I think maybe he was a year ahead of you. But he remembers dancing with you at a party after he graduated. He said you were an amazing Shag dancer. I didn't know you liked to dance!" Charlie's words were tumbling almost faster than Jennifer could follow them.

"My goodness, Charlie, slow down!" said Jennifer, her own mind spinning, her heartbeat quickening, and her breath now only coming in short spurts. "What is Shane's dad's name?" she asked, stalling for time to think.

"Case Reynolds, and his wife's name is Julia" answered Charlie. "He was the catcher for the Monarchs and, after college, he was in the Army. Do you remember him?"

She felt trapped and was regretting her decision to look for a signal to resolve all the secrecy of the past two decades with the appropriate players. This was certainly a signal but, at this point, she had no idea of what other things Case and Charlie might have talked about in Michigan. She looked at her son, feigning some confusion, saying, "Case Reynolds? Case Reynolds ... well, of course, I remember him. He was one of the most popular men on our campus, and he wasn't just a catcher. He was one of the stars of the Monarch team, just like you are. What a coincidence!"

"So, do you remember dancing with him at some party?" continued Charlie.

"That was a long time ago, Charlie, but ... yes, I think I remember that dance. Case could do a dance called the Shag well, and Grandma Floe had taught me how to do the dance when I was a little girl. Case and I were probably the only two kids in Indiana that knew how to do a dance invented in Myrtle Beach, South Carolina."

Breathe! she told herself. *Try to look normal. Find an exit from this conversation - to think!* she thought, but Charlie was persistent.

"That is a coincidence, then," said Charlie. "Did you know that he had a son who was coming to the college?"

To herself, she thought, *I knew he had a son at the college, but I had no idea that he would be sending another son to the school.* Instead of telling Charlie what had gone through her head, she said, "No, Charlie. I had no idea. I haven't seen Case or talked to him since he left the campus over 20 years ago. It's a small world after all, isn't it?"

"I guess so," answered Charlie. "I thought the whole story was kinda neat, Mom. Mr. and Mrs. Reynolds are terrific folks, and it was nice to hear that Mr. Reynolds had a good memory of you as well."

Back in Indianapolis, the Reynolds unpacked the Suburban and critiqued their trip to Michigan. "Don't think I've ever enjoyed a family trip more," stated Case. "As usual, dear, thanks for taking care of most of the meals. I had envisioned dining out more than we did, but it seemed like the boys just wanted to hang at the cabin every day after skiing."

"I enjoyed cooking for them, Case," answered Julia. "Both of them were so appreciative ... they made me feel like I was Indiana's best chef."

"Well, I think you are!" smiled Case. "It's nice to be recognized occasionally, though."

"Did you notice that I did no laundry the entire week?" asked Julia. "By the time I was up every morning, the boys had already started a load ... both our stuff and theirs," said Julia.

"That's new," replied Case. "Laundry has never been Shane's strong suit. Must be something rubbing off from Charlie."

"Maybe," said Julia. "Charlie certainly seems like a positive influence in many areas."

"Yep. I like that boy ... well, really ... he's a man," said Case. "Did you hear us talking about our business?"

"Yes, I did," said Julia. "What was that about? You trying to recruit him already?" Julia said, smiling.

"Wouldn't be the worst thing I could do," said Case. "I didn't start any of the conversations about BRET or BRIC, Julia. Charlie initiated those. I think he had a sincere interest in knowing about our businesses. He's getting an Accounting degree, but he has taken a lot of Science courses. He had lots of questions about the different alternative energy technologies."

"Well, he graduates in May," said Julia. "What are you thinking?"

Case smiled and said, "Not really thinking anything yet. Let's see how the baseball season goes. I'm sure we'll find out what Charlie has in mind for after graduation as we get to know him and his family better this spring."

"Sounds like a plan," she replied. "Now, I'm tired, and I'm going to bed unless you have anything else that would require my company."

"No," smiled Case. "I'm tired too. I'll be up in a few minutes."

After Julia had gone upstairs, Case went to the other side of the house where he had a small office. After booting his computer up, he entered a series of queries from the online records available from Hancock County, Indiana. With the help of Google, it only took a few minutes for him to get the information he was seeking. In front of him, next to the blinking cursor, he read:

As he scrolled down the pages, he came to March 10th, 1991:

3/10/1991
Time of Birth: 6:58 AM
Sex: M
Weight: 6 lb. 10 Oz
Disposition: Healthy
Name: Charles Claude Hamilton
Mother's Name: Jennifer Elizabeth Hamilton
Father's Name: Unnamed

That solved the lingering question that Case had relative to Charlie's father. During the ski trip, no conversations that related to Charlie's family had occurred after the first evening. The online public record in front of him would indicate that Jennifer had not been married at the time of Charlie's birth. Furthermore, if the identity of Charlie's biological father was known to Jennifer, she was unwilling to list it on the birth certificate. Case thought back to the brief time he had known Jennifer at Lefton College and decided there was no way that she would not know who the father of her baby was. She was too buttoned down as a student and certainly didn't seem the type that would have had multiple sex partners. In fact, as he remembered back, the only attempt at intercourse that Case and Jennifer had made, which had occurred at her parents' house after that dance at the VFW, had been amateurish on both his part and hers. Neither of them seemed to have had much practice at that point in their lives.

BUT ... there it was! There *had* been that one awkward encounter!

Case got a calendar out of the top desk drawer and counted nine months back from March 10th. June 10th stared back at him. He graduated during the first week of June, and the party in which he had danced with Jennifer was a few days after that. Less than two weeks after that, he had reported to Fort Benning.

Case's hands felt a little sweaty as he considered the remote possibility that was now floating around his head. It was probably just coincidental timing but, in Case's business, he had learned that very little was coincidental. He now had more questions than answers, but he was at a roadblock. He couldn't badger Charlie with questions. He wasn't about to pick up the phone and start asking Charlie's mom questions either. His progress seemed to be checked for the time being. The baseball season was just around the corner, though. There would be other opportunities to make some additional casual inquiries.

"Jennifer," said Tim, "don't jump to conclusions. A very natural sounding conversation between Case and Charlie occurred, and Charlie discovered that Case had danced with you a long time ago. So far, that's all anyone knows. If Case had developed real anxiety about the timing of that dance, don't you think you'd have heard from him by now?"

"No, I don't," said Jennifer. "He's a smart man, and I think he's a good man. No matter what he may be thinking, he would not be the type to potentially insult me with prying questions of such a personal nature. He may have concerns, and maybe even some theories, but he doesn't know enough yet, to be able to come to verifiable conclusions."

"Okay," said Tim. "I agree, so what makes you think this is a signal?"

"I don't know, Tim," answered Julia. I have felt that, at some point, I would know whether my secrets could remain secrets, or whether they would have to be revealed. I think this is the signal that, sooner or later, they *will* have to come out. If I don't do it the right way, the truth could come out in the wrong way. I've got important responsibilities to both Case's family and mine to make sure things are handled well, and not poorly. Right now isn't the time to act yet, but I think the question of IF I act is answered. Now, the only question remaining is WHEN."

"Jennifer," said Tim, "I'm so sorry that a series of random coincidences has created this situation for you. What were the odds of Case settling back in Indiana after recovering from his injuries in Texas? What were the odds of his superstar son not going to Indiana University and coming to Lefton College instead? And what were the odds that Case's first son, who he doesn't even know about yet, and his second son would be close enough in age to attend the same college at the same time?"

Jennifer answered, "I don't know, Tim. I'm not an overly religious person, but I leave room in my beliefs for the possibility there is something powerful and divine that has a master plan for our lives and our universe. It seems like a lot of coincidences have led us to where we are. Maybe that trail was made for a purpose. I don't know, and I don't know how this will turn out, but I need to do everything I can to try to make it turn out well for everyone."

"So, what do you think is next," asked Tim.

"I think that sometime after the baseball season starts, the right opportunity will present itself. If something happens to expedite that schedule, I'll be prepared," said Jennifer.

Charlie's academic load in the second semester, with the addition of the two Physics courses, was significant for a senior. That, however, didn't impact his workout schedule. As the first day of baseball practice got closer, his excitement for the coming season got greater. That feeling seemed to be shared among the rest of the players as well. The pitching sessions were more intense and lasted longer. The batting cages were occupied for increasingly longer hours after classes. The gym always had a baseball player in it who was lifting weights, doing pull-ups, or running the bleachers.

Knowing that their weekend social schedule would soon be curtailed by baseball activities, ballplayers were also enjoying some of their last GIGIFs for the year. On one Friday near the end of the month, the usual group of friends had gathered at Frocks. A band named Rotogilla was providing the entertainment and Charlie was watching Jill and Shane on the dance floor. Standing next to him were Jud and Danny. When the music stopped, Shane and Jill started edging through the crowd toward Charlie. On the way, Shane got bumped pretty hard by another student who had appeared to lose his balance. Shane had started to react, but Jill pushed him toward Charlie and Jud. As they arrived, Charlie heard Jill say, "It isn't worth it, Shane. Ignore it."

"What's going on?" asked Charlie.

"Oh nothing," answered Jill. "Just an immature jerk trying to make a point."

"Who? Shane?" asked Jud.

"No, not Shane!" said Jill. "Chuck Waters. He's still mad that I'm dating Shane and not him. He's constantly trying to goad Shane into some kind of macho fight."

Chuck Waters was a linebacker on the football team who had dated Jill briefly before Shane. He was from the same town as Jill and the two had gone to some events together during the past summer. He had presumed that the relationship was more than it was and continued to call Jill after she started dating Shane. Jill had made it plain to him that her current interest was Shane.

"I'm not looking to fight with him," said Shane. "That's grade school stuff, but I'm getting tired of him 'accidentally' pushing me at the campus post office, the grill, and now here."

"I get that, Shane," said Charlie, "but I agree with Jill. Just let it roll off! You already won the prize and we don't need you getting hurt in some moronic scuffle with a 6'2", 200-pound linebacker."

"Okay, okay," said Shane. "You're right. I just don't want him, or anyone else, to think I'm afraid of him."

Jill answered that. "Only idiots would assume that. Most realize that you're just a lot smarter than him."

"Have a beer, Shane," said Jud, smiling.

"Good idea," said Shane, giving Jud a fist bump.

Linda Hawkins joined the group, surprising Charlie a little. After the Homecoming activities, she had become a regular member of a larger group of Charlie's friends that hung out together. Charlie hadn't seen her at a GIGIF since her fiancé, Doug Jennings, graduated the year before.

"Hey Linda," said Jill, "I haven't seen you at one of these since last year!"

"I know," said Linda, "I've missed them! Doug says 'Hi' … he also says that if I forget how to dance he's not going to marry me." She laughed and grabbed Charlie's hand before he could resist.

Seven PM came too early for this GIGIF to end and, even though the two kegs of beer had been depleted 30 minutes earlier, the crowd convinced the band to play for an extra fifteen minutes. By the end of the encore set, all in the large room were dancing with a partner, with several partners, or by themselves.

Jill, Shane, Jud, and a girl named Susie were heading for the parking lot and looking for the Renault. The little car wasn't where they parked it, though. As they looked around, a bit confused, they finally saw their car. It was sitting on top of the garbage dumpster at the back of the parking lot. As Jud walked toward the dumpster, wondering how the vehicle could have gotten there, Chuck Waters and three other football players appeared from among the crowd departing Frocks.

"Oh crap, Jud," said Chuck, slurring his words, "that looks like a hard parking place to exit."

Jud, with Shane, Jillian and Susie behind him, said, "Very funny, Chuck. Elgin, Conley, Burke, did you help Chuck with this?"

The other three football players scuffled a bit, looking sideways, and Chuck said, "Shouldn't be a problem for that skinny-assed pitcher and you to get it down, Jud."

Jill spoke now, saying, "You're a moron, Chuck. You're also drunk, and I think you're in a lot of trouble now."

"That so?" said Chuck. "Your man going to teach me a lesson?"

"Probably will," said Shane, "but not with my fists. You're so drunk it wouldn't be a fair fight."

At that moment, Charlie, Danny, and Ten Ton joined the group. "What's going on here?" asked Ten Ton.

"Oh, nothing much," said Jud. "Chuck and his football buddies thought it would be fun to steal my car and park it on the dumpster."

"That's not funny," said Ten Ton, looking at Chuck. "Let's get it down."

"Oh," said Chuck, "I get it. You got your own 'boy' here to help you get it down."

Nobody breathed for a few seconds after that ill-conceived comment, and most in the group were glancing sideways at Ten Ton to gauge his reaction. Ten Ton was staring at Chuck, with 200 years of hatred, violence, and suppression working its way through his giant body to the top of his head... and his eyes. It was cold outside and, perhaps it was just the condensation created by his breathing, but smoke appeared to be coming from Ten Ton's eyes, giving the appearance of a volcano that was about to erupt. "What did you say?" he asked Chuck.

Chuck, even in his inebriated state, felt the danger and answered, "I don't want any trouble with you, Denton. I simply asked if you were going to help them get their car down."

John Stribling, Dean of Academics, arrived on the scene and asked the group, "Have we got a problem here?"

Jud answered, "No, sir, but I think you just saved someone's life."

Stribling replied, "Well, glad I got here when I did then. What seems to be..." then he noticed the car parked on the dumpster. "How did that car get there?"

"Ask Chuck," said Jud.

"Chuck?" said Stribling.

"Oh, it was just a prank..." started Chuck.

"Shut up, Chuck," said Stribling. "Do we have enough guys to get this car back on the ground before the Lefton Township Police Department gets here?"

"Yes sir," said Jud. "We can get it down."

"Good," said Stribling. "After you have the car down, can I have several of you follow me to the admin building to get some additional information?"

Several from the group nodded and Stribling said, "Chuck, Elgin, Burke ... get in my car. Who else helped you put the car up there?"

Elgin Stivers answered, "Conley Daniels, but he already left."

"Okay," said Stribling. "Get him on your cell phone and tell him to meet us at the admin building."

"But, Dean Stribling," said Chuck, "my car is down here. Can I follow you up to the campus?"

"No Chuck, you can't," said Stribling. "You can walk down and get your car tomorrow morning. Now, either get in my car, or I will leave you to talk to the police who will likely be here any minute. How old are you, Chuck?"

"I'll be twenty-one next month," said Chuck.

"What I thought. You better get in my car."

As Stribley drove back to campus, he made a call on his cell phone. When his car arrived at the college, he went past the admin building and proceeded to the gym. When he stopped the car, he told the three football players that Coach Donning, their football coach, was waiting for them in his office. As the three sat down in front of Donning's desk, Donning asked them where Conley was.

"Coach," said Elgin, "Conley had a date. I called him from Dean Stribling's car and he didn't see any reason that he had to be involved in this."

"Okay," said Donning. "He doesn't. I'll turn his name over to the Lefton Police Department tonight and they'll take care of him. If any of you can get in touch with him, though, you might tell him that, if he isn't at my office within the next thirty minutes, he won't be enrolled at this college by tomorrow. I'll also make a call to his parents and let them know they'll be able to pick Conley up tomorrow morning at the Hamilton County jail."

"Whoa, Coach!" said Chuck.

"Shut up, Chuck!" said Donning.

"Coach," said Chuck, "this is getting blown out of proportion."

"I said shut up, Chuck," said Donning. "I meant it!"

"I can get Conley on the phone," said Elgin.

"Good. He doesn't have much time to get here. Men," said Coach Donning, addressing his three players, "I have notes here from a conversation I had with Dean Stribling, and I'm shocked. Grand theft auto, public drunkenness, malicious mischief, underage drinking. You've had quite an evening!"

"Coach, this is a bunch of horse shit ..." said Waters, when Donning cut him off again.

"Chuck, this is the last time I'm going to tell you to shut up. The next time you speak, unless I have specifically asked you to speak, I will excuse you from this meeting. I will then turn both you and my notes over to the Lefton Township Police, who will pick you up here and process you downtown. By the time you finish down there, you will no longer be enrolled at this college. Do you understand me?"

"Yes sir," said Waters, meekly.

"Good. Dean Stribling will be sending me statements from six other witnesses in the next hour. While I wait for those and Mr. Daniels, I would like you each to write your own statements about this incident. I will compare your statements to the other witnesses' and, if I find any discrepancies, will turn the files over to the Lefton Police to sort out. In other words, it is in your interest not to lie about anything. One other stipulation I will make is this: As you prepare your individual statements, whenever you refer to your actions relative to Jud Long's car, you will use the terms, 'steal' or 'stole'. I will not accept statements from any of you that characterize what you did in any milder terms. Do you understand me?"

All three responded in the affirmative and Elgin wondered if he could ask a question.

"Yes, Elgin," replied Donning, "what is your question?"

"It appears, Coach, that you are asking us to basically sign a confession to a crime," said Elgin. "This seems pretty serious. Should we talk to an attorney before we do that?"

"Good question, Elgin," said Donning, "but here's the thing. In this country everyone has a right to a fair trial and to be represented by an attorney. If you would prefer to exercise your rights in the court system, and not keep this incident confined to the College, you may. At the point that any of you would like to do that, my work here is done. I will simply turn you and this paperwork over to the Lefton Police Department. Unfortunately, if that happens, you will no longer be protected by the sanctity of this college, because you won't be a part of it anymore. It is evident that each of you participated in an incident significant enough to be expelled from this institution. Because it is our desire to build good citizens at this college, not destroy them, both Dean Stribling and I, with the approval of the President of the College, have agreed to try to keep this a college issue. Frankly, this is extremely generous on our part. So, what is your decision?"

"Sorry Coach, I'll stick with keeping it at the College," said Elgin.

"Me too," said Burke.

"I guess, me too," said Chuck, "but this makes it seem like we don't have any rights at the College."

"Chuck," said Donning, "when you start playing with the Devil, you are forced to play by the Devil's rules. In this situation, you have put yourself in a position where, indeed, your rights are limited. If, however, you are lucky and smart, this may be the most important lesson you will ever learn from college. You will find in life that, if you are a bully, there is always a bigger bully waiting for you. In this case, I'm the bully, and I don't have to use my fists. By the way, Chuck, am I reading these notes correctly? Did you refer to Denton Jones as a 'boy?'"

"I may have said something like that," said Chuck, "but I didn't mean anything by it."

"My God, Waters!" exclaimed Donning. "Do you have some kind of a death wish?"

"Honestly, Coach," said Chuck, "I'm not prejudiced. I guess I wasn't thinking."

"Apparently not," said Donning. "I know quite a bit about Denton. Did you know he's here on a full academic scholarship and that he was recruited to play football?"

Elgin said, "Really? Why has he never been on the team?"

"Because," said Donning, "some very caring folks from his community advised us, after he had been recruited, that the programmed violence of football would not be healthy for Denton or for any players competing against him. It was good advice and I turned Denton over to Coach Blevins. Suffice it to say that Denton is someone you should keep as a friend … and not have as an enemy."

At that moment, Conley Daniels appeared at the coach's office "Good evening, Mr. Daniels," said Coach Donning. "I will let your friends review with you what we have discussed, so far, this evening. If you have any problems with the instructions I have provided them, come back and see me. Otherwise, when all of you have finished your statements, meet me at the bottom of Dread Hill."

Fifteen minutes later the four football players were standing with their coach at the bottom of the hill behind the football stadium referred to as, Dread Hill. Cross Country track athletes used the hill for training and had named it long ago. "Men, it is 8:30 PM, and you have two hours to complete twenty round-trip circuits to the top of this hill and back. if any one of you is unable to complete this task, I will expect others of you to compensate with additional trips. To summarize, I expect 80 completed cycles up and down this hill in the next two hours. When you are done, report back to my office."

At about 10:45 PM, four exhausted and muddy athletes were back at Coach Donning's office. The coach was waiting with a small stack of papers. "It has been a long evening, men, and I'm ready to go home. I have reviewed your written statements, and each corresponds sufficiently to the statements made by the other witnesses. Congratulations. Your signed statements will remain in my desk drawer for the remainder of your respective enrollments at this College. They will not become a part of any record unless you commit additional infractions while at Lefton. Additionally, I am holding each of you responsible for the potential actions of your friends. If there is any attempt by either you or any of your friends to exact revenge on any of the victims of, or witnesses to, this incident, I will make your statements a part of your permanent records. Life will offer you few opportunities like this one to escape the severe consequences of mistakes you make; Remember this one."

All four stood to leave, but Chuck Waters waited behind. "Coach," he said, "can I talk to you for a minute more?"

"Certainly, Chuck."

"I'm sorry," he said. "This isn't me tonight, and it isn't who I want to be. I sobered up during the runs up that hill and thought about a lot of things. I appreciate that you and the College are giving me a chance to get beyond this. I owe Denton, Jud, Shane, and Jillian an apology as well."

"Well said, Chuck," said Donning, "and sounding much more like the athlete I recruited two years ago. I think you've learned several important lessons this evening." The two shook hands and the long night was finally over.

January sped by and, in the first week of February, baseball practice officially began at Lefton College. Opening Day was just three weeks away.

Blevins saw his old friend, Claude Hamilton, hanging over his usual spot at the fence on the third-base line. Charlie's grandfather and Stu Blevins went back quite a few years, to Stu's first years at Lefton College. After Stu had received the coaching offer from the college, he immersed himself in the community's baseball culture. He volunteered as a Director for the township's Little League Board and, within two years in Lefton Township, had been voted Chairman of that board. He had met Claude, first, when Claude was a volunteer coach for one of the League's T-ball teams. Claude and Stu became good friends as their Little League interactions had continued over the past two decades. Stu's favorite charity was the Little League, where he continued to serve as the Board's unpaid Chairman, and Claude had continued to serve as a volunteer coach on various Lefton Township Little League teams, even after his own grandson had progressed past the local Little League levels.

Even before Charlie had walked on as a freshman catcher at Lefton, Claude had become a regular fixture around the fence at practices and in the stands during games. Claude loved baseball and Blevins had found ways of turning that enthusiasm into productive activity for the College, as well as satisfying side work for the affable Claude. For the past five years, Coach Blevins had given Claude a list of other Division III rivals to scout whenever he had the opportunity. There was, of course, no pay in any budget at Lefton College for this, but Claude seemed happy with a good steak dinner once or twice per year with his friend as compensation.

Charlie's numbers during high school as a player weren't overly impressive and, as an undersized catcher, no college or University programs had recruited him to play baseball. Blevins was delighted when Charlie had tried out for the Lefton College team three years earlier and made the team as a walk-on freshman. In the years since then, Charlie had more than proved his value as a quality player for the College team. Sometimes outstanding high school players don't get noticed because they play for mediocre teams. That seemed to have been the case for Charlie. Nobody was prouder of the way Charlie had answered his baseball challenges since then than Coach Blevins, except perhaps Charlie's grandfather and his stepfather.

As Blevins strolled over to the fence, Claude yelled over to him, "Great day for baseball, isn't it, Coach? Your team is looking pretty good."

Coach Blevins laughed. 'Great day for baseball' was a line that Claude Hamilton was famous for. Local folks in town remembered him saying the same thing decades ago as a high school catcher at Lefton Township, and it was the mantra for every team Claude had coached at the Little League. Truth was, for Claude, every day ... any day ... was a 'great day for baseball,' and Blevins had to agree that, compared to almost anything else one could do on any given day, baseball was a good alternative. "Claude," he replied, "You say that every year about this time! This year, though, we might have a contender!"

"Shoot, Coach, you had a contender last year! Going to the Mid-East Regionals is nothing to sneeze at," said Claude. "Junie looks like he's got more pop in his bat this year, and Pudge appears to be down a size," observed Claude. Junie Moore, the team's shortstop, and Pudge (Davey) Cowan, the regular second baseman, were local boys who had played in the Lefton Township Little League system. Claude had coached both boys, as well as his grandson, Charlie, at different times during their Little League years.

"Yeah. Junie wore out the batting cage this winter. Pudge has been in there a lot too, which might have something to do with the weight loss. He looks a lot faster, doesn't he?"

"How do the pitchers look?" asked Claude

Blevins stared at Claude and laughed. "Claude Hamilton! You know the answer to that question as well as I do. Do you think I don't know that you get a detailed report from Charlie after every workout?"

Claude smiled, and said, "That's true, but maybe you don't see the same things Charlie does. Charlie seems pretty happy with the group."

"He should," replied coach Blevins. "He spent most of the winter working with them. He says it's the best pitching group we've had since he's been here, and I tend to agree. Hey Claude," continued Blevins, "... I want you to watch a kid hit when we start batting practice in a few minutes, will ya'?"

"Okay, which one?" Claude replied.

"The new kid," answered Blevins. "The walk on. His name is Luis Spedimente. He doesn't weigh a buck thirty soaking wet with all his clothes on and a backpack full of books. He says he's 5 feet 2 inches, but my tape measure says he'd have to be wearing three-inch heels to be that tall. He grew up in one of the Hispanic barrios in Indianapolis, and he's here on an academic scholarship. Just watch him hit in a few minutes."

"Okay," said Claude. "Anything in particular I should be looking for?"

"Nope. No hints. Just watch," answered Blevins

About 15 minutes later, the smallest player on the field entered the batter's box against Coach Blevins, who was throwing batting practice from behind a screen in front of the mound. Blevins threw approximately 15 pitches, and the hitter didn't hit a single one out of the infield. Then the small hitter went to the other side of the plate, taking about 15 more pitches from Blevins as a left-hander. Again, none of the batted balls left the infield, and none were hit particularly hard.

When Blevins returned to the infield fence after practice, Claude was still standing there. "Not sure what I was supposed to be watching there, friend," offered Claude. "Looks like you've got an undersized player who can't hit a lick, and he's equally bad from both sides of the plate."

"Right," said Blevins. "Did you notice anything else?"

Claude thought for a moment, hoping to come up with what he might have missed. He finally said, "No, Stu, I didn't."

"Claude, I threw that kid 30 different pitches, to 30 different places around the plate. Many of the pitches were balls, not strikes. While they weren't thrown at full speed, they were thrown from only 40 feet away, which would simulate a modest college fastball. Luis didn't miss one!" finished Blevins.

"Sorry, Stu, I should have noticed that," said Claude. "That *is* somewhat impressive. How do you use that in a game, though?" questioned Claude.

"I don't know yet," said Blevins, "but that's why I picked him up from the tryouts. He's also as fast as lightning, so I might use him as a late-inning pinch-runner. If I just needed to drive a runner home from third base with a ball hit to the right side, he might also be my guy. I don't know yet."

"Where does he play in the field?" asked Claude.

"He doesn't," said Blevins. "At least, not yet. I'm not sure he's ever played baseball with an actual glove. He has an old glove that he used during the tryout, but ... get this ... he fields like he hits! Every ball I hit to him at second base during the tryout, he knocked down, then recovered from the ground and threw to first base. Because of his speed, he was able to knock down balls well to his right and well to his left, but he didn't field a ground ball cleanly during the entire try-out!"

"Interesting. Sounds like he hasn't played much organized baseball."

"I would guess ... none," said Blevins. "I think he played stickball in the barrios and that nobody used baseball mitts there. He's a good kid, with a personality that's three times as big as he is. He's obviously grown up with nothing, but I have met few more positive people."

"Sounds like a good project for you," said Claude.

"Right, like I need a new project this year," answered Stu.

"Your projects usually work out," said Claude.

"Thanks, Claude."

When Charlie got home from practice, both his grandfather and his mother were waiting for him. "How was practice?" said Claude, before Charlie even had time to drop his backpack on the couch.

"Granddad, you were there! Why are you asking me?" laughed Charlie, good-naturedly.

"Well, I was impressed from where I was standing," said Claude. "Jack Ryan looks like an animal, both as a hitter and a pitcher. That new outfielder ran down everything hit near him ... but I didn't see him hit, though. Shane looks 'lights out' on the mound."

"We didn't throw that hard today, but Shane is the real deal, all right," said Charlie. "Jack is a great addition as well. Did you notice how much weight Pudge lost? He's way faster this year and doesn't seem to have lost any power."

"And how about the chemistry," asked Jennifer, equally interested in how the first practice had gone.

"It seemed good, Mom," said Charlie. "Everyone has been working together all winter, and the new guys ... well, the new guys don't even seem like new guys. They fit right in. We only have one guy on the team, because of the tryouts, who hasn't worked with us all winter. He doesn't know everybody that well, but I really like him."

"Was that the little Hispanic kid?" asked Claude. "Coach Blevins was telling me about him. He sounds like he's had an 'interesting' life."

"I think that's probably an understatement, but you'd never know that by talking to him. He hasn't played much organized baseball, but he has some natural talent which can be developed, I think."

"What's his name?" asked Jennifer

"Luis Spedimente," answered Charlie, "...but he's already got a nickname. We call him Louie Speed."

"Meaning, he must be fast?" questioned Jennifer.

"Very!" said Charlie. "We're working him out at second base, but he hasn't quite got the hang of wearing a glove yet."

"Maybe he's got the wrong kind of glove," said Claude.

"What do you mean, Granddad," asked Charlie.

"Seems like I remember another walk-on player who wasn't too good with a fielder's mitt on the first day of practice," said Claude, smiling at Charlie.

"Funny, Granddad," said Charlie. "I think this might be a slightly different case. Truth is, even without great glove work, he can get to everything hit near him. He uses his glove as sort of a weapon to knock the ball down and can usually retrieve it quick enough to throw a normal runner out. If he can learn how to use a glove, he could be an amazing infielder."

"Can he hit?" asked Jennifer.

Claude answered before Charlie had a chance, "Not a lick, Honey. He's a switch-hitter who hits equally bad from both sides of the plate ... but, here's the thing. He can get the bat on the ball, and put it in play, no matter where the ball is thrown around the plate. He has no concept of balls or strikes and treats every thrown pitch as if it might explode if the catcher touches it."

"That's funny, Mom, but accurate," agreed Charlie. "It will be interesting to see how Coach Blevins might use him in games."

Claude told Charlie he had gotten a call from the clinic before practice was over and hadn't stayed until the end. He asked whether the infield had worked on the 'special' drills Charlie had developed the previous year. Claude was particularly interested in these exercises because the roots of these drills lay in the coaching Claude had provided Charlie, starting when Charlie was about five years old.

"Charlie," he would tell his grandson. "Baseball is a game of opportunities, and many of the opportunities occur when average players aren't looking for them. As an example," he would say," most runners on base don't get serious about where they are until the pitcher steps onto the rubber to pitch to the next hitter. Unless timeout has been called, though, the game doesn't stop between pitches. Keep your eyes open for runners who are daydreaming. You can throw to a base anytime, not just when you're making a play on a batted ball."

Charlie had earned a reputation during his Little League days for unexpected snap throws to different bases, and he had worked with his pitchers to make them aware of unusual opportunities that existed to catch unaware baserunners off guard from the pitching rubber. Over the course of his years behind the plate, Charlie had developed a series of practice exercises for infielders that Coach Blevins had allowed him to institute at the end of regular practices the previous year. The exercises comprised of some simple hand signals from either the pitcher or catcher that all in the infield understood. These signs would alert infielders to an impending pick-off play to be initiated by either the catcher or pitcher. To underline the importance of these exercises, Charlie changed the routine method for tossing the baseball around the infield before innings and after third strike pitches. Each of these 'throw around' opportunities offered another chance to practice a potential real-time gameplay. It seemed senseless to Charlie to not take advantage of the practice opportunity. The unusual routine confused opposing teams, who didn't understand its underlying purpose. Coach Blevins loved the routine because it forced ballplayers to keep their head in the game at all times.

The three weeks of practice had gone quickly, and Coach Blevins was more than satisfied with how the team looked. It was apparent that all the pitchers had worked out over the winter, as all came to the first practices with no rust from the off-season. While he would still not allow extended pitch counts during the first several games, Blevins felt that the pitchers were nearly at mid-season strength to start the year. Luis Spedimente continued to amaze the coach with his ability to hit a thrown ball delivered anywhere within two feet of the plate, and the freshman Hispanic had made great strides in learning how to properly use a glove in the infield. The starting infield players were all back from the previous season, except for first base, where Jack Ryan fit perfectly. Blevins tried to avoid using starting pitchers as position players, but he had to make an exception for Jack. The Junior College transfer had too much to offer at the plate to keep him out of games. Joining senior outfielder, and returning lead-off man, Danny Colovito, in the outfield would be sophomore, D'Ante Billings in left, and senior, Jud Long, in right.

In addition to Shane Reynolds and Charlie Hamilton, Coach Blevins' team now officially consisted of:

Jack Ryan - Junior. Transfer from Riordan Junior College. Right-handed pitcher / first baseman

Jack arrived at Lefton College via Riordan Junior College and would start the season as either the number one or number two pitcher. He had good command of three pitches, including a fastball, slider, and a change-up. His fastball was generally in the 90 + range, and his slider wasn't much slower. His change-up was also a curveball that could break eighteen inches or more, as well as drop. Jack could hit for both power and average and had played as an outfielder in Junior College when he wasn't pitching.

Coach Blevins would move him to first base to protect his arm at Lefton College.

Luis Spedimente - Freshman; walk-on

If, and when, Luis played in the field, it would probably be second base. The diminutive 5-foot 1 inch, 125 lb., Hispanic kid from the slums of Indianapolis had played limited, if any, organized baseball and was uncomfortable even wearing a fielder's mitt. He had made the team because of his ability to get a bat on virtually any pitch thrown to the plate, ball or strike. He had only hit a few balls out of the infield during all of spring practice but, with his speed, he could beat out most balls hit to the left side unless the infield played him to bunt. He had a positive personality and a willingness to learn. Blevins believed he could eventually be developed into a quality second baseman. He would use him in unique situations during the player's freshman year.

Hayden Piper - Freshman; outfielder

A right-handed hitting outfielder who had played at one of the Wisconsin's largest high schools in Oshkosh, Hayden was a good-fielding speedster. Only 5 feet 9 inches tall, and 150 lbs., he still had the potential to develop muscle in college. If he did, he could become a dangerous hitter.

Josh Stine - Sophomore; left-handed pitcher

Josh had joined the team as a freshman, seeing limited playing time in his first season. He currently lacked the pitch arsenal or stamina to be an everyday starting pitcher, but Blevins believed he could be an efficient short inning, left-handed, relief pitcher for the Monarchs. His fastball was in the 85 miles per hour range, and he had a reliable curveball. As he got older, and if he continued to work out in the weight room, he might improve his fastball. He would start the year as the #5 pitcher on the team.

Alexander James – Sophomore; outfielder

Nicknames sometimes accrue to kids for obvious reasons; sometimes the evolution is more convoluted. Such was the case for Alexander. His parents still called him Alexander, but on his first T-ball team, his coach had shortened it to Zander. His teammates, by the end of the season, were referring to him as Zander-Man, which in high school had been further shortened to Z-Man. The Z-Man was known for his solid defense and steady bat. While not a power hitter, he hit the gaps and had the speed to leg out doubles and the occasional triple.

Samuel Casey – Sophomore; pitcher

Samuel (AKA - Sammy C) had seen minimal action during his freshman year but would probably pitch many innings this season. Sammy's dad had played college ball as a pitcher, and it was apparent that Sammy had been well coached during his Little League and high school years. He had excellent control of three pitches and good overall mechanics. The only thing holding him back at the college level was strength. At 6 feet 2 in and 170 pounds as a freshman, he had been a bit of a string bean, with a fastball that topped out in the mid-80s. This year, he looked to have added 10 lbs. to his lanky frame, and he had spent much of the winter in the weight room working on leg strength. Coach Blevins had convinced him that, with his long arms and lanky frame, arm strength probably wouldn't hold him back as much as the need for more muscle in his hips and thighs.

Louis Phillips - Junior; third baseman

Phillips had held down the third-base position since walking on as a freshman. He'd won the starting role at third base halfway into his first season when the regular senior who played the position had suffered a minor sprain. By the time the senior was well enough to play again, Louis had nailed down the starting position for himself. Phillips didn't stand out in any specific aspect of baseball but did everything well ... except for fielding ... which he did *exceptionally* well. No ball hit to the left side of the infield seemed out of his range, and he seldom finished a game with a clean uniform. Whether fielding or running the bases, Phillips seemed to spend quite a bit of time on the ground, either diving for balls or sliding into bases. He wasn't fast enough to beat out an infield hit, but he still managed to steal his share of bases. He was an alert and opportunistic base runner. He was also the ideal number two hitter because he could lay down a bunt, he could hit to the other side, and he was willing to look at a lot of pitches. While he had the strength to occasionally loft a baseball out of the park, his best hits were to the gaps, and line drives over the infield.

Junie Moore and Pudge Cowan – Seniors; shortstop and second baseman

Junie and Pudge had been playing with, and against, Charlie's Little League and high school teams for over a decade. Neither Junie nor Pudge had attended Charlie's high school, but the three were friends from years of playing on the same or opposing teams with each other. Part of Charlie's success with his special pick-up plays was because his two middle infielders had seen these plays for years. Pudge had been the victim of at least three pick-offs by Charlie during his Little League years, that he still complained to Charlie about. As a child, Pudge had been a little 'round' ... hence his nickname ... but he was always one of the Little League's power hitters. He had slimmed down significantly at Lefton College but had not lost his power. During the previous season he had hit 20 home runs, and he would return this year as the team's clean-up hitter.

Junie was about as opposite his second baseman friend as a ballplayer could be. At 5 feet 8 in, and 140 pounds, Junie didn't appear to have a muscle in his body. He did though, and most of it seemed to be in his right arm. He was a dazzling infielder and, like Phillips, could cover a lot of ground. Coach Blevins would often play Junie up the middle so that he could cover some of Pudge's area as well. This allowed Pudge to cover the hole between first and second base. Junie was a relatively weak hitter, usually hitting in the nine hole, but he was an exceptional bunter. Whatever he lacked at the plate, he more than made up in the field.

Jake Grimsley – Senior; right-handed pitcher

Jake had been the Monarchs' 'ace' the previous year, on a team with a relatively weak pitching staff. This year, with the addition of Reynolds and Ryan, it appeared that Jake would enter the season as the number three starter. The consummate team player, Jake didn't seem bothered by the ranking. He was a solid, veteran, right-handed pitcher with excellent control of 3 pitches. His fastball could touch 90 on a hot day, and his curveball caused right-handed hitters to often bail out at the plate. His change-up was effective when it was in the dirt ... although a little too inviting for hitters if it stayed above the belt.

Denton Jones – Senior; right-handed relief pitcher

Denton, aka 'Ten Ton,' Jones was one of two black players on the Monarchs' team, and his role was specific. He was a short inning relief pitcher. He was big at 6 feet 6 inches and 250 pounds, and he was scary! He had one pitch, a fastball that could reach into the mid-90s, but his control of that pitch wasn't reliable. That fact made the pitches that he threw all the more frightening. At the plate, Denton looked imposing, but that was where his effectiveness as a hitter ended. He couldn't hit. He was the funniest player on the team, and he kept the dugout loose with his hilarious banter and relentless commentary. Coach Blevins used him in late innings when the bases were empty, and he wanted strikeouts.

Jessie Clapper – Sophomore; outfielder

Jesse, a left-hander, had also been a walk-on player in his freshman year. He had played outfield and pitched for his high school team, and though he hadn't been a stand-out player, he had shown good versatility. Coach Blevins had been impressed with his hustle during the tryouts, as well as his left-handed power as a hitter. He was a good outfielder with a better-than-average arm, who could provide good outfield backup and a left-handed hitter in the lineup on occasion.

D'Ante Billings - Sophomore; outfielder

D'Ante was African-American and fast. He had played high school baseball in St Louis, where he had led his conference in stolen bases, but he'd gotten little or no attention from any D1 or D2 schools to play baseball. His family didn't have much money, but D'Ante was determined to get a college education. He had taken it upon himself to create a video package and a player portfolio, which he sent to over a dozen Division III colleges. Coach Blevins had not received one of these packages, but his friend, Coach Williams from Manchester University, had forwarded him a copy. Blevins had a spot open for a speedy outfielder and was able to provide D'Ante a financial aid package with a partial academic grant. D'Ante was able to obtain student loan financing to cover the difference in tuition, room, and board. He had a great attitude, was a hard worker, and had not yet reached anywhere close to his peak potential.

Oxton Silver - Senior; outfielder

Ox had been a walk-on player three years prior, the same year that Charlie had joined the team. He was big and strong and could handle anything hit his way in the outfield. Because he wasn't very fast, however, he wasn't able to cover as much area in the outfield as others. Coach Blevins had added him to the varsity team because, in an emergency, Ox could also pitch. He had been a high school pitcher, as well as an outfielder, and while his fastball was only in the mid-80s, he also had a reasonably good curveball. He could chew up some innings if needed and provide a good backup at the outfield positions. Ox was an average hitter with occasional power.

Judson Long - Senior; outfielder

Jud would most likely move into the right field position, vacated by Doug Jennings, who had graduated. At 6 feet 2 inches and 190 lbs., Jud was big, but still relatively fast. He also had the best arm among all the outfielders on the team. At the plate, Jud was a patient hitter ... sometimes *too* patient. He was choosy about the pitches he liked to hit, and he struck out looking a few too many times for Coach Blevins. When he did hit the ball, it was hard. With relatively little playing time over the past three years, he had still managed ten home runs at Lefton College. Coach Blevins had hopes that Jud would become a bit more aggressive at the plate this year. Jud was a popular teammate for two reasons. One, he was intelligent, affable and unselfish; two, his little sister, who had started at the college last year, was one of the prettiest girls on campus. Her name was Jillian.

Roger Ball – Sophomore; catcher

Roger was the heir apparent to Charlie's position at catcher, and there was no doubt in anyone's mind that he would do a good job. Much larger than Charlie, at 5 feet 10 inches and 200 pounds, Ball had the more prototypical catcher's build. He was a good defenseman with an excellent arm, and he had readily embraced Charlie's philosophy relative to the pick-off plays. Roger also seemed to have a mystical ability to guide an airborne baseball from the pitcher's hand to just the location over the plate where he wanted it. Besides catcher, he could fill-in at first base and third base when needed.

Danny Colovito – Senior; outfielder

Danny had been the starting center fielder for the past two years and had become the team's leadoff hitter the previous year. With his speed, he could track down anything in center field, from gap to gap, and while his arm wasn't the strongest, he could easily hit the cutoff man. Since the cutoff man was usually Pudge, who had a superior arm, their relays from center to home were seldom a problem. Danny could beat out an infield grounder and had a good drag bunt. He also was willing to take pitches until he had two strikes, which made him a good leadoff hitter. If he got to first, he could often steal second.

The first game of the season for the Monarchs was at home on a Saturday afternoon in late February. The weather in Eastern Indiana during this part of the year was unpredictable, but this day had turned out to be as nice as a late winter day could be in that part of the world. The temperature at the 2 PM start time was almost 55°. On the mound for the home team, was freshman rookie, Shane Reynolds. Opposing him, for the Manchester University Spartans, would be their senior ace pitcher, John Simmons.

As the warm-ups for each school were completed, Coach Blevins and Manchester Coach, John Williams, met at the plate with the home plate umpire. Blevins and Williams, old friends as well as rivals in their Division III conference, exchanged line up cards and pleasantries.

"Jeez, Stu!" said Williams. "Did you have to start my year off with Reynolds? He shouldn't even be playing at the D3 level this year!"

"Might as well run him out there for the home fans," said Blevins. "Everyone around here wants to see him. I see you got your ace starting too. Should be a good game. Good luck!" The coaches shook hands; the umpire dusted the plate, and the Monarchs took the field.

Tim and Jennifer had taken seats behind the home team dugout on the third-base side. They both noticed when Case and Julia had arrived. The Reynolds had taken seats directly behind home plate. Most baseball dads of sons who are pitchers like to position themselves behind the plate, where they can evaluate and, at times, criticize, the umpire's calls. At the Lefton College baseball field, seats in this area were easy to find in February. The Lefton College students loved their team but watching a nine-inning game in chilly February weather required a little more than just team spirit. The small baseball complex was sparsely populated today, with mostly family members of players, and a few dedicated girlfriends in attendance. Behind the Manchester dugout were some Spartan fans who had made the short 1.5-hour trip south to watch their team's opening game.

Down in front of Jennifer and Tim, was Claude. He was as close to the Monarchs' dugout as he could possibly be and still be in the stands. When he saw Tim and Jennifer seat themselves, he waved. Jennifer and Tim both waved back. Claude seldom sat with his daughter and her husband during Charlie's games, feeling a slightly greater baseball loyalty to Coach Blevins. Claude felt that he needed to be in an area near the dugout where Blevins could easily talk to him if that were required.

"Have they noticed us?" asked Jennifer to Tim, avoiding glancing in the direction of the seats that Case and Julia now occupied.

"I can't tell," said Tim, casually glancing in that direction, as if he was trying to gauge the sun's trajectory in the sky. "Okay ... there goes!" he said. "Case is definitely looking around the stadium.... Bingo! He sees you!"

"Tim, don't stare!" admonished Jennifer." I don't think now is the time to talk to him, or for us to be introduced to his wife."

"Okay," said Tim. "Now that he's found you, I don't think he'll come down here right away. He's back to focusing on his son on the mound, who is warming up."

"Good," said Jennifer. "If you notice him coming this way, warn me."

"Okay," said Tim. "But don't you think that's sort of inevitable? Eventually, he and his wife are going to come down here."

"Yes," said Jennifer. "I do. I just hope that it's after the game is over."

As all in the stands settled in, and as Case, Julia, Jennifer, and Tim all squirmed in anticipation of personal introductions that had not yet occurred, the umpire yelled the directive that officially, and annually, restarted the motors of true baseball fans all over the world. "Play Ball!"

Shane retired the side in the top of the first, striking out two and forcing a weak ground ball out to the right side. The Spartans' pitcher matched him with three consecutive ground ball outs in the bottom half of the inning. Shane, throwing fire, struck the side out in the second. Simmons allowed a lead-off single to Pudge in his half of the inning but then got Charlie on a fly-out to left, before Jud grounded into a double play. Shane walked a hitter in the third, before striking out the next two. After another deep count, the Spartans' leadoff hitter had grounded into a force at second to end that inning.

The Spartans' pitcher remained solid through the 4th, with two more ground-ball outs, and a monster shot from Jud Long that was caught at the fence by the left fielder. At 0 - 0, starting the 5th, Coach Blevins had a short conversation with Charlie before the pitcher and catcher went to the field. "I know, Coach," said Charlie. "Shane doesn't have a good feel for the pitch count, and this isn't something we could work on over the winter. This is my first opportunity with Shane in a game situation."

"I'm not finding fault with either you or Shane," said Blevins. "I just wanted to make sure you and I were on the same page. Shane's pitch count after just four innings is almost 75 pitches. He's throwing a no-hitter, and a shutout, but I'm not letting him go past 85 pitches this early in the season, period. Even if he is pitching a no-hitter! Sorry."

"I understand, Coach," said Charlie. "I also agree. I'll have a chance to talk to Shane after this game."

"Okay," said the coach. "I'm going to have Grimsley start loosening up in the bullpen. Ryan is throwing tomorrow, and we don't have another game until next Thursday, so I can spare Grimsley as a reliever today."

When Shane took the mound, he noticed Grimsley throwing on the side, and motioned for Charlie to visit him on the mound. Charlie called timeout and trotted out to talk to Shane. "Hey Charlie," said Shane. "What's Grimsley doing warming up? I feel fine."

"You are fine," said Charlie. "You've got a no-hitter going, you've already struck out nine, and you're in a nothin' nothin' game. I also haven't noticed any less velocity on your fastball so far."

"So, why does Coach have Grimsley warming up?" asked Shane.

"Because you're at 75 pitches already," said Charlie. "This early in the season, Coach won't let you go past 85, no matter what."

"Even if I feel fine?"

"Yep, even if you feel fine. This is only the first game of the year, Shane," said Charlie, "... and you're an important piece to our team this year. Coach isn't going to jeopardize your arm to win one game. Let's get through this inning so that you can qualify for a win if we can squeeze a run out during our half of it."

"Okay," said Shane. "Sorry, Charlie. I've still got some things to learn at this level, I guess."

"No problem." said Charlie. "Make them hit the ball this inning!"

Shane responded as requested, and recorded two ground ball outs, as well as another three-pitch strikeout. Shane's first college baseball game ended for him after pitching five scoreless innings, striking out ten players, and throwing 84 pitches. The Monarchs couldn't score in the bottom of the 5th, which officially made Shane's first college game a non-decision. This meant that, despite giving up no runs and no hits in a scoreless game, it was impossible for Shane to record a win. It was also, however, impossible for him to take a loss if that occurred.

Grimsley, the team's best starting pitcher from last year's team, who was now the number three pitcher on the current team, pitched like a veteran. Allowing two hits over the next three innings, while striking out three hitters with his sneaky curve, he had held the Spartans' hitters in check. On the other side, John Simmons continued to be impressive for the Spartans. Through seven innings, he had only thrown 85 pitches, allowed two hits, and struck out three. He had allowed only one walk and was still throwing hard when the bottom of the eighth began.

Danny Colovito started the inning with a bloop single. Lou Phillips then grounded out, forcing the speedy Colovito at second. Charlie connected for a ground-rule double down the left-field line, which had taken a hop into the bleachers. The Monarchs had runners at second and third with only one out, when Coach Blevins called timeout. He brought his lineup card to home plate, and after a short conversation with the home plate umpire, substituted the speedy freshman, Hayden Piper, as a pinch-runner for Phillips, who occupied third base. He then entered Luis Spedimente as a pinch-hitter for outfielder, Jud Long.

At second base, Charlie watched these maneuvers and smiled. The coach, in the 8th inning of a 0-0 game, was taking a gamble and 'going for it' with an extremely unorthodox move. Louie Speed, as the team called him, was an unknown commodity to his own team, much less the rest of the league, including the Spartans. Certainly, the opposing team couldn't begin to guess Coach Blevins' strategy as the diminutive hitter stepped into the batter's box. Hayden Piper, at third base, had been given the signal from the first base coach to 'run on contact.' Luis, batting right-handed, stepped into the batter's box as if he had been doing it for years. Simmons, with an open base at first and not sure what the opposing team strategy might be in this scenario, played it safe. He threw a low fastball to the outside of the plate. He couldn't have known that Luis never took a pitch. Luis slapped the ball on the ground to the second baseman who, despite playing shallow, had no chance to throw out the speedy Piper, who had broken for home plate on the pitch. It wasn't exactly a traditional 'squeeze play', but it had the same effect. Charlie advanced to third on the play, and Luis was safe at first. Luis easily stole second base on the next pitch, with the catcher making no attempt to throw down with a runner on third base. Simmons then intentionally walked Billings to load the bases. Moore hit into a double play to end the inning but, for the Spartans, the damage had been done. The Monarchs now led the game by the slimmest of margins, 1 - 0.

When the Monarchs took the field in the 9th, Charlie brought the ball out to Grimsley on the mound. "OK Jake," said Charlie, "just keep throwing the way you have been. We've got the #8, #9 hitters up, and then back to the top of the order. At the bottom of the order, they'll be taking at least a pitch before they're green-lighted. Don't waste that free strike. The Spartans will probably pinch hit for their #9 hitter. We'll figure out what to do with him when we get there. Let's just finish this soon ... it's too cold out here to keep playing!"

"Got it, Charlie," acknowledged Grimsley. As expected the #8 hitter took the first pitch, which Jake threw for an easy strike. On 0 - 2, the left-handed hitter swung poorly to protect the plate, nubbing a fair ball to the left side, just inside the foul line. The third baseman, Phillips, fielded it on the run but had no play at first.

Bad luck, thought Charlie.

The pinch hitter was a large and ominous looking player. Charlie visited the mound, saying to Grimsley, "Forget that last one, Jake. Just dumb luck, but I don't like the looks of this hitter coming up. Let's see if we can get rid of the baserunner before this beast they sent to pinch-hit has a chance to hurt us. Let's go with the third pitch. The base runner has no intention of stealing. If he tried, with nobody out in the ninth, his coach would crucify him. So, don't even glance at him for the first two pitches. Make him feel really comfortable," finished Charlie.

"Got it," said Grimsley. Charlie then held up one hand, with three fingers up, as if signaling to the outfielders. All in the infield caught the signal, as well as their coach, who knew that on the third pitch of this at-bat, Grimsley would throw an outside pitch, which Charlie would 'snap-throw' to Jack Ryan at first, in an attempt to catch the runner on first off the base. The big pinch-hitter took the first pitch for a strike, and let the next pitch go high for a ball. On neither pitch had Grimsley even glanced at the runner at first base, and the runner had stepped off a slightly bigger lead as a result. Jack Ryan seemed to be a born actor. While holding the runner as he would be expected to do, he was totally nonchalant. Anybody watching would figure that a pick-off throw to him was the last thing on his mind.

On the third pitch, Charlie received the fastball to the outside of the plate. Retrieving the ball in this area allowed him to move naturally to his right, toward the first base line. His snap throw to Ryan was a bullet, catching the base runner completely by surprise. Ryan applied the tag before the runner could even get back to within two feet of the bag.

"You're out!" shouted the umpire.

"That's one," thought Charlie. On 2 - 1, the big pinch hitter lofted a long fly ball to center which the replacement center fielder, freshman Hayden Piper, ran down for out number two. Both Charlie and Jake looked at each other smiling. That ball could have easily gone out of the stadium, and they both knew their 'instincts' had been right about the big pinch hitter. While the scoreboard now showed two outs, under slightly different circumstances, it could have shown the Spartans leading 2 - 1. To finish the game, replacement second basemen, Luis Spedimente, knocked down a hard ground ball hit to his left with his glove, recovered it, and threw to first for the final out.

The Monarchs had won a close one in their opener and, as Coach Blevins looked around the locker room after the game, he couldn't help smiling. His new ace had pitched well, and the Monarchs' defense had been rock solid. The heroes of the game, however, had been two unlikely suspects. Jake Grimsley, his senior pitcher, got the win, and the winning RBI had been delivered by a small Hispanic kid who had just played in his first organized game of baseball. The Baseball gods were truly creative and entertaining, he thought.

After the players showered, and before they drifted off to waiting families and girlfriends, Blevins gathered them in the team meeting room. "Good game, guys," he started. "John Simmons is one of the best pitchers we'll face this year, and he just pitched a heck of a game. Complete game, allowing only three hits, one walk, and only one earned run. You guys got out-hit and very nearly out-pitched, but you didn't get out-played. In this game, it doesn't matter how many hits you record, or how many strikeouts you get in a game. It only matters that by the end of nine innings you get one more run than your opponent. We did that today and it was a team effort. I'm proud of you. Game time is 1 p.m. tomorrow. Be here by 11:30 AM. Jack, you're starting. Shane, you'll be at first."

"And what about me?" said the ever-enthusiastic Luis.

"Luis, you'll be on the bench, next to me, where I can protect you. I can't let anything happen to my secret weapon hitting machine. You should have seen the look on Coach Williams' face when you hit that horrendous pitch. I think Simmons was trying to waste it, and I'm not sure the catcher would have even caught that ball if you hadn't hit it." The team laughed good-naturedly, and all parted out the door except for Shane and Charlie.

Shane started the conversation, "Sorry, Charlie. I guess I lost focus on what was important today."

"What do you mean?" asked Charlie.

"I was only able to go five innings because I let my pitch count get too high early on," he answered.

"That's true, but that isn't something we could work on during the winter. It isn't something we have even talked about. Most pitchers ... not just high school and college pitchers ... most pitchers, think their job is to keep opposing players from hitting the ball. The great Sandy Koufax says that he didn't become an effective pitcher until he realized his job was to make hitters *hit* the ball. A ground ball or a fly ball can take a single pitch or two, while the minimum number of pitches for a strikeout is three, and usually a few more," said Charlie.

"I get it, Charlie. The next game will be different," said Shane.

"Shane, you were awesome today while you pitched! In some cases, you were just too awesome. All hitters aren't created equal, and you don't have to throw your best stuff to every batter. Strikeouts are sometimes overrated. There's a time and place for them, but you need to save your best stuff for the times you really need that stuff. Coach Blevins would rather have you lead the league in wins than lead the league in strikeouts."

"OK," Shane said. "Like I said, next weekend will be different." The boys walked out of the building together to meet two different sets of families who were waiting for them. Case invited Charlie to join Shane at the Village Inn for pizza, but Charlie, glancing at his granddad, declined. "Thanks, Case," he said, "...but my granddad and I have sort of a post-game tradition. Will you be at the game tomorrow?"

"Probably so, see you then."

When Grimsley had recorded the last out, Tim warned Jennifer that Case and Julia were headed down the rows of seats in their direction. "Here goes," said Jennifer. "Don't get any funny expressions, and just follow my lead."

"Got it," agreed Tim.

As Case got closer, he said, "Jennifer Hamilton! You haven't changed a bit! You might not remember me, but I'm Case Reynolds, Shane's dad, and this is my wife, Julia."

"Well, Case Reynolds!" replied Jennifer. "Look at you! It has been a long time. My last name is actually Drake, now. This is my husband, Tim." All shook hands, and Jennifer said, "Charlie had such a good time with your family in Michigan. Thank you for taking him along."

"That was our pleasure," said Julia. "What an outstanding young man you have!"

"Thank you," replied Jennifer. "We're proud of him. He and Shane seem to have become good friends here at Lefton."

Case again took the lead in the conversation, "They sure have!" he said. "Everything we hear about in Shane's reports seems to have something to do with Charlie... or Jill Long!"

"Well, Charlie and Shane have spent a lot of time this winter working together. Judging by the game today, their efforts seemed to have been worthwhile. Shane pitched great!" said Jennifer.

"Thanks," said Case. "I think he probably wishes he could have gone a little deeper than five innings, but his fastball was sharp for this early in the year."

Tim said, "From what I have seen the last couple seasons, Coach Blevins doesn't like his pitchers to throw more than 70 or 80 pitches in the first few games of the season. Shane shouldn't feel bad about only going five innings."

Claude had now joined the group from his spot near the dugout. "Dad," said Jennifer, "these are Shane's parents, Case and Julia Reynolds. Case, Julia, this is my dad, Claude Hamilton. As you can probably see, my dad is Coach Blevins' main Bleacher Coach."

All laughed at Jennifer's joke, including her dad who continued to look at Case. "Nice to meet you, folks," said Claude. "Your son is one heckuva pitcher." Claude paused as he examined Case, and said, "You look familiar to me, Case. Have we met before?"

Case answered slowly, "Probably so, sir. I was a catcher on this very team about 20 years ago. I was a year ahead of your daughter at Lefton."

"Now, all that makes sense!" Claude said. "You knew Blevins, and that's how we got Shane here at Lefton this year, right?"

"Yes," said Case. "Blevins was my coach 20 years ago."

"Right!" said Claude, "...and you're the one that Blevins is always comparing Charlie to. He keeps telling Charlie that Charlie reminds him of another catcher who played for him a long time ago."

"Charlie and I talked a little about that in Michigan," laughed Case. "Apparently, Charlie had the same problem convincing Coach Blevins that he was big enough to play catcher as I did."

"Right," said Claude, continuing to look at Case. "When you were his age, you were probably about the same size as Charlie."

Tim and Jennifer were both uncomfortable with the direction of the current conversation, and Jennifer broke in abruptly, "Dad, you and Case can feel free to continue to review the ancient history of the College, but I'm going to try to find a warmer place. Julia, you look like you're shivering as well. It was great meeting you and good to see you again after all these years, Case. I think we'll have plenty of opportunities to catch up a little more this spring when the weather is warmer."

Case laughed, and said, "You're absolutely right! Great to see you again, Jennifer, and nice to meet you, Claude and Tim." As the group separated, Claude continued to watch Case and Julia as they left the stadium. Something was bouncing around his brain, and his head shifted back and forth between his daughter and Case. He finally shook his head, still deep in thought, and walked toward his car.

When they got back home, Jennifer said to Tim, "I think dad has it figured out."

Tim answered, "Well if he doesn't, he will soon. He's no dummy, Jennifer. You never told me how much Charlie looks like Case; and now that I've met Case, I see a resemblance between Shane and Charlie, too."

"Tim," Jennifer replied. "I haven't seen Case in over 20 years. Until I saw him today, I didn't realize how much Charlie looked like him either." She started to cry softly.

"Jen, we're okay," said Tim. "We knew that we were going to have to start unraveling this soon, anyway. Today didn't change any of that."

She looked at him with teary eyes, and said, "I know we did, but I just didn't expect that the similarities in appearances would be so obvious. Now, I wonder if Coach Blevins has already figured this out as well. He was the faculty advisor at the dance at Henson's after Case's graduation. And what about Charlie? Or Julia? Don't you think she's noticed it too?"

"Jen, your dad has been looking at every new face he's met for the past 20 years hoping that he might get a clue as to who Charlie's father might be. It's different for the others. Unless you have a reason to look for resemblances, I don't think you notice them as much," said Tim. "I know the whole story now, so, naturally, I noticed the resemblance and, of course you would notice. I don't think Shane, Charlie, or Julia have thought twice about it yet."

"What about Case?" she asked.

Tim replied, "I think he's starting to put it together, Jennifer. I was watching his face as he talked to you, and I saw a lot of concern."

"There's a game tomorrow and Case and Julia will probably be there," said Jennifer. "If you don't mind, I'd like to find an excuse not to attend. I'm just not quite ready for this to go any further, yet."

"No problem," said Tim. "I'll go. You just figure the reason you can't is and let me know so that our stories match. Case and Julia wouldn't approach me at the game without you being there."

"No," said Jennifer. "I don't think they would. Thank you, Tim."

The following morning, Jennifer told Charlie she had gotten a call from the college's independent auditor, and that the audit team was planning to be at the school on Monday. She felt she needed to spend Sunday afternoon getting ready, and she asked Charlie if he minded if she missed the game. Her story, for the most part, was true. The auditors were, in fact, going to be at the school on Monday afternoon, but she had known this for two weeks now and she was already totally prepared.

Charlie was okay with her plan and Jennifer wished him luck on the game. To add credibility to her story she spent the afternoon at her office idly filing and rearranging furniture. She was surprised when her office phone rang at 4:30 PM and wondered who would be calling the Controller's office on a Sunday afternoon. She let the call go to voicemail, then dialed her code to listen to the message a few minutes later. Her heart went into her mouth when she heard the familiar voice of Case Reynolds.

"Hi, Jennifer. This is Case. I found this number in the college directory. Hope it's the right one ... anyway, the game just ended, and I was wondering if I could stop by your office tomorrow morning sometime. Julia is heading back home in the morning, and I'm heading to Columbus for a meeting later in the day. I don't have to leave until around lunch, though. Call me on my cell at 314-244-1111 if this doesn't work for you. I'll call this number again tomorrow morning to see if I can get an appointment. Thanks."

Strike three! thought Jennifer.

Jennifer arrived at her office early and waited for Case's call. The conversation she had been dreading since last fall now seemed imminent, and Jennifer was surprised at how calm she felt. Perhaps the thousands of scenarios she had played out in her head over the past five months had drained any remaining anxiety. Dinner the evening before, with Tim, Charlie and her dad, had been animated as the three men replayed the day's game for her. The Monarchs had easily defeated Manchester on Sunday, 8 - 3, with Jack Ryan delivering eight strong innings of pitching. Josh Stine, the team's sophomore relief pitcher and spot starter, entered the game in the ninth in relief of Ryan and had allowed three runs, but the game was already out of reach for the Spartans by then. The whole team had hit well, and Charlie finished the game 2 for 4 with two RBIs. He and his granddad had been more excited about one of Charlie's special pick-off plays that had worked early in the game than they were about his RBIs. Jennifer had slept well and, this morning, felt ready for whatever was going to happen.

When the phone rang at 8:15 AM, she answered it herself. "Jennifer Drake, how may I help you?"

"Oh ... hi... Jennifer. It's Case. Did you get the voicemail I left yesterday?"

"Yes, Case, but I just got here, and hadn't gotten around to calling you yet."

When Jennifer said no more, Case asked, "Would you have time to meet me for a few minutes this morning? Julia has already left for Indianapolis, and I have to go the other direction, to Columbus, a little later."

"Sure, Case. I've got a little time this morning with no appointments. I have some auditors coming in from out of

169

town this afternoon, but I'm already prepared for them. What time would you like to meet?"

He replied, "I can probably be there in about fifteen minutes if that's okay. You are in the admin building, right?"

"Yes," she said. "Just park in the visitor area at the back of the building. I'm on the second floor."

"Okay. See you in a few minutes," he said.

When Case stepped into Jennifer's office on campus, he looked uncomfortable. Jennifer greeted him warmly and asked him to have a seat next to her desk. He did this and began fumbling with the framed photo on her desk of herself, Charlie, and Tim.

"What a nice photo," he said to break the silence. "You have a wonderful family, Jennifer. I guess you know how fond we are of your son."

"Thank you, Case," replied Jennifer. "We have enjoyed Shane as well. His athletic reputation preceded him to the college, but that isn't the only quality that defines him. He is a fine young man! You should be proud."

"Oh, we are," replied Case, relaxing a bit as he and Jennifer talked about their boys. "Shane is the best part of our lives, and every age has brought different adventures to enjoy."

"I understand, believe me," said Jennifer. "What is it that you wanted to meet me about?"

Case knew the time for pleasantries had now ended. knew. Jennifer had metaphorically just announced, *Play Ball!* He started awkwardly, "Sorry, Jennifer. I know you're busy ... it's just that ... well ... after the trip to Michigan when Charlie joined us, I've been thinking a lot, and .... well, frankly ... that evening I spent dancing with you after graduation was one of the highlights of my college years!"

Jennifer blushed noticeably, surprised at the direction Case's initial statement seemed to be going. "Thank you, Case," she replied. "I've always remembered that as a special evening as well. Is that what you wanted to talk to me about?"

Case searched Jennifer's face for a clue and wondered if her comment relative to the 'special evening' had some deeper underlying meaning for her. If it did, her face didn't show it, and he still seemed to be on shaky ground. "No," said Case, "not really ... well, maybe to some extent," he stuttered, "but ... excuse me for just a moment, Jennifer. I seem to be babbling. Let me get my thoughts together."

Jennifer felt sorry for Case. She knew for a fact, what he only suspected. He was forced, out of politeness and integrity, to gently probe. She could relieve the tension at any time. She didn't want to make him uncomfortable, but the more he told her under these circumstances, the better she would be prepared to provide him the right answers, in the right way. She waited patiently for him to continue.

After a moment, Case reestablished eye contact with Jennifer. He seemed to have strengthened his resolve, and began speaking, "Jennifer, I didn't come here today to try to rekindle a brief romance from over 20 years ago. I feel, however, that it is important that you know I remember that evening very well ... and I remember *you* very well. It was one of the more memorable evenings in my college-era life ... because of the fun I had dancing with you ... and not because of how that evening ended."

Jennifer smiled at Case, saying, "And what was wrong with the way it ended?"

"Sorry," said Case. "I didn't mean that the way it sounded."

"No apology necessary," said Jennifer. "I know what you meant ... and nothing happened that evening that should still make you embarrassed today. We were a couple of kids, high on an evening of fun, doing what many other kids did, and still do, in the same situation."

Case visibly relaxed, and said, "Thanks for remembering that so kindly." He smiled for the first time in several minutes, and continued, "As I recall, neither of us seemed to have had much experience in what we were doing."

Jennifer laughed and agreed. "Yes, your recollection is correct ... but in some ways, that's one of the things that still makes the evening memorable. We did something that was a bit irresponsible, and we didn't do it very well ... because we were both young, naïve, and still somewhat innocent."

"Right," said Case, becoming serious again. "Sometimes that kind of naïveté and irresponsibility can have bad consequences, though. As I research dates and birthdays, and .... well ...., uh ...," and his voice tapered off.

Jennifer could no longer let him 'twist in the wind' and knew that the full count pitch she had been waiting for had now been delivered. She held her hand up to the stuttering Case and stopped him from talking. "Yes, Case," she said. "I became pregnant that evening, and Charlie was born about nine months later."

She watched Case's face and tried to imagine what was going through his mind. He showed no immediate emotion, keeping his eyes on Jennifer as if waiting for her to say more. When she didn't, Case finally said, "Jennifer, I am so sorry. Why didn't you tell me?"

"I tried, Case," she said. "Believe me, I tried. By the time I knew I was pregnant, you had already left Fort Benning for Saudi Arabia. When I figured out how to track you down and contact you at Eskan Air Force Base, you had already been medically evacuated back to Beaumont Hospital in Texas. I tried to reach you several times at the hospital, but the first two times you were only allowed to take calls from immediate family. The third time, I found out you'd been discharged and were living somewhere at Fort Bliss. When I called that address, a female answered the phone. She indicated that you weren't available when I called but offered to set up a time when I could call back. During that short conversation, she let me know that she was your nurse ... and that she lived with you. Would that have been Julia?"

"Yes ... yes. That had to have been Julia," said Case. "Did you leave your name or a number for me to call back?"

"No, Case," said Jennifer. "I didn't. I wasn't looking for you to provide financial support ... or anything else. I just felt that you should know there would soon be another human in the world with similar DNA to yours. While I was talking to Julia, I decided to 'let it go.' You had already been through a lot with the accident. Why should I potentially mess up your relationship with another woman with the news that you had fathered a child with someone else? It may not have been the right thing to do and, for that, I am sorry. At the time I felt that I could handle raising a child on my own and that you should be left alone."

"It appears to me," said Case "... that you've done a pretty good job of raising a child on your own."

"As they say, Case," she replied, "...it takes a village, and I had plenty of support from my parents and Tim."

"I don't know what to say ... or even think," said Case after a long pause.

"Are you angry?" asked Jennifer

"How can I be angry?" replied Case. "Every decision you made back then seems to have been made to protect me, to the great disadvantage of yourself. I feel that I have a large bill due from you, and I want to know how I can start paying that."

"No, Case," she said. "You don't owe me anything. Charlie and I have had a good life and have needed nothing. Charlie's grandparents helped a lot, and so did my husband, Tim. Charlie has no psychological hang-ups that I know of, or that are apparent, relative to not knowing who his real father is, and he has had few questions about it growing up. When he was young and asked, I simply told him that his father had been a soldier who had gone off to a war and had not returned. This seemed to satisfy him then; as he has gotten older, I think he has avoided the subject out of respect for me."

"He's an amazing young man, Jennifer," said Case. "Sitting here talking with you about Charlie ... well ... one of the many things I'm feeling guilty for ... is this completely undeserved feeling of pride I have at being connected to Charlie."

"Don't feel guilty," said Jennifer. "Charlie has good genes. There's no denying that. I feel guilty as well ... for never even giving you an opportunity to be a part of his life or allowing you an opportunity to participate in it."

Case looked at Jennifer and surprised her by reaching across the desk and grasping her two hands between his. "Yes, Jennifer, I've missed a little time, but Charlie's life is still near the beginning. I've got time to catch up, and I'm going to start doing that right now!"

Jennifer gently pulled her hands back from Case's and said, "That may not be so easy. How will Julia take this news? And what about Shane? Is he going to understand?"

Case thought for a minute and looked at Jennifer before answering. "You've thought about this a lot, haven't you?"

"Case, it's all I've thought about for about 20 years! You've only had a few minutes. Why don't you take some time to absorb all this, and let's talk again in a couple of weeks. From what you have said, I believe your desire to be a part of Charlie's life, and that touches me. We need to think responsibly this time, though. Many innocent lives other than our own will be impacted by this news."

"Okay," said Case. "I understand, and I guess I agree. Nothing that has happened yet demands any immediate action, and perhaps planning how to unravel this is a better idea than just plunging ahead. I want to get Julia's opinion, and I hope that it will be okay if she attends our next meeting."

"Of course!" replied Jennifer. "How will she take this?"

"Julia?" asked Case. "She'll be fine, Jennifer. She's a wonderful and intelligent woman with a beautiful heart. I have never given her a reason to mistrust me, and I'm not going to start now. I think she will understand the situation and have good ideas on how to handle it. How much does your husband know?"

"He's the only one who knows everything. My own father doesn't know who Charlie's father is. I told Tim my history right after Charlie met Shane. When I heard Charlie mention the name, 'Reynolds,' I looked in the admissions records for the names of Shane's parents. As soon as I saw your name there, I knew that a circle was about to be completed."

"I'm sure that was a bit traumatic for you and, again, I apologize," said Case. "Thank you for meeting with me and thank you for your honesty. I think you are an amazing woman and that I owe you much. For now, though, let's just continue to talk and to think this out together."

"That's a deal, Case," said Jennifer. "Let me know when you and Julia want to meet."

After Case left her office, Jennifer relaxed in her chair and looked at the photo of her family on the desk. A tremendous weight had finally been lifted from her, and she felt better than she had in a long time. Case was a good man, and he couldn't have taken the news she had given him any better. As she remembered her thoughts from the previous day, after she had heard the voicemail left by Case on her office phone, she realized that she might have been wrong. She had not taken the 'Strike Three' pitch she had imagined; she had delivered a 'hit' ... and maybe even scored a few RBIs. Baseball ... and life ... were funny.

Case returned from Columbus and immediately asked Julia if she would sit with him in the den before dinner. When Case finished the long story, Julia sat for a long time looking out the window. She had listened without interruption, as Case had requested, for the length of Case's dialogue. Now, she sat quietly. Unsure of what she might be feeling, after a few moments, Case asked, "Julia, are you okay?"

Julia turned towards him and said, "Yes, Case. Sorry. I'm fine. I just can't get it out of my mind that I was the one who answered at least one of Jennifer's calls at the hospital, and I'm certain I'm the one who took the call from her at Fort Bliss. I remember that call! That poor girl! I feel awful!"

Case came from around the couch and put his arms around his wife. "Julia, you couldn't have known why Jennifer was calling and, according to her, she never left her name or number with you for me to call back."

"No, that's right," said Julia, now sniffling slightly into a tissue. "She didn't. As I remember it, however, I wasn't exactly hospitable to her, or overly inviting about her leaving that information. Honestly, Case, I assumed that it was just some old girlfriend trying to catch up … and I figured that this girl needed to know that I had officially taken you off the market for myself."

"Which," answered Case, "…is exactly how Jennifer interpreted your message. She wasn't looking for money or other support. Your answers gave her the closure she needed to abandon her efforts to notify the biological father."

"I'm sorry, Case! That wasn't fair to you; it wasn't fair to Jennifer, and it wasn't fair to Charlie."

"Thinking about what could have been, or might have been, is wasted energy, Julia," said Case. "I wish I had been more responsible in my personal actions after the dance. Jennifer wishes she had been more persistent in notifying me of her condition. You wish that you would have allowed Jennifer a better opportunity to talk to me. None of that history can be changed, though. How do we move forward in the most positive way now?"

Julia sniffled onto Case's shirt a few more times, then regained her composure. "I don't know, but I'm on board. We owe Jennifer a lot of money for starters," she said. "She has raised Charlie by herself, with no support, and done a great job of it!"

"I agree, Julia, but the money thing is a non-starter for her. She says she's had plenty of help from her parents and her husband. She's had a good job with Lefton College since she graduated, and, because of that, Charlie has never suffered from missing the things he needed."

"But, don't we now want him as a part of our life?" asked Julia. "Now that we know he is part of our family, don't we want to help him, and participate with him?"

"Yes, I do," answered Case. "I'm glad you feel that way, too. Many wives in your position wouldn't."

"Case," said Julia, "... this is life, not some kind of soap opera! Charlie is connected in the most intimate and personal way to you. You are connected to me in ways that are equally important, and just as strong. And Shane is connected to Charlie in ways that he doesn't even know yet! We have a larger family than the one we thought we had a week ago and, as I see it, the additions are positive. Where do we go from here?"

Case and Julia talked for several more hours, well into the night. By the following morning, both felt comfortable with a plan. Case emailed Jennifer, proposing a meeting after the next Lefton home game, two weeks away.

The auditors sat comfortably in one of the building's conference rooms and Jennifer checked on them at around 3:00 PM. She asked if they thought they would need her that afternoon. The lead accountant of the three-person team glanced at the other two on the team, then told Jennifer that she believed they had everything they needed. She further indicated that their group anticipated being completed with their work by early the following afternoon. After that, the audit team would want to have a short debriefing with Jennifer. She thanked them and indicated that she had a meeting off campus ... if attending that meeting would not impact their work. They assured her that it wouldn't, and she left the college headed for her father's veterinarian clinic. On the way, she called Tim on her cell phone and told him her plan.

Since way back in 1990 when she first informed her parents of her pregnancy, she had promised herself that, as soon as Charlie's father knew about Charlie, she would inform her parents. Now, over 21 years later, she could finally keep that promise ... at least for her father's sake. When Jennifer asked the receptionist if her dad was available, Claude came to the front. "What's up, Jen? Is everything OK?" he asked.

"Yes, Dad. Everything's fine. I just wanted to speak to you for a few minutes in private. Do you have a little time?"

"Sure, Jen. Come on back to my office," answered Claude. "Let's sit over here near the coffee table."

After they had taken seats, Jennifer took a deep breath and started to speak. "Dad, back in 1990, when I told you and mom about being pregnant, I told you that I couldn't yet reveal to you who the father was. The reason was that I didn't feel anyone should know that information until Charlie's actual father knew. There were reasons I couldn't get that information to that man ... until today. After over 21 years ... the man just found out about Charlie a few hours ago. You were my first stop after my meeting with Charlie's father."

Jennifer paused for a moment gathering her thoughts, when Claude asked, "Did you have a meeting with Case Reynolds today?"

Jennifer gasped and quickly looked at Claude with some alarm in her eyes. "Dad, how did you know?"

"Don't panic, Jennifer," Claude said. "It's OK. I didn't figure everything out until I met Case yesterday after the game. My God, Baby! Charlie looks just like him. Charlie and Shane also resemble each other. I still couldn't be certain though and thought my old eyes might be playing tricks on me, until I got down your yearbook. Once I realized that Case graduated in 1990, I was fairly certain I had solved the mystery. You have to know though, Sweetheart, I'd have never mentioned it to you, Charlie, or anyone else!"

Jennifer listened to her dad, then hugged him. "I know you wouldn't have, Dad, and you have been so patient. I have felt guilty for not sharing the information with you and mom since the evening I told you I was pregnant." Jennifer then gave her dad the short version of the story relating to her difficulties in communicating the news to Case until today.

"Sounds to me," said Claude, "...like you were the martyr in all of this ... trying to negatively impact the fewest number of lives possible. How did Case take the news today?"

Jennifer replied, "He was great! It was such a relief to finally unload the burden. Case had started to figure things out after the ski trip to Michigan. He felt terrible that he had not helped me financially and he wanted to make that up. I told him that wasn't an option."

Claude asked, "What happens now? Will you tell Charlie?"

She replied, "Case will talk to his wife, Julia, when he returns to Indianapolis tomorrow. The adults .... Case, Julia, Tim and I, will then meet again two weekends from now when Case and his wife come to the College for the Monarchs' next home series."

"I assume Tim is up to speed on all of this?" asked Claude.

"He's the only one, until today, that has known everything."

Claude asked, "How will Case's wife react?"

"I don't know," said Jennifer, "... but Case says she'll be fine. We have to think about Shane as well as Charlie."

"Of course!" said Claude, "... although I have to believe that, for those two, this is going to be good news, not bad. They already act like brothers ... and they don't even know they actually are!"

"That's something isn't it?" mused Jennifer. "What are the odds that all of this would ever happen?"

"I think that depends on who you really believe is controlling this whole game," said Claude, smiling. "We aren't all that sure, are we?"

"No," smiled Jennifer "... but that's why I leave some room in my personal beliefs for the things I don't understand or can't comprehend. Something has defied the odds to move our lives to the meeting I had today with Case. Inside, I feel like it was supposed to happen."

"I agree, Honey," said Claude. "Case seems like a gentleman, and I'm glad to know him. Keep me posted ... and ... of course, I won't say anything to anybody."

"I will, Dad. Thank you for everything," she said and paused. *"Everything!"*

Shane's second start was the following weekend at an away game against Taylor University. The Trojans were also in the Heartland Collegiate Athletic Conference (HCAC), so this was a critical early matchup between two of the conference's better teams from the year before. The Monarchs had taken an early 1-0 lead on Pudge Cowan's second-inning home run. The team manufactured a second run in the seventh when Junie Moore beat out a drag bunt for a base hit, stole second, and advanced to third on a groundout by Colovito. He tagged on a long fly ball from Philips, before Jack had ended the inning with another long flyball out to center.

The Trojans could not get any grip on either Shane's fastball or his occasional curve. While the game was still a tight one at 2 - 0 in the bottom of the ninth, Shane seemed to be coasting. He had only thrown 87 pitches entering the ninth, and Coach Blevins was giving him a chance to record his first collegiate win with a complete game shutout. Shane had only struck out three hitters during the game, and each of these had taken no more than four pitches. He had allowed two weak hits, no walks, and seemed in complete control.

The first hitter for the Trojans grounded out to Pudge on the second pitch thrown to him, but Shane nicked the second hitter on the arm with an inside fastball. The third hitter flew out to Colovito, and Shane only needed one more out to seal the game. On the third pitch of that at-bat, the left-handed hitter, very late on a swing on Shane's fastball, chopped a weak ground ball to Phillips at third. Phillips had been playing in on the hitter and, as the dribbler came toward him, it appeared that the ball would go foul. The play would have been a difficult one due to the speed of the lefty hitter, and Louis pulled his glove hand back at the last moment to let the ball proceed over the foul line. After the baseball had crossed the line, and just before going beyond the bag, it took a peculiar hop back toward the playing field ... and hit the bag. Base hit.

Charlie came to the mound to calm his pitcher, and said, "The righty pulled one of my stunts, Shane, and tried to get hit. The lefty was just lucky. Don't worry about it. Get the hitter!"

Shane, pitching from the stretch, got ahead of the large hitter at the plate with two fastball strikes. Charlie then called for a curveball from Shane, placing his glove on the outside of the plate and low. He hoped that the hitter, not wanting to make the game's final out, would take the bait he was offering on the curveball. And he did. If the ball had been the fastball that the hitter expected, the hitter's swing would have been well under the ball, and probably late. Unfortunately for Shane, his curveball literally curved into the head of the swinging bat. As soon as the bat met the baseball, there was no question about where it was going ... the only question was how far it would go. It left the playing area in dead center field, bouncing well beyond the fence in the parking lot. It was last seen hopping for Illinois.

The game was over on the walk-off, three-run homer, and Shane took the loss. In the locker room, all were trying to make Shane feel better, but it wasn't working. Charlie said, "I shouldn't have called for the curve. We should have stuck with the fastball."

"Don't you start trying to take the blame, Charlie," said Shane. "I wasn't supposed to throw an 0 - 2 curveball in an area that the hitter could get to it!"

Coach Blevins strolled over to the lockers where Charlie and Shane were sitting and, in an upbeat tone, said, "Great game, Shane! That's the kind of pitching that's going to take us some places this year. By my count, you only threw 94 pitches in a nine-inning game."

"Well, thanks, Coach," said Shane, glancing at Charlie, and then saying to his coach, "... but in my first two collegiate games, I'm 0 - 1 with a non-decision. I don't see how that's going to get the team where we want to go."

Blevins then gave Charlie a quick nod, indicating that Charlie should leave, and sat down next to his freshman pitcher. "Shane," he said, "next to baseball, my favorite game is poker. I play with a group of guys about once a month, and I win my share of pots. But here's the thing, Shane ... poker is a game of luck, enhanced by skill. Baseball, on the other hand, is a game of skill, enhanced by luck. Over the course of a long season, the teams with the best players are going to win the most games. Occasionally, a team without the best players gets lucky. That's all that happened today. I couldn't be happier about the way you pitched. You may be 0 - 1, but the team is 4 - 1 so far, and you're going to win your share of games this season if you keep pitching the way you did today."

He continued, "Shane, I don't want to minimize what we do out here, but you have to remember, this is just a game. In the grand scheme of things, whether we win or lose isn't going to make much of a difference in your life, my life, or anyone else's life. Once in a while though, the game produces a moment that you'll remember forever ... or a lesson that you'll remember forever. When that happens, you have to have the good sense to appreciate it. The home run that kid hit off you today was a monster! Maybe the longest I've ever seen in college ball, and I've been in college ball a long time. I'm sorry that it happened to be off you but, my God, Son! That drive was a thing of beauty that I'll remember the rest of my life!"

Shane listened, then laughed. For a few seconds, he couldn't even speak because he was laughing so hard.

Finally, he looked at the old coach, and said, "Coach, I'm glad I was able to provide that kind of epic memory for you, but you can probably understand why I wasn't able to appreciate what a sight it was when it happened. You're right though. I'll remember that home run the rest of my life as well. Boy, it went a long ways, didn't it!" Then, Shane reached over to shake his coach's hand, saying very seriously, "I'll also remember this conversation the rest of my life. Thanks, Coach."

"You're welcome, son." Blevins replied, "Now, let's get outta' here! The rest of the team is already on the bus."

As Shane headed out of the locker room, he saw his dad waiting in the parking lot. "I know you have to get on the bus," Case said, "but are you okay?"

"I'm fine, Dad," said Shane cheerfully. "Coach and I were just talking about the game. That was some home run wasn't it?"

"Oh ... yes ... it was ... but...," Case's voice trailed off.

Shane answered quickly, "Coach was happy about the way I pitched today, and when he made me put things in perspective, I felt pretty good about it, too."

"Okay, Son," said Case. "I was just going to tell you that I thought you pitched a heckuva game. Looks like someone else already gave you that news."

"Thanks, Dad," said Shane. "Are you staying for the two games tomorrow?"

"No," said Case. "I just drove over for this evening's game. Your mom and I will be in Lefton next weekend for your home games there."

"Great! See you there," Shane said, and he boarded the bus.

The following day, the Monarchs played a doubleheader against Defiance College. In college, doubleheaders were generally played as seven-inning games, and Jack Ryan had started the first game, with Jack Grimsley taking the second one. Jack won his game easily, 7 - 1, with a complete game. He had also connected for one of the Monarchs' three home runs. Pudge and Charlie had the other two, going back to back in the second inning.

The second game was a little more competitive, with Jake having to pitch out of trouble in two of his first three innings. One of Charlie's pick-off plays in the third had mitigated the damage that inning, but heading into the fourth, the Monarchs were down 2 - 0. After Colovito walked to lead off the inning, Phillips lined a double to the right-field gap. With runners on second and third, Pudge connected for his fourth home run of the young season, and his second of the day. Up 3 - 2 at that point, the Monarchs continued their hit attack that inning and headed to the bottom of the fourth up by a score of 5 - 2. Grimsley pitched an uneventful fourth and managed to get through the fifth, leaving the bases loaded. Sam Casey pitched the last two innings allowing one run on two hits, gaining a save and preserving the win for Grimsley. The Monarchs left Defiance with a 6 - 1 record and looked forward to the next four games at home.

The Monarchs were back at Lefton for a series of four games to be played between Friday evening and Sunday. On Friday, they would play Earlham College, followed by two games on Saturday with Hanover University. The team would finish the weekend on Sunday with a third game against Hanover.

Coach Blevins had looked ahead at this series of games and, even though it was still early in the season, considered them somewhat pivotal. All four games would be conference games, and Earlham was annually one of the conference's powerhouse teams. The Hanover Panthers were also a competitive rival, and, by Sunday of that series, the Monarchs would not have one of their three main starting pitchers available. Either Casey or Stine would have to make the Sunday start. After some deliberation, Blevins decided on Jack for game one against Earlham, with Shane and Jake Grimsley for games two and three against Hanover. He would wait to decide on who would get the start on Sunday.

Jack pitched a strong game against the Earlham Quakers, going eight innings before needing relief help in the ninth. The Monarchs were up 3 - 1, and Jack had only allowed four hits with one walk, but his pitch count was 94. It was still early in the spring, and Blevins refused to bend his personal rule for limiting early season pitch counts, no matter how tight the game might be.

Wanting to save both Stine and Casey for Sunday's game, Blevins told Ten Ton to get loose at the top of the eighth. Before the big righty went to the mound in the ninth, the coach stopped him at the steps. "Denton," he said, "you know your job here. It's a tight game, but this team has not been able to hit Jack's fastball all night. I don't think they will be able to hit yours either. We just need three outs, and they're at the bottom of their order ... 6, 7, 8 and 9. Stay within yourself and don't get fancy. We can't afford walks!"

"Got it, Coach," said the always affable big man. "Now, you just have a seat and relax. Me and Charlie got this," he said smiling.

If anything ever bothered Ten Ton in a game, it wasn't apparent. The team's clown on the bench, Ten Ton was a different person when he took the mound. If his sheer size didn't intimidate opposing hitters, the perpetual sneer on his face when he pitched did. The fact that Ten Ton's fastball reached velocities into the mid-90s and that it wasn't entirely reliable added to the concerns of hitters.

Ten Ton was finishing his warm-up tosses with Charlie, as the Quakers' first hitter watched from the on-deck circle. When Charlie yelled, "Comin' down!" Ten Ton launched his last warm-up throw towards Charlie. It was only vaguely toward Charlie, however, whistling over the catcher's head at 94 miles per hour and hitting the wall in front of the stadium seats loudly. Charlie fielded the ball cleanly off the wall, completing his throw down to second, and laughing under his mask, "Ten Ton, you are too much!"

The hitter stepped gingerly into the batter's box, still considering what he had just witnessed. To him, the batter's box didn't seem to be a particularly safe place to be at the moment. He was now hoping to see a pitch, somewhere away from his body, that he could hit early in the count. Ten Ton made quick work of him, throwing three pitches to the outside of the plate which the hitter swung at. None of the pitches was thrown to the exact spot where Charlie held the glove, but they were effective nonetheless.

The next hitter, number seven in the Quakers' order, did not fare much better. After looking at a called first strike the hitter was late on an outside fastball. Ten Ton moved the hitter away from the plate on the third pitch with a chin-high fastball. On the fourth pitch the hitter had one foot out of the batter's box as he took a third strike fastball on the inside corner.

Ten Ton's masterful performance was blemished when he hit the third batter squarely on the back of the hitter's thigh. The pitch had been inside, and the hitter had correctly turned his body toward the umpire to take the pitch where it might do the least damage to his body. He went down in a heap holding his thigh. Time was called as the young man was attended to, and he was eventually able to get on his feet and limp down to first base. On his way to the base, he heard Ten Ton apologize for the pitch that had gotten away.

In the on-deck circle, the number nine hitter looked toward his dugout, wondering if, and probably hoping that, his coach might want to pinch hit for him. With no relief coming from that quarter, he proceeded timidly to the batter's box. His tentative stance seemed to indicate that his primary goal in this plate appearance was to escape the at-bat without injury ... rather than try to extend the game with a hit or a walk. He struck out on three successive swings, and the game was over.

As soon as the out was recorded, the sneer on Ten Ton's face turned into a broad grin. He no longer looked like a dangerous or psychopathic criminal, but more like a younger version of a kindly James Earl Jones. Charlie met him halfway to the mound and congratulated him.

"Sorry about that third hitter, Charlie," he said. "That was tighter than I had planned."

"What about the one you threw over my head in the warm-ups?" Charlie asked.

Ten Ton grinned, winked, and said, "Oh ... *that* one went exactly where I planned!"

Shane was scheduled to start the first game of Saturday's doubleheader against Hanover College. He would face the Panther's ace, Derek Stemple. Derek was a junior, who had set a conference record the previous year for most strikeouts in a season and lowest earned run average ever recorded in a season. He was a hard-throwing lefty, like Shane, with much collegiate experience. It was a beautiful day in March, with clear skies and no wind, and a temperature of almost 70 degrees. It was unseasonably warm for this time of the year, and nobody on the field or in the stands was complaining.

Shane started the game with three consecutive groundouts. Stemple answered with two strikeouts and a fly out. Shane came back with a fly out, another groundout, and a four-pitch strikeout. Stemple responded by striking out the side, which included Jack, Pudge, and Charlie. The three best hitters on the Lefton team hadn't been easy strikeouts ...two had taken the count full, and Charlie had connected for a long foul ball that had almost been a home run.

In the third, Shane allowed a runner on a passed-ball strikeout. Charlie simply couldn't handle one of Shane's sharp breaking balls that had dived a foot in front of the plate and was well outside. The hitter, already down 0 - 2 in the count, had swung at the pitch, and it skittered to the backstop. The runner was eliminated when the next batter hit into a double play. Shane got the third out on a five-pitch strikeout. In the bottom half of that inning, Stemple retired Billings on a groundout before Shane singled up the middle for the Monarchs' first hit. The light-hitting Moore sacrificed Shane to second, which brought Danny Colovito to the plate.

The senior center fielder had flied out on the first pitch of the game, and he resolved to see more pitches during this at-bat. Remembering Danny's anxiousness in his first at-bat of the game, Stemple started him with a fastball out of the zone, and outside. Danny took it for a ball. Danny flinched at the left-hander's next pitch, a curveball that started in the middle of the plate. He held back in time to take the ball inside for ball two. Colovito called, "Time!" and stepped out of the box, thinking. *Stemple is down 2-0 in a tight game; he doesn't want to go to 3-0; his best pitch is a fastball ... I'm getting a fastball on this pitch,* he thought. Colovito stepped back into the box and prepared himself for something near the middle of the plate and about 90 miles per hour.

The veteran collegiate player had figured right. While his swing was slightly behind the pitch, the bat connected solidly, launching a scorching line drive toward the right-field corner. Shane had taken a substantial lead from second base and, with two outs, was running on contact. He easily scored, with the throw from the outfield being cut off to hold Danny to a double. Phillips followed with another patient at-bat that ended with a long fly ball out to left field. Going into the fourth, Shane had a one-run lead to protect and the top of the Panther line-up to face. After the warm-ups, Charlie visited the mound for a word with his pitcher. "Okay, Shane, my man," he said. "We've got a good game going. We only go seven innings for doubleheaders, so this could be the last time we see the Panther's best hitters until the last inning of the game. You've only thrown 25 pitches for the first three Innings. Stemple has already thrown around 60. He might be around by the 7th, but I doubt it. Continue to pound the strike zone, but our strategy should be strikeouts this inning ... if we can get them."

Shane complied, delivering two strikeouts and a foul ball out caught by Charlie. Only one of the strikeouts had occurred on a 3 - 2 count. The other one was on four pitches. His pitch count after four complete was a healthy 43.

The Monarchs could do no additional damage in the fifth despite mounting a threat. Jack flew out on a 3 - 2 pitch before Pudge walked and Charlie was hit by a pitch. Jud hit a rocket to second base which was knocked down by the second basemen in time to record an out at first, while the runners advanced to second and third. Shane drew a walk on a 3 - 2 count, loading the bases before Junie struck out to end the inning.

In the 6th, Shane struck out the number four hitter on five pitches, before walking the number five hitter on six. Charlie visited the mound, and Shane met him halfway. "I know, Charlie," said Shane. "Just getting a little too fine there. I figured the number five hitter would be a little more aggressive in a tight game, but he seemed fine with just taking a walk."

"Okay," said Charlie, "I agree. The bottom of their order is fairly weak, but I'd prefer not seeing the middle of their order in the 7th."

"Agree," said Shane. "Let's go with a pickoff on two ... if we don't get the runner, I'll strike out the hitter."

Charlie gazed at Shane for a moment and said, smiling, "In a perfect world, sounds great. I'll get back to you." Charlie held up one arm toward the outfield with two fingers extended. Outfielders moved around a bit in the charade, and infielders looked oblivious to the signal. From the stretch, Shane threw a first-pitch curveball for a strike. On the next pitch, he delivered a fastball to the outside of the plate, which Charlie caught and immediately threw to Jack at first. Though close, the runner had gotten back to the base just ahead of the pick-off attempt. Shane's next pitch was a blazing fastball to the inside corner for a called strike. On 2 and 2, the hitter swung weakly, resulting in a ground ball to Shane, who turned it into a double play.

Everyone on the bench knew … and everyone in the stands knew. Shane, himself, knew. Going into the last inning, Shane had a no-hitter going. Nobody said a word to him, though. Stemple came back to the mound for the Panthers at the bottom of the six. He'd thrown over 90 pitches already but had only allowed two hits and was just down by a run. His coach decided he deserved the chance to win the game. Colovito sliced a line drive to right field that was caught. Phillips walked on five pitches before Jack hit a hard ground ball to third which was converted to a double play.

Top of the seventh and Shane needed three more outs. Before he left the dugout, his coach stopped him. "Shane," Blevins said, "I think this may be one of those moments we talked about last week. Don't think about anything else but enjoying it!"

"Got it, Coach," said Shane.

After completing the warm-ups, Charlie visited the mound. Retrieving the game ball from Phillips, he handed it to Shane, saying, "I got nothin' to say, Shane. This is your game. You got seven, eight, and nine up … and I'm guessing in a 2 - 0 game, we'll see at least one, or maybe two, pinch-hitters. You're at 65 pitches. You can tell me what you want to throw."

"Okay," said Shane. "I feel good. My fastball is still live, and the curveball has been pretty reliable today. That's the number seven hitter in the circle, and I struck him out twice today. Doesn't look like they're pinch-hitting him, so let's go after him early."

Charlie returned to his position, and the hitter stepped into the batter's box. The left hander's first pitch was hard and fast to the center of the plate, and the hitter swung, hitting a soft line drive toward third base. Phillips moved to his right before launching himself horizontally to spear the foul ball before it hit the ground. *One out*, thought Charlie.

A pinch-hitter entered the game for the Panthers' and, after looking at his coach, Charlie again visited the mound. "Coach doesn't know anything about this hitter, Shane," said Charlie, "so I don't know what to suggest. He looks big, so I'm guessing he's a power hitter."

"Right," said Shane. "I've been throwing almost all first-pitch fastballs, so let's start him with a curve to his fist. We'll go from there."

Shane's first pitch started exactly to the area of the plate that the hitter was hoping, and he was already too far committed in his swing to pull back when the pitch attacked his fists. The result was a weak ground ball to Jack at first which he fielded, throwing to Shane covering the base for out number two.

Another pinch hitter arrived on the on-deck circle and, again, after glancing at the bench, Charlie trotted to the mound. "No information on this guy either," said Charlie. "Looks like he's strong and can drive the ball. My guess is that this is their last hope to tie. How's the tank?"

Shane said, "The tank is full!"

The big hitter stepped in, and Shane started him with a curveball breaking toward the right-handed hitter's hands. This time, unlike the last pinch hitter, the hitter's hands never moved. Shane tried the opposite approach on the next pitch, going for a fastball on the outside corner. While close, again the hitter's hands never flinched, and the umpire indicated "Ball two!"

"Okay," thought Shane, "...with your team down a run, and two outs in the last inning, you're looking for a walk? Not going to happen!"

Shane delivered his third pitch to the big hitter, a 93 mile-per-hour fastball near the center of the plate. The ball was met by the bat a tad early ... and was deposited in the parking lot to the left side of the foul line in left field. *Whoa!* thought Shane. *That was close! Okay, what are you looking for on 2 and 1? I think you're looking for a fastball, because you know I don't want to go to 3 - 1 on you.*

Shane shook off the sign just displayed by Charlie, and while Charlie's glove wasn't in the exact location Shane wanted, he started his windup. The pitch started outside the plate and, had it been a fastball as the batter expected, would have been a ball. The curveball broke for the plate however for a called strike. At 2 - 2, Charlie called for the same pitch again, this time running it from the center of the plate to the hands. The hitter took it for a ball, 3 and 2.

Wow, thought Shane, *This guy is <u>good</u>.* Charlie was trotting out to the mound and Shane greeted him, "What now, oh wise one?"

"I don't know," said Charlie. "I wish you had perfected the change-up we've been working on. This guy has patience, seems to be on your fastball, and I'm not sure why he wasn't in the starting lineup. At this point, I'd be okay with walking him and go after the leadoff hitter. You've already struck him out and forced him to ground out in this game."

"I hear you, Charlie, but I'm feeling it. Let's strike this guy out and end it."

"Got it!" said Charlie, with no amendments.

The batter was at a slight disadvantage because he knew the next pitch could be either the curveball or the fastball. He also knew that the pitcher could afford to walk him in this situation. In his mind, he guessed, *curveball toward the hands.* The pitch was a fastball to the outside corner. The hitter tried to adjust his swing in the microseconds between the time the pitch left Shane's hands and the time it arrived near the plate. The bat missed the ball by some millimeters, and the ball struck safely into Charlie's mitt for strike three. The umpire called, "Strike three! Game!" and his teammates surrounded Shane. He just won his first collegiate game, and it was a complete game, no-hitter. As he left the playing field, Coach Blevins offered a hand.

"Another memorable moment offered by this great game I suspect?" said Blevins.

"Yes, Coach," he said, "It is a great game, isn't it?

"Yes, Shane. It is. "

After the game, Shane and Charlie stayed at the Village Inn, celebrating their seventh win with the rest of the team. Jill had joined them, and Charlie was surprised that Linda Hawkins had come with Jill. Charlie had seen her at the game and had wondered what the attraction was for Linda, now that her fiancé, Doug Jennings, had graduated. He was worried that he, himself, might now be the attraction for Linda.

Case, Julia, Jennifer, and Tim used the opportunity to get together back at Tim and Jennifer's house. When she entered the house, Julia went straight to Jennifer.

"Hi, Jennifer," she said. "Case told me everything, and I'm sorry... I'm so sorry! I was the one you talked to at Fort Bliss, and I'm the one that blocked your efforts to talk to Case. I was so wrong, and I'm so sorry!"

"Julia, Julia ..." said Jennifer. "Stop! You did exactly what any other normal woman would have done! I could have, and probably should have, been more persistent. I could have tried harder, but you gave me the excuse I was looking for, *not* to try harder!"

"Thank you for trying to make me feel better," said Julia. "I still feel responsible."

Glancing at Tim, Jennifer said, "The only one among us who has absolutely no responsibility for our current predicament is Tim. He can be totally objective, and he has some thoughts."

All turned to Tim, who began, "Thanks, Jennifer. Nobody in this room loves Charlie more than me, and I've become quite a fan of Shane as well. These are two great boys, well raised by great families. At this moment, they believe they are just friends. When they find out they are brothers, I want to be there!" Tim continued, "I don't think either Shane or Charlie will pass judgment on their parents and I don't think they will feel cheated that they didn't know about each other earlier. I think they will feel that a miracle has come true for them. My suggestion to Jennifer is that perhaps this miracle be revealed after the baseball season. Let their current personal relationship carry them through this next few months of baseball, unenhanced ... or unimpaired, by any other potentially larger dynamic."

"I think you're right, Tim. That's a good plan," said Case. "Nothing is going to change for either over the next couple months. Let's don't give them anything new that might distract them." Looking now at Tim, Case asked, "I have to ask you, Tim, with the greatest respect, how do you feel about all this? You and Charlie's grandfather have been Charlie's male support group for many years. How do you feel about a late-to-the-party interloper like me, now?"

"That's a good question, and a fair question, Case," said Tim. "I have thought about it quite a bit. Charlie and I have been as close as any man and boy can be since he was five. My relationship with him is special and, I believe, permanent. That won't change. I know Charlie too well. You aren't an interloper, Case. You are Charlie's father, and I welcome both you and Julia to his growing family."

"Thanks!" said Case. "You set a high benchmark for being in that select company."

Jennifer had gotten a calendar off the refrigerator and was looking at it. "The Monarchs' last home game is on May 6th, and if they make the Mid-East Regionals, the championship game is on May 20th. If we agree, I think our full family conversation should follow the team's last game."

Julia responded first, saying, "I think that's a good plan. I agree with Tim that both boys will receive the surprising news well, but let's don't give them anymore to think about until after the school semester and after the baseball season."

"Sounds good to me," said Case

"Me, too," said Jennifer. "Can I tell you all how much better I feel with everyone else helping to make these decisions, versus just me?"

"You deserve a break, girl," said Julia. "We're all in this together from here on out!"

"Sounds like a good reason for a beer to me," said Case. "Tim, do you keep any of that in this house?"

"Only about two cases," said Tim. "Think that will be enough for this evening?" All laughed and enjoyed one of the least stressful evenings that any in the group had had for several weeks.

When he saw Case in the stands, Charlie had been surprised. Shane wasn't scheduled to pitch that weekend, as Coach Blevins was holding him for the more important away conference game against Earlham College on Wednesday. Case had made the trip to Columbus to watch the team, anyway. Charlie knew that Case traveled frequently to Columbus and it was always nice to have home fans for distant games. After the first game against the Capital University Crusaders, which Josh Stine had won 6 - 4, Case stopped Charlie in the parking lot. He inquired whether Charlie could possibly visit him at the hotel later that evening. Since Case was staying at the same hotel as the team it wasn't a problem.

Charlie was rooming with Jud that weekend and, when he left the room to see Case, he indicated to Jud he'd be right back. Case met Charlie at the door of his room and Charlie was surprised when he didn't see Shane in the room. Case said, "Come on in, Charlie. This won't take a minute. I wanted to talk to you about something ...and give you some information." Charlie entered the room and, less than 15 minutes later, exited with a folder of papers.

The Monarchs had a successful weekend in Ohio, going 3 - 1 in the four games played against strong Ohio teams. On Saturday, they had split the doubleheader with Ohio Wesleyan, with Jake Grimsley winning the first one, 3 - 1, and Jack Ryan taking a tough 4 - 3 loss in the second game. Sam Casey pitched the Monarchs to a 5 - 2 win against the Ohio Dominican Panthers, with some help from Ten Ton in the ninth.

Shane got the start against the Earlham Quakers on a Wednesday evening. Earlham College was only a short drive from Lefton Township, so the game was almost like a home game, except that on this evening few Monarch fans were in the stands. Few Quaker fans were either. It was cold and misting something that was too heavy to be fog, too light to be rain and not white enough to be snow. Ten Ton swore it *was* snow and he was wrapped in a blanket at the end of the bench. Mercifully, the game only lasted five innings. With the Monarchs ahead by a score of 11 - 1 after the fifth, the umpires called the game. Shane had only allowed two hits, but one was a home run in the bottom of the fourth to the Quakers' clean-up hitter. After the game, on the short bus ride back to Lefton, Coach Blevins had asked Charlie and Luis to join him in the front seats of the bus.

"Charlie," he began, "another good game for you. Three for three with a dinger at the plate and three pick-off plays in the field."

"Thanks, Coach," said Charlie, with a suspicion that the compliment wasn't the coach's only reason for inviting Charlie to sit with him at the front of the bus.

"You're welcome, but I'd like you to think about something with me," said the coach. "An army's most effective strategy is the 'ambush,' and its most effective weapon is the one the enemy doesn't know about. The team had three pick-off outs tonight, including the timed play from Shane that you called. Great plays ... and all well-executed. The problem is that, in a game we were winning 7 - 0 from the top of the second inning, we didn't need those plays to win. There is a balance in using the plays enough in real game situations to keep them sharp ... and overusing them to the point that they no longer surprise anybody. This evening was too awful a night for anybody in their right mind to be scouting us but, if you aren't careful, your reputation for using the unconventional pick-offs will be socialized around our league ... and even beyond. If teams start to expect these plays, runners will be more careful on the bases and pick-off outs will be harder to get.

For the rest of the season, I want you to be more discreet about showing other teams all the tricks we have in our bag. I think we have a good chance to go to the Mid-East Regionals again … and maybe even further. Let's keep some of our weapons a secret if we can."

"I understand, Coach," said Charlie. "I never even thought about that before, but what you say makes sense."

"Luis," said Blevins, "the same thing goes for you. You're playing well enough to be getting more playing time than you are, but you have a unique gift that few teams know about yet. Pudge graduates this year and, if you keep working the way you have been, you'll be tough for anyone to beat out for the second base position next year. This year, though, I want as few teams as possible to know about either your speed or your ability to make contact with just about anything thrown to the plate. Those slap ground balls to the infield aren't going to work for hits once teams know that's all you can do. They'll just play you in every time you bat, and those ground balls will be easy outs. Next year, that's not all you're going to be able to do … but this year that may be all you need to do in certain key situations to help the team win a game or two."

"Thanks, Coach," said Luis. "I think I know what my role is this year and I'm just glad to be part of the team."

"What about Shane's change-up, Charlie?" asked Blevins. "Any progress?"

"Yes sir," said Charlie. "Quite a bit. Jack showed him a weird pitch that he used to use in high school for a change-up. It's more like a big, drop off the table, curveball, but the pitch is also at least 15 mph slower than Shane's fastball. Rather than gripping the baseball in the back of the hand like most change-ups, the pitcher only grips about half the ball, with the other half sticking out of the back of the hand. Jack quit using the pitch when hitters got used

202

to seeing so much of the baseball exposed on his delivery. If the hitter knows what's coming, he can either lay off it, or wait, and hit it like a slow-pitch softball."

"Can Shane throw it for a strike?" asked Blevins.

"Most of the time, now," said Charlie, "but the nice thing about the pitch is that it's even more effective when its thrown for a ball. It is so slow that hitters think they can tee off on it … until it drops into the dirt in front of the plate. Shane isn't ready to use it in a game yet, but he's getting close."

"Sounds good," said the coach. "So far, he hasn't needed a third pitch, and nobody thinks he has one. That might be another weapon we keep under wraps for a while."

The bus had arrived back at Lefton College and, as the players began hauling their gear to the locker room, Shane saw Jill waiting by her car. She waved at Jud, then called to Shane," Sorry I didn't drive over to Earlham tonight. How'd you guys do?"

"Don't blame you a bit," said Shane. "Sitting in the stands would have been even more miserable than playing in the game was. We won 11 - 1. Jud was two for three with another home run. I was one for three at the plate and got the win, pitching. I gave up a monster home run in the fourth inning, though."

"That was my fault," said Charlie, catching up to Shane. "By the fourth inning, and up 10 - 0, I was just calling for center cut fastballs to keep the hitters swinging. I think everyone just wanted the game to be over."

"Well," said Jill, "the weather is supposed to be nicer this weekend. Shane, it's already 11:00, so I'm going to go back to the dorm. I just wanted to say 'hi'. I'll see you tomorrow for lunch."

It was the bottom of the sixth against a conference team, Anderson College, and the two sides were locked, 1 - 1, in a classic pitcher's duel. In the first game of a late March Saturday doubleheader at the home field in Lefton, Jake Grimsley was matching all-conference left-hander Dick Needles out for out and pitch for pitch. Dick had allowed only a run on three hits through the first five innings for the Ravens. His pitch count was still under 70 despite walking three hitters. Jake had allowed four hits and a run through six innings, walking none; his pitch count was nearing 80 pitches, though.

Due up for the Monarchs in the bottom half of the inning were Hamilton, Long, and Billings. If the team managed to get anything going, Jake was due up as the fifth hitter in the inning. Either Hayden Piper or the Z-Man would probably pinch-hit if the inning went that far. Blevins had Ten Ton loosening up in the bullpen for the Monarchs.

Charlie was one for two on the day with a double in the second inning. He flied out in the fourth. In his third at-bat, he grounded sharply to third base. The third baseman made a good play, throwing Charlie out by a step from deep behind the bag for the first out. Jud Long, also one for two on the day, was due up. He was responsible for the Monarchs' only run, driving in Charlie from second base with an opposite-field single in the second. He was struck out by Needles in the fourth on an ugly curveball from the senior lefty. Jud had pleased Coach Blevins this season by not being quite as selective as in previous seasons at the plate. While still a patient hitter, who very rarely began to swing until he had a strike, Long seldom struck out looking at pitches anymore.

As he stepped to the plate in the sixth, Jud mentally reviewed his previous two at-bats against Needles. The Ravens' pitcher had started him with a center-cut fastball in the second, which Jud had taken for a strike. He'd then looked at a serious curveball that broke on his hands for a ball. He'd stroked an outside fastball to right for a single on the third pitch, which had scored Charlie from second base. In the fourth, Needles had again started him with a fastball strike, belt high and to the outer edge of the plate. Jud had laid off the second pitch curveball but, this time, the baseball had caught the inside of the plate for strike two. From that point in the bat, all Jud could do was try to foul off curveballs to keep the at-bat alive. He did this for two more pitches before striking out on another sweeping curveball towards his hands. Whatever happened on this at-bat, thought Jud, he knew he wanted nothing to do with Needles' curveball. Swinging at the first pitch was against Jud's normal routine, but the big right fielder thought that Needles' first pitch might be his best opportunity for a good pitch to hit.

As in Jud's first two at-bats against Needles, the left-hander started Jud with a fastball near the center of the plate. Surprising Needles, Blevins, and everyone else on the Monarchs' bench, Long took a ferocious swing, meeting the baseball cleanly. The baseball left the stadium on a line drive over the fence in right-center field, and Jud started his trot around the bases. He had put his team ahead by a score of 2 - 1. A cute girl in the stands that had a resemblance to Jud was the loudest cheerleader. Jill was jumping and screaming and when she heard Ten Ton out in the bullpen start chanting in his big booming voice, "Here come da' Jud!" "Here come da' Jud!" She picked up the chant as well. By the time Jud reached third base, the whole home side of the stadium had joined in the chant. The senior right fielder, who had never started a game for the Monarchs until this year, was smiling. As he rounded third, he pointed to his sister and touched the brim of his cap.

Billings grounded to first, and Moore struck out to end the inning, but the Monarchs were now up by a run. Blevins gave his senior starter the ball, and Grimsley trotted back out to the mound for the seventh. He was able to retire the first hitter on a foul ball pop fly which Phillips retrieved from the first row of the bleachers. He walked the Ravens number two hitter on four pitches, and Charlie visited the mound. "I'm OK, Charlie," said Jake. "That guy has two of the team's four hits against me, and I was just a little too careful. My arm still feels good."

"OK," said Charlie. "This next guy hasn't got a hit today, but he's backed Jud to the wall twice on flyballs. He's their number three hitter so he can probably hit. He's a lefty; keep the ball low. Ground ball to Pudge for a double play would be my preference," Charlie said, smiling.

Jake smiled and said, "Comin' right up!"

That's not exactly what came up, though. After taking a close pitch on the outside corner for a ball, the hitter uncoiled to hit a vicious line drive that just barely eluded the leaping Jack Ryan's glove at first. Jud was racing at full speed from his right-field position to try to cut the ball off before it disappeared into the right-field corner. With his long, left arm extended fully, he was able to snag the hopping baseball in full stride. Planting his right foot on the next step toward the foul line, he pirouetted away from the plate and toward the outfield fence as he transferred the baseball from his glove to his throwing hand. As he completed the full turn, he was already bringing his throwing arm back and transferring his body weight from his right foot to his left foot.

Pudge had moved out toward the outfield and was lining himself up with Charlie at the plate. Jack had left first base and was standing just to the left of the mound, about 45 feet in front of the plate. Grimsley had run at full speed to back up Charlie behind home plate. Jud had several options in this scenario, depending on a variety of dynamics. The runner at first was speedy and was already nearly to third when Jud completed his turn. The hitter wasn't as fast and was just starting his turn around first toward second. It would take a perfect throw to home to nail the runner from this deep in right-field. If instead, Jud threw to Pudge, the team would likely record an out on the advancing hitter, or perhaps force the hitter to be hung up between first and second base. The Monarchs would then have two outs and nobody on ... but the game would be tied.

Jud chose the riskier strategy, firing a bullet over Pudge's raised arms toward the plate. The throw never achieved a height of more than seven feet as it approached Jack and the first baseman heard Charlie yell, "Let it come!"

Jack dropped flat to the ground to avoid obstructing Charlie's view, and the ball flew past him toward Charlie. As the ball took one bounce toward the plate, Charlie stepped into the baseline to retrieve it. He simultaneously stooped into a defensive position to receive the inevitable collision with the baserunner. Runner, ball, and catcher all seemed to arrive at the same spot at the same time, approximately 3 feet up the third base line, away from the plate. Checking to ensure that the catcher had retained the ball during the collision, the umpire made a dramatic gesture, proclaiming, "You're out!" and Charlie jumped to his feet. In Charlie's mind, this play, as dramatic as it had been, wasn't over yet. As he had expected, Charlie saw that the hitter had reached second base on the play and had gone slightly down the line towards third in the event Charlie dropped the ball during the collision. Like all in the stands, the hitter had become a spectator and hadn't expected the catcher involved in a violent collision to jump to his feet and fire a strike to second base. Junie Moore, the shortstop, did expect this, however. He was standing on second to retrieve Charlie's throw, made the easy tag for the third out, and the game was over.

As Jud trotted toward the infield, the chant from an inning before began again. "Here come da' Jud! Here come da' Jud!" This was Jud's game for sure. He had single-handedly delivered the win to Grimsley by providing the first run and then the winning run. He had then prevented the game from being tied with an outstanding defensive play. Shane, who was sitting on the bench next to Coach Blevins, said, "Looks like another one of those moments this game gives us, huh, Coach?"

Blevins looked at the freshman pitcher, and said, "Yep. Gotta love it, don't you?"

"Sure do," said Shane.

Sophomore pitcher, Sam Casey (Sammie C), pitched the second game of the doubleheader and, though he pitched well, took a tough 4 - 3 loss. Jud was again the offensive leader for the Monarchs, going two for three with a double in the fourth that drove in two runs. Ten Ton pitched a strong seventh inning, striking out two Ravens, but the Monarchs could not rally in the bottom half of the inning. Despite the loss, Lefton College remained in first place of the HCAC with an 11 - 2 Conference record, and 14 - 4 overall.

Between the first and second games, Case and Julia made their way to where Janine and John Long were sitting. Tim Drake had pointed out the Longs to Case earlier in the day. The Longs had been at the opening home series, but Case and Julia hadn't had an opportunity to introduce themselves, and the Longs had missed the next home series of games.

"John Long," said Case, "I'm Case Reynolds, and this is my wife Julia. Your daughter has made quite an impression on our son, Shane, and on us as well. It is evident from the last game that you have more than one star in the family. What a game Jud had!"

"Thank you, Case!" said John, "This is my wife, Janine. It is great to meet you two. As you might imagine, we have heard quite a bit about your son at our house over the past six months. He is as charming in person as Jill has made him out to be in her legend of him."

"Thank you, John," said Julia. "Because of Jill's internship at Indiana Psychiatric, we have had several opportunities to visit with her at our home. She is a remarkable young woman on many levels."

"Jillian has told us about her trips to Indianapolis and about how nice you all have been to invite her to dinner," said Janine.

"That's the least we could do to repay her for her taxi service bringing Shane home for some weekends. As you know, freshman at Lefton College can't have cars, and we have seen Shane much more than we anticipated we would in his first year there," said Julia.

"I have a feeling that the taxi service wasn't a hardship on Jillian," John said, laughing.

"And we're pretty sure that Shane's reasons for coming home on those weekends had less to do with seeing us than it did on who his driver for the trips was," answered Case. "Whatever the reason, we thoroughly enjoyed seeing both of them. Jill seems to have a good plan for what she is going to do in life."

"That she does," said John, "and Jillian has always had a way of getting what she wants."

"And from what I understand, one of the things she wanted to do was attend the same college as her brother, while he was still there, even though she was three grades behind him in high school," said Case.

John and Janine laughed, and Janine answered, "Yes, that's true. We didn't think she could do it, but she proved us wrong. As you have probably heard Judson and Jillian have a close personal relationship."

Julia said, "I think that is so sweet, and it seems that Jud has ensured that she has a battalion of bodyguards on the baseball team."

"It seems," said John, "and you will find this season, as you get to meet the rest of the boys, this is a special group of young men. I can't imagine a better peer group."

"We can't wait," said Julia. "We have gotten to know one of the boys, the catcher, Charlie Hamilton, pretty well and my husband already wants to hire him when he graduates."

"It would be a good choice," said John. "Charlie will be an asset to any team he plays on, any organization he participates in, and any company he works for. I'm glad that Jillian and Jud can call him a close friend."

"That seems to be a rather universal sentiment about Charlie," said Julia.

"It is, and it is well-earned," chimed in Janine. "From what Jillian tells us, Charlie has sort of adopted Shane this year and he couldn't have a better mentor in his first year at college."

Case glanced briefly at Julia and winked. "Between him and Jill," said Case, "Shane is being well cared for. As parents, we feel fortunate. Looks like they are getting ready to start the next game. We just wanted to introduce ourselves and tell you how much we have enjoyed getting to know your daughter."

The Monarchs were almost at the halfway point of the regular season, with a road trip to Indianapolis scheduled for the following weekend. The team was 12 - 3 in the HCAC conference and 15 - 6, overall. This gave them a two-game lead for first place in the conference, and they would play one of the weaker teams in that conference in a doubleheader in Indianapolis. Coach Blevins called a team meeting for 4 o'clock on Monday afternoon.

"Men," he began, "we're off to a good start. If we play the second half like the first half, we'll be in a good position to get another invitation to the Mid-East Regionals. I'm not here to talk about baseball today, though. I'm here to talk about this." He was holding up some papers. "These are mid-semester academic reports. Charlie, Jud, Jake, Jack, Shane, Sam... Good job! Excellent reports. Many of the rest of you have also done very well... a couple of you haven't."

"At this College," Blevins continued, "our focus is to ensure a quality education. If you have a quality athletic experience here, that's a bonus. Only 2% of all players who play college baseball ever play in the pros... and that includes Division I and Division II players. Of that percentage, only a small number get to the major leagues. If you make it to the majors, the average career is 5.6 years long. Gentleman, your education will last a lifetime. There should be no question where your priorities are here at Lefton College. We'll practice tomorrow and Wednesday, and the bus will leave at 9:00 AM on Friday morning for Indianapolis. That's all I have. D'Ante and Hayden stay here for a few minutes."

The two players looked guilty even before Coach Blevins started talking to them. "D'Ante," said Blevins. "you're a sophomore, and you're our starting left fielder this year, but these grades wouldn't get you hired as a dogcatcher. You aren't in any danger of flunking out, but if this is the best you can do academically, you're wasting your time at this school. *Is* this the best you can do?"

"No, Coach," said the young ballplayer. "I'm not proud of these grades so far this semester. Neither are my parents. I've just lost a little focus I guess with my excitement for the team."

"Okay," said Blevins, "good answer. I want you to get your focus back, and I've arranged some help. Your worst grade is the D in accounting 202. Charlie's mother, who is also the Controller for this college, has agreed to tutor you for two hours per evening for the next ten days, including this weekend. You are excused from practices until next Thursday, and you won't make the trip to Indianapolis with the team."

"Hayden," said Blevins, "what do you have to say?"

Hayden Piper, a freshman, looked like he might pass out and, in a trembling voice, said, "No excuse, Coach. I did well first semester and just got out of a good study routine, I think."

Blevins replied, "I would say! Halfway through this semester, you've got two 'D's, two 'C's, and a 'B.' Last semester, you made the Dean's list. One of your 'D's is in biology, which is your stated major. Professor Gunderson has agreed to tutor you for an hour before classes, starting every morning at 7:00 AM. He will do this every day, except Sunday, from tomorrow until next Thursday. Let's see if you can pull the two 'D's up. You are also excused from practice during this time and won't be making the trip to Indianapolis."

"Sorry, Coach," said Piper. "I appreciate your helping me out."

"Okay," ended Blevins. "I'll look forward to seeing you back in uniform next Thursday. You've both made contributions to the team this year, and we need you if we're going to continue to be competitive. You owe yourselves *and your teammates* your best efforts to improve your academic performance."

If the punishment seemed harsh, Blevins knew that at least this was the right week to make the point about academics. Of the four games in Indianapolis, two were nonconference, and the other two were against the league's weakest team, the Franklin Grizzlies.

Case and Julia had invited Jennifer and Tim to stay at their home in Indianapolis for the weekend, and Jennifer had accepted for Saturday evening. Due to her commitment to Blevins, relative to D'Ante Billings, she couldn't leave Lefton College until 10:00 AM on Saturday morning. She had scheduled D'Ante's Sunday tutoring for 6:00 PM, so that she could still see most of the Monarchs' game against Butler University.

Sam Casey pitched on Friday evening, and the Monarchs easily defeated Marian College, 8 - 2. Shane started the first game on Saturday against Franklin College. The game only lasted five innings, as the umpire called the game due to the mercy rule at the bottom of the fifth when the Monarchs were up 12 - 0. Shane had allowed a single in the second inning, precluding his second no-hitter of the season.

The second game on Saturday afternoon had only been slightly more competitive, as Jack Ryan had gone the distance in an 8 - 1 win. Alexander James, the Z-man as he was called by his teammates, played left field for the suspended Billings. He had made several good plays in the outfield and hit respectably, going three for eight so far for the weekend.

Case had made reservations for four at the famous St. Elmo's Steakhouse in Indianapolis, and the four adults enjoyed a relaxed evening of great food and stimulating company. Case also made sure the drinks kept coming, surprising everyone with the announcement that he'd made arrangements for one of his employees to pick the group up when they had finished dinner. He and Julia would come downtown the next morning to retrieve their car.

Since the trauma of discussing the 'big secret' had passed, Jennifer, Tim, Julia, and Case were becoming good friends. In the process of visiting during games and dining together after, the group discovered that they shared more than just a bond with Charlie. All were intelligent and well-informed relative to world events. Tim and Case both participated in fantasy baseball leagues. Julia and Jennifer were each great cooks. Both couples placed the value of 'family' above all else.

During the meal, and after the obligatory reviews of the three games that had been played, the adults shared ideas about the impending conversation with the boys. All were now looking forward to the event. As Jennifer glanced around the table, her thoughts made her teary-eyed. Julia noticed this and asked, "Jennifer, is something wrong?"

"No," Jennifer said, a little embarrassed by her show of emotions. "Something is right. I was sitting here thinking how much I enjoyed this group ... and how glad I am that we met ... or re-met."

Julia replied, "It is sort of funny, isn't it? If someone wrote a book about it, nobody would believe it!"

The evening ended with the two couples riding back to the Reynolds' residence in the back of a large suburban driven by one of Case's employees. If the young driver minded the singing coming from the back, he didn't show it as he occasionally smiled into the rearview mirror.

The double-header on Saturday against Franklin College had finished earlier than most expected, giving the team members and their friends more time before the 10:00 curfew than usual. The Best Western, where team members were staying, was well situated inside a large mall, among a variety of fast food restaurants. It was a beautiful and warm

April evening, and many of the team were still congregated at the picnic tables near the entrance to the motel.

Jill had made the road trip to watch the games and had been invited by Shane's parents to stay at their house on Saturday evening. Jennifer and Tim Drake were also staying with Case and Julia on Saturday evening. The Drakes would be staying in the large mother-in-law guest suite. Jill would be in Shane's old bedroom. Tim and Jennifer had offered to bring Jill in their car, but Jill thought it would be more comfortable for everyone if she weren't dependent on others for transportation during the weekend. She had driven the Renault to Indianapolis.

As ballplayers started drifting off to the area dining options, Charlie, Shane and Jill decided to play 'paper, rock, scissors' to determine who would walk to the Pizza Hut next to the hotel to bring back a pizza to be eaten at the picnic table. Shane lost. Charlie promised to keep Shane's girlfriend safe while he went to get the pizza.

Shane left the picnic table to get the pizza, leaving Charlie and Jill. Charlie opened a conversation that he'd wanted to have with Jill for some time. "Jill," he said, "I know that you are good friends with Linda Hawkins. Can I talk to you a little about her?"

"Of course, Charlie!" answered Jill, "She really likes you. I guess you know that."

"Sort of," said Charlie, "and that's the problem for me. She's beautiful and fun and I like having her in our group, but she has made some remarks that make me think she wants to be more than friends with me."

"Duh!" smiled Jill. "Has it really taken you three months to notice that? Yes, I can confirm that she'd like to be more than friends with you, Charlie."

"What about Doug?" asked Charlie.

216

"Well," answered Jill. "I think she's a bit conflicted about Doug, and she isn't sure what to do. She's engaged and feels a little guilty about her feelings for you. She doesn't want to hurt Doug but, at the same time, isn't sure she should be getting married either."

"I understand... I guess," said Charlie, "but I need to let her know, in a nice way, that I can't be a part... or a reason... for those decisions."

"You don't like her?" questioned Jill.

"I *do* like her," said Charlie, "and if she weren't engaged to a good friend of mine, I might try to explore the relationship more, to see if it could develop to be something more than 'like.' She's engaged though so, for me, having anything other than a casual friendship isn't possible."

"What if she broke off her engagement?"

Charlie looked at Jill for a long time before answering. "This probably makes me sound really stupid or naïve... or something... but, it would not make a difference to me if she broke off her engagement. I wouldn't be able to date her seriously until a lot of time had passed since her relationship with Doug. I'm not sure why, but I just couldn't do it."

Jill smiled and picked up Charlie's hand. "It isn't stupid or naïve. It is just noble to a fault," said Jill. "You are so much like Shane that it's scary, but those 'noble' instincts are one of the reasons that I love both of you so much! Are you sure you two aren't related?" she said laughing.

"No, don't think so, but thanks. What do I do about Linda?"

Jill retracted her hand and thought for a few minutes, then said, "I'll help, Charlie, but I think you just have to have a friendly conversation with her. She's a good person and she's going to understand. Your problem is going to be that your conversation is just going to make her want you more. I think your answer is simply that 'life is funny... we'll see what happens down the road.'"

"Thanks, Jill," said Charlie. "I can do that, and you're right. Under different circumstances, Linda and I might be perfect for each other."

"Right," said Jill. "Here's my theory, want to hear it?"

"Absolutely, Jill! You're one of the smartest girls I know, so I'm interested in any theories you have," said Charlie, smiling.

"Well, not sure I'm 100% right on all this, but I don't believe there is just one right person for me, or anybody else, in the world. If that were the case, what are my odds of actually finding him? I think there are probably thousands of 'right ones'... but out of the tens of millions of men in the world, how likely is it that I might actually meet one of the few thousand that are among the 'right' ones for me? I think Shane *is* one of those. There may be others but, while trying to find that out, I could lose the one I did find. I'm not taking that chance. My parents seem disappointed that I'm not using my college years to 'play the field' more but, in this case, I think they're wrong. I like the way Shane looks ... and I like the way he looks at me. Our values are similar; we make each other laugh; he likes to dance. He's honest and loyal and he cares about me. If there are others out there just as good, I doubt there are many, if any, better. I am committed to investing quality time on this relationship versus wasting time looking for a different one. In my opinion, Linda hasn't found one of her 'thousands' yet. If she had, she wouldn't be having the feelings she has for you. She needs to keep looking. You do, too."

"Shane is a lucky man, Jill," said Charlie.

"He knows that," laughed Jill, "but I'm a lucky girl, too. I sincerely hope that I'm still on the periphery of your life somewhere, Charlie, when one of the right women bumps into you. That woman, also, is going to be one lucky girl!"

"Thanks, Jill," said Charlie. "I have a feeling that, even after I graduate this year, you and Shane and I will stay connected. There's something unique about our relationship."

"Here comes Shane with the pizza, and I'm hungry," said Jill.

"Me too," said Charlie. "Thanks for this talk!"

"You're welcome, Charlie."

The three friends enjoyed a boxed pizza together as the sun set over Indianapolis. When they finished, Jill offered to drive them over to the mall, but Charlie said he had some studying to do back in the motel room. Two hours remained before the team curfew, so Shane and Jill got in the Renault and headed for the mall. As Charlie watched them depart, he realized how much he really loved these two people ... and as much as he loved each one of them individually, he loved them even more as a couple.

The Cincinnati road trip was an annual trip for the Monarchs, and the team usually stayed at the same Holiday Inn Express east of Cincinnati and Covington. The team played Transylvania University on Friday evening, winning behind a three-hit complete game shutout from Jake Grimsley. Pudge and Jack each had home runs in the game and Lefton College won the conference game, 6 - 1.

On Saturday, the Monarchs faced the Mount St. Joseph Lions for a conference doubleheader. Jack pitched the first game and, despite not needing any relief help in the sixth inning, Coach Blevins went to the mound after Jack had retired the first two hitters. Denton Jones was warming up in the bullpen.

Jack and Charlie both seem confused when Blevins joined them on the mound. "Great game, Jack. We've got a 5 - 0 lead, and you're pitching a three-hit shutout. We only need four outs, and I have a reason for wanting to get Denton in the game now. He's got a fan club out there in the bleachers, and you're the second hitter due up at the bottom of the inning, Jack. I want to make sure Denton's fans get to see him hit *and* pitch today."

Jack was smiling and immediately relinquished the ball to his coach, "No problem, Coach," he said. "Good idea, too!"

Earlier in the day, while the team was warming up before the game, Charlie had seen several police officers come into UC Health Field, on the campus of Mount St. Joseph College, with 40 or more children. Coach Blevins had stepped to the rail on the first base side of the diamond to speak to one of the officers. He had also given an attractive older black woman, who was with the group, a light hug over the rail. Ten Ton, who was in the outfield with the rest of the team doing stretching exercises, had waved at the group.

When Ten Ton came to the mound, his fan club became loud and excited. After the big pitcher struck out the first hitter he faced on three blazing fastballs to end the inning, his fans were all standing, yelling and applauding. As Ten Ton came to the bench, he thanked Coach Blevins. "Coach, I know you didn't need me out there, but I appreciate you getting me in this game. My mama and those kids appreciate it too!"

Coach Blevins said, "No problem Denton, but you aren't done yet. We've got an inning to go, and you're up second this inning to hit."

"You want me to hit?" questioned Ten Ton.

"Yes, I want you to hit!" said the coach. "I don't care if you strike out on three pitches … just look good doing it." Coach Blevins was smiling at Denton.

After Phillips flied out to left, Ten Ton stepped to the plate. He had picked the largest bat he could find from the rack, but it still looked small in his hands. As he walked to the plate, Denton looked more like he was hunting fresh meat with a club than approaching a batter's box to hit. His large frame took up most of the batter's box and, if he wasn't a good hitter, he still looked formidable.

Ten Ton's first vicious cut at a belt-high fastball would have easily stopped a charging rhinoceros, but it did no damage to the seemingly tiny baseball. His second cut at an outside fastball was no closer to connecting. To informed or knowledgeable observers, it would seem that Ten Ton's chances of actually hitting the baseball might be only slightly better than a blind man's. It didn't matter to the kids in the bleachers who had come to watch their hero. They loved seeing the big man's swings and continued to cheer him on.

Sometimes life imitates art ... and sometimes things really happen in life that should only happen in a fairytale. Denton Jones ... and his fan club ... were about to have one of those surreal moments that would create a lifelong memory for all of them. On the third pitch, Ten Ton swung at a fastball which would have been over the head of most hitters. On Denton, it was only chin-high. The bat did not connect with the baseball cleanly, but the sheer force of the swing sent the ball screaming skyward. It seemed to go out of sight in the clear blue sky before coming back into view on its trip back to earth. The ball, on the long triangular flight from the plate, had just enough forward momentum to drop several feet over the center field fence. It had traveled over 800 feet on its way up and then down, to clear the fence 412 feet away, and Denton had just hit the first home run of his entire life! He had watched the ball go out of the stadium at the plate, just as everyone in the stands and on the field had. The umpire finally said to him, "Son, that's a home run, but you still have to touch all the bases."

Coming out of his daze, Ten Ton said, "Oh, sorry sir, I don't have a lot of experience in this part of the game." As he approached first base the coach gave him exaggerated motions directing him to second. "This way, Ten Ton," he said, "and when you get to second base look at the third-base coach. He'll show you where to go after second." The third-base coach provided the same progressive instructions, and Ten Ton smiled as he trotted home. He was greeted there by most of the team.

To complete his day, Ten Ton retired the side in order in the seventh with two more strikeouts and a groundout. Coach Blevins then had Ten Ton act as the first base coach in the second game of the doubleheader. Shane pitched a four-hit, complete game, shutout, which the Monarchs won, 4 - 0. Much of the entertainment during the game, however, had been Ten Ton's animated gestures as the first base coach and his hilarious chatter throughout the game. At the game's conclusion, Blevins told Ten Ton to go visit his fans and his mother, who were gathered behind the first base dugout in the stands.

As Charlie and Coach Blevins watched Ten Ton disappear into the massive crowd of kids, Blevins said, "Those are kids from the inner city who Ten Ton works with in the summer. Most of them have a pretty tough life, and they need a few heroes like Denton."

One of the police officers was motioning Blevins to the rail and Charlie was close enough to hear the short conversation. "Thank you, Coach," said the officer. "This was really special for the kids. I've got the money to pay you back for the tickets."

"You don't owe me anything," said the coach. "Thanks for bringing them out here." Then Blevins slipped into the dugout before the officer could say anything more.

Charlie watched the coach disappear and remembered the framed quote that Blevins had on his wall back at the college. There was much more to this man, he thought, than most people knew. He felt privileged to have had him as a coach … and a mentor … for the past four years.

The framed quotation that hung from the wall behind Coach Blevins' desk at Lefton College:

Do all the good you can,
By all the means you can,
In all the ways you can,
In all the places you can,
At all the times you can,
To all the people you can,
As long as you ever can.

John Wesley

The Monarchs finished up the regular season in championship style, winning nine of their last eleven games. With a 25 - 5 conference record, they earned the automatic invitation to the NCAA Mid-East Tournament as the HCAC Champions. The closest team to Lefton College in the Conference was Anderson College with a 21 - 9 conference record. With no need for a conference play-off game, Coach Blevins also had an extra week to prepare for the Mid-East Regionals. The tournament was being played in Washington, Pennsylvania.

He spent much time thinking about the brackets he had received for the tournament. The Monarchs had earned a number two seed, which meant their first game would be against the number seven seed, DePauw University. Lefton College had played DePauw recently, near the end of the regular season during the team's Terre Haute trip. Sam Casey had pitched for the Monarchs, and Blevins' team had won that game handily, 6 - 1. Blevins knew, however, that since the game was not a conference game, the Monarchs had not seen DePauw's best pitcher. That would not be the case in the first game of the Mid-East Tournament. Conventional strategy would dictate that both teams start their best pitchers. All coaches knew that it was difficult to come up through the losers' bracket in a double elimination tournament to win a championship after dropping the first game. Even after winning their first game in last year's Mid-East Tournament, Lefton's pitching wasn't strong enough to get the team past three games after losing the second game of the tournament. Blevins was thinking strongly about going against conventional wisdom and starting the same pitcher who had earned a win against DePauw earlier. While the Monarch hitters undoubtedly had success against the Tigers' number four or number five pitcher, the Tiger hitters had been held well in check by young Sam

Casey. The Monarchs would face a better pitcher this time, but the Tiger hitters would probably be the same ones who Casey had faced just a few weeks back.

If Lefton could earn a win with Casey in the first game, the team would be well set up for the next three games. Shane, Jack, and Jake would start these games and, with some luck, those would be all the games that the Monarchs would need to play in the tournament. Blevins knew his critics would be plentiful and loud if his strategy backfired; he'd won the debate against himself, however. He was going to start the Mid-East Tournament with Sam Casey.

Washington and Jefferson College was the host team for the tournament, and was also the number one seeded team in the eight-team tournament. Washington, Pennsylvania, was outside of Pittsburgh and an easy four-hour drive on I-70 from Lefton Township. While many family and friends of teammates made the trip for the four-day tournament, all team members were required to take the team bus. Players were also required to stay as a team at the same hotel, a Marriott Residence Inn, located several miles from the Washington and Jefferson College campus.

The first games of the tournament were scheduled for 2:00 PM on Thursday, May 17. The Monarchs would play DePauw University at Consul Energy Park, the home field for a semi-professional team, The Wild Things. If they won, game number two would be on Friday at 2:00 PM. If they lost, they would play a second game on Thursday evening at Ross Memorial Park on the campus of Washington and Jefferson College.

The team bus pulled into the Marriott on Wednesday a little before 5:00 PM. Before getting off the bus, Coach Blevins told the team that they were free to dine at any of the restaurants within walking distance of the hotel, but that they were to be back at the hotel lobby for a short team meeting at 8:00 PM that evening. When all were assembled in the lobby later that evening, Coach Blevins addressed them:

"Okay, guys ... we've done what we needed to do to be able to play a little more baseball this week. No matter how we fare over the next few days, I'm proud of each of you individually... and all of you collectively. In fact, as I look out among you, I don't even see individual faces ... all I see is a team. We start the tournament against a team we have seen before, DePauw University ... and we beat them out in Terre Haute a few weeks ago. Sam pitched a great game with Ten Ton helping him in the ninth, so we're going to give the ball to Sam again tomorrow. We're going to see the Tigers' ace tomorrow, a senior by the name of Pewsey. I don't know much about him except that he's got a 10 - 2 record this year and he's been a starter for DePauw for four years. I expect he's pretty good ... but we've been seeing everyone's best pitchers all year. I do not doubt that our lineup will do fine against him. Going into these games, only the DePauw and Ohio Wesleyan teams know much about us ... and neither of these teams knows everything about us. We made one pickoff against DePauw and had another one in one of the games against Ohio Wesleyan, but none of these teams know anything about Luis. I don't expect any blowout wins at this level, but if we do get any substantial leads, I'm going to do anything I can to save some innings from our starters in case we need them later in the tournament. The championship games in these types of tournaments are usually decided by the number four or number five pitchers on any team. We're going to try to stay as strong as we can for as long as we can with pitching. Get some sleep and, above all, enjoy this weekend. Not all ballplayers get an opportunity like this. We'll leave the hotel around 10:30 AM, and I'll have box lunches delivered to the locker room at Consul Energy Park."

At game time, the weather was beautiful in southwestern Pennsylvania, with the temperature a comfortable 72°. Consul Energy Field was a professional level baseball field used in the summertime by The Wild Things of the independent Frontier League. Fans occupied the lower level seats on the first base and third base sides of the field behind the dugouts. The Monarchs occupied the third-base side dugout and, based on their higher tournament seed, were the designated home team.

Sam Casey threw his first pitch of the game ... and the tournament, a called strike, at just a few minutes after 2:00 PM. He retired the side in order on just nine pitches in the first. Bill Pewsey, DePauw's senior right-hander, did the same in his half of the inning. The Monarchs clawed for a run in the second and then two in the fourth before the Tigers broke through against Casey in the sixth. After retiring the first two hitters on ground balls, Casey walked the third hitter. The Tigers big left-handed cleanup hitter then hit a first-pitch fastball past Jake Ryan at first for a base hit, which put runners on the corners with two out. DePauw's right fielder watched two curveball strikes from Casey before jumping on a fastball, that was high and out of the strike zone, sending a towering fly ball toward Danny Colovito in centerfield. Danny leaped at the fence, but the baseball went over his glove by just a few inches for a three-run home run. Sam struck out the next hitter for the third out, but the game was now tied. Coach Blevins visited Charlie and Sam as they came to the dugout.

"How's the arm, Sam?" asked Blevins.

"I feel good, Coach," said Sam. "I need to use the curve more to the guys in the middle of their lineup, but what I feel the worst about, is the walk!"

Charlie said, "His velocity still seems good and, except for the cleanup hitter's single, he's hitting his spots.

The home run was sort of a fluke. The guy made a good cut on a pitch he shouldn't have swung at."

"Okay," said the coach. "You're only at 60 pitches so far with the bottom part of the order coming up. Six through nine have done nothing against you in this game or in the one three weeks ago. We'll try to get one of those runs back this inning."

The Monarchs threatened in both the sixth and seventh but couldn't score. Sam retired the side in order in the seventh and, after allowing a leadoff single in the eighth, struck out the next three hitters.

When he came to the bench, everybody was standing to greet him. The sophomore righty was obviously done for the day with a pitch count of 102, but he had pitched the game of his young career. While allowing three runs in a tie game, he had only allowed three hits, one walk, and had struck out six. Coach Blevins waited for Casey to sit down on the bench before coming over to them. "Great game, Sam," Blevins said. "You put us in a position to win ... and I think we're going to do that for you ... this inning!"

Ten Ton was warming in the bullpen to pitch the ninth and Sam Casey, the pitcher, was due up at the plate. All on the bench knew Blevins would send a pinch-hitter to the plate for Sam, but most were surprised at the hitter Blevins chose. "Luis!" yelled Blevins. "Get a bat. You're pinch-hitting for Casey." If others wondered about the strange move, Charlie didn't. He smiled a bit as he thought about the cagey coach's strategy. Before Luis left the dugout, Blevins had a lengthy conversation with him.

The diminutive Spedimente was an unknown quantity to the Tigers. As a freshman, Luis had no college history that could be sourced, and he had not played in the game between the two teams in March. As he stepped to the plate as a left-hander, the Tiger catcher looked toward the

DePauw bench and his coach. The coach sent the 'got me ...
I don't know' signal back to his catcher.

To waste a pitch to feel the hitter out, Pewsey sent a
fastball to a location several inches outside of the plate.
This, of course, was the perfect spot for Luis, who slapped it
for a weak ground ball toward shortstop. The speedy
Hispanic was already two strides up the line to first base
before his bat hit the ground. When the shortstop fielded
the slowly bouncing ball, he didn't even attempt a throw to
first.

The Monarchs' strategy was more apparent now, and
Pewsey held the runner close to the bag at first with several
throws in that direction before the first pitch to Colovito.
Coach Blevins originally wanted Luis to steal on the first
pitch, but now changed his signs to both the runner and
the hitter. Colovito was to bunt, but only on a good pitch.
Luis was to stay on first until he saw the sacrifice go down.

The Tigers were expecting a sacrifice and had moved
the third baseman in. The first baseman, holding Luis,
couldn't move until after the pitch was delivered. Pewsey
tried to make Colovito commit on a bad pitch. It didn't
work, as the senior center fielder pulled the bat back on the
pitch that landed well outside. The second pitch, a
curveball to the inside of the plate, was also taken by
Danny for a ball. Pewsey was now in some danger of
making a very manageable situation an unmanageable one.
He delivered the next fastball to the center of the plate,
which Danny easily laid down toward third base. Danny's
speed made the play close, but he was out on the sacrifice.
Luis was in scoring position at second with one out.

Lou Phillips stepped to the plate, then called time,
stepping back out to review the signs coming from the
third-base coach. Hitter and runner watched intently; then
both tapped their jerseys to indicate they understood. All
players on the Monarch bench watched the silent

communication as well. They all knew the team's signs, and each of the Monarchs was interested in understanding what Coach Blevins' strategy would be. When the third-base coach raised two hands to the runner as the final part of the signal, Charlie knew what the coach had in mind. Blevins had basically called for a hit and run on the second pitch of the at-bat ... subject to change, depending on what the first pitch was. It was a strange strategy with a runner at second base. Usually, the hit-and-run was used when a runner occupied first. The idea was ... on a given pitch, the runner on first would take off for second in an apparent steal attempt. This would cause the second baseman to move toward the bag to receive the catcher's throw ... which would open a hole on the right side of the infield to punch a ground ball through. In a best-case scenario, the hitter could deliver the ground ball, getting a cheap base hit, and the runner would advance to third. In a worst-case scenario, the hitter would miss the pitch, and the runner might get thrown out on the steal attempt.

With the runner on second, Charlie figured that the only possible strategy was that Blevins would have Luis take off for third on the pitch that the hitter would attempt to hit to the right side. If the hitter was successful in getting a ground ball to first or second, Luis, who would already be near third base, would continue to run to attempt to score. As Charlie looked at the hitter, he understood the strategy more fully. Nobody on the team was better than Phillips at the hit and run ... and nobody was more reliable at taking the ball the other way. He just needed a pitch near the center of the plate or out. He couldn't go the other way on an inside pitch.

Pewsey, from the stretch, and watching Luis closely, delivered a curveball to the hands of Phillips, which the hitter took for ball one. Hitter and runner looked at the coach, who signaled that the original plan was still on. This was the pitch, thought Phillips, and when it was delivered to the outer third of the plate with no wrinkles, he was relieved. He chopped a ground ball toward second base which the second baseman easily fielded. Glancing toward the runner, who had begun running on the pitch, it was apparent there was no play at third. The second baseman threw the ball softly to the first baseman to record the ground ball out on Phillips.

Throwing softly turned out to be a bad idea, as Luis never slowed up when he reached third-base but continued at warp speed toward home plate. The Tiger first baseman recognized this immediately and, after recording the out, fired the baseball to home plate. The Tiger catcher also realized that Luis had not stopped after rounding third base. He stepped up the line toward third-base and stooped down in front of the base path to block the plate, awaiting the throw from his first baseman.

Luis, recognizing the roadblock, slid around the catcher toward the inside of the diamond, on his stomach. The catcher had to reach back toward the plate for the first baseman's throw, and all watched as the runner tried to touch the plate with an outstretched hand before the catcher could touch some part of the sliding runner's body.

The umpire made the call—*Safe!*—even though it appeared that the catcher might have gotten a tag on Luis before Luis' hand touched the plate. The Tigers coach was already advancing onto the field when the home plate umpire called timeout ... and motioned for all players and coaches on both benches to remain where they were. He then summoned the third-base umpire to join him halfway between third-base and the plate. After a short conversation with his umpiring team member, he confirmed that the runner was safe and that the run had scored. He then immediately signaled for both the Tigers' coach and the Monarchs' coach to join him on the field.

As the two coaches arrived, the young umpire explained, "Coach Riley, Coach Blevins ... the run scored because of catcher's obstruction. A catcher cannot block the plate without the ball. He may move into the baseline to retrieve a thrown ball but, in this case, the thrown ball was obviously behind him, not in the baseline. Our primary goal in this game is to keep it safe for players and, while I believe that there was no intent by any of the players involved in this play to hurt anyone, I feel compelled to warn each of you that a flagrant violation of the obstruction rule is grounds for expulsion from the game ... and this tournament. Do we all understand that?" The right answer to that question from the umpire was obvious. Both coaches acknowledged with no further discussion.

In the top of the ninth, Ten Ton struck out the first two hitters and retired the third one on a weak ground ball to Phillips. The Monarchs had won their first game of the Mid-East Regional Tournament. The heroes of the game had been their number four pitcher, a freshman hitter who had only recorded ten total at-bats for the entire season, and a veteran team player who could hit a ground ball to the right side of the infield. Later that afternoon the Monarchs found out they would face Widener College in game number two.

In game two of the tournament, Jake Grimsley started for the Monarchs. He was opposed by the Widener University's junior left-hander, Jesse Cooler. Widener had a challenging first game against their cross-state rival, Keystone College, squeaking out a 5 - 4 win in 12 innings. The team had used four different pitchers in the game, including their number two starting pitcher, who eventually earned the win. Hank Solden had only pitched two innings, and could undoubtedly pitch a few more in the tournament, but the Widener coach had chosen to go with their number three pitcher, who was still fresh with no innings pitched in the tournament.

Cooler was no match for the Monarch lineup, and the Widener University hitters were no match for Grimsley. Lefton was up by seven runs by the sixth inning, and Grimsley was pitching a three-hit shutout. Despite this, Blevins substituted Josh Stine for Grimsley in the top of the seventh, electing to save Jake's arm for some future innings in the tournament... if it were needed. The Monarchs went on to win the game easily, 9 - 3.

Game three was played back at Ross Memorial Field on the campus of Washington and Jefferson College. The game featured Jack Ryan for the Monarchs against a sophomore named Neil Ellis for the Ohio Wesleyan Battling Bishops. Ohio Wesleyan had handed Jack one of his two losses earlier in the season, and the big right-hander was anxious to avenge that loss. Since Shane was scheduled to pitch the next game, Roger Ball was playing first base for the Monarchs.

In a game of unbeaten teams, both looked deserving of Champions as the afternoon wore on. Jack was perfect through five innings allowing no runs, no hits, and one walk. Neil Ellis was almost as good allowing no runs on four hits and two walks. The Monarchs had at least a runner on base in each of the first six innings but had not managed to push one across the plate. In the seventh, Jack allowed the first base hit against him, a week pop fly that fell between Billings, the left fielder, and a diving Phillips, the third baseman. That runner was erased two pitches later when he tried to steal on Charlie. Jack then struck out the next two hitters to end the inning.

In the bottom of the seventh Jack led off the inning with a base hit up the middle. Pudge advanced him to second base with a sacrifice bunt, bringing Charlie to the plate. After taking two outside pitches for balls, Charlie took a 90-plus fastball squarely on the right thigh. As he started to run to first base, the umpire called him back. Instead of awarding first base, the umpire called *Ball Three.* Coach Blevins immediately came to the field to confer with the home plate umpire, asking why his hitter, who had clearly been hit by the pitch, was not awarded first base.

The umpire replied, "Coach, the hitter did not attempt to avoid the pitch."

Hearing this explanation, Charlie told the umpire, "Sir, I didn't *try to avoid* the pitch *because I was planning to hit it!*"

"Son," said the umpire, "that pitch was far too inside to hit, and you never moved the bat to attempt to hit it. I admire that you have the courage to take a fastball on the thigh to help your team, but I can't award that courage with a free base."

"Thank you, sir," replied the ever-respectful Charlie, "but I thought the pitch might be a curveball, and I was waiting for it to break toward the plate."

"Nice try, Kid," replied the umpire, "but this pitcher hasn't thrown a curveball all day, and we're in the seventh inning. I don't think he has a curveball!"

"That's what I was thinking too, Blue," agreed Charlie, "but I didn't want to look stupid when he threw his first one to me!"

"Get back in the box, Kid. *Ball three!*" countered the ump.

On a 3 - 2 pitch, Charlie knocked a fastball to somewhere over the bleachers, putting the Monarchs ahead 2 - 0. As he touched the plate, he winked at the smiling umpire and said, "Thanks, Blue, guess you were right about the curveball."

The umpire replied, "No problem ... how's the thigh feel?"

Charlie answered, "Hurts!"

With the lead, Jack pitched 'lights out' in the eighth, retiring the side on three ground ball outs. In the Monarchs' half of the eighth, the backup catcher and sometimes first baseman, Roger Ball, added to the Monarchs lead with a two-out home run to right field, ending the day for the Battling Bishops' junior pitcher. Jack struck out the side in the top half of the ninth to finish his complete game shutout with a flourish.

Most of the Monarchs remained at the stadium to watch the game between Washington & Jefferson College and Ohio Wesleyan. W & J had battled through the loser's bracket to put themselves in a position to go to their second Mid-East Championship game in as many years, but they couldn't quite pull it off this year. The Battling Bishops' number four pitcher, a sophomore by the name of Dukes, was still fresh, having pitched no innings in the tournament yet. The W & J Presidents, having already lost to Ohio Wesleyan earlier in the tournament, were forced to use three different pitchers in a game they lost 7 - 2 to the Ohio team. This set-up a rematch between the Battling Bishops and the Monarchs. Back at the hotel, Coach Blevins addressed his players in the lobby where they had gathered.

"Guys," he said, "we've seen Ohio Wesleyan three times already this year. Tomorrow, we play them for the Mid-East Regional Championship. I like our chances. Shane is fresh and hasn't thrown an inning yet this week. Ohio will be forced to start their number five pitcher, Shelby, who we faced back in March. We've already beaten their number three guy, and their number one and number two guys have already pitched at least eight innings a piece this week. We can't take anything for granted, though. This is a good team, and they will do whatever they have to do to be competitive tomorrow. And remember, to win this Championship, the Bishops are going to have to beat us twice tomorrow. Records and statistics and history all go out the window in Championship games. The wins usually go to the teams with the most heart. We've got as much of that as any team in the country. I'd rather not play two tomorrow, so get a good night's rest and let's take care of business in the first game."

The following day, a good crowd was on hand for the Championship game. Most of the teams who had participated in the tournament had booked accommodations for the length of the tournament, and many of these teams had hung around to see who would take the trophy home. Through the course of the weekend, friendships were made among the teams, and fans had become familiar with teams other than their own.

Shane made the first pitch at 2:00 PM and the game was underway. He was perfect in the first, retiring all three hitters he faced on ground balls. First up for Ohio Wesleyan in the second inning was their clean-up hitter, Matt Barnes. The junior first baseman had led his conference in both batting average and home runs the past season, and on Shane's third pitch to him, Matt powered a line drive home run over the centerfield fence. With the Battling Bishops leading the game 1 - 0, Ron Shelby, their sophomore starter, managed to keep the Monarch hitters off balance through the first four innings with his unusual arsenal of breaking balls. Lefton broke through in the bottom of the fifth when Jud Long delivered a two-out double to the wall, which scored Charlie and Jack. Shelby was done by the middle of the seventh, but the Bishops brought in Neil Ellis, the right-hander Lefton had seen the day before. Despite the number of pitches thrown a day earlier, Ellis was still effective in keeping the Monarch hitters in check for the rest of the seventh inning and then the eighth inning.

Down by a run 2 - 1 in the top of the ninth, Ohio's pinch hitter for their pitcher singled up the middle against Shane. He advanced to second on a sacrifice by the lead-off hitter, and then to third on a ball hit to Pudge at second base. With two outs and the tying run at third, the Bishops' number two hitter hit a line drive over the bag at third. Phillips dived for the ball, knocking it down and managing to keep the baserunner from scoring, leaving runners at the corners with two outs. Shane lost a long battle with the number three hitter, finally walking him on a full count. That brought the dangerous Matt Barnes to the plate.

So, there it was. A charmed season filled with heroics had put the Monarchs in position to advance to the Division III College Championship for the first time in the school's history. That chance, however, depended on one more out and that out had to be extracted by a rookie pitcher, and delivered at the expense of one of Division III Baseball's best hitters. With the bases loaded, any hit would put the Bishops ahead; a walk would tie it. Charlie glanced at his coach on the bench and trotted to the mound.

Shane appeared calm, but Charlie knew that, in this case, appearances were deceiving. "Great day for baseball, huh?" said Charlie.

That brought a glimpse of a smile from Shane as he replied, "I think I'd rather be watching baseball right now."

"Are you kidding me?" asked Charlie. "This is what we live for! Bottom of the ninth, a run up, only need an out to go to the Big Show next week, and there isn't anyone on our bench I'd rather have with the ball right now than you, man!" Charlie continued, "I'd really like to stay and chat with you, but let's finish business here first. The coach thinks we go right after him with heat ... stay away from the middle ... err to low versus high ... try not to let him get ahead in the count."

"Is that what you think, too, Charlie? Matt already hurt us back in the second with one of the best fastballs I've thrown all day," said Shane.

"I know, and then we gift-wrapped a walk to him in the fifth 'cuz we were afraid to pitch to him," said Charlie. "The guy's got a good eye, and he isn't going to swing at junk, so he'll take the walk to tie the game ... but that isn't what he wants to do. He wants to be the hero and win the game. I agree with Coach ... let's go after him with your best stuff! Realistically, if he walks and we go into extra innings, our chances aren't as good. You're at your inning limit right now, so let's win it or lose it on this batter."

A little dust cloud exploded when the catcher's mitt smacked the fielder's glove as the two friends parted. Glancing again to the dugout to ensure that he was still on the same page with his coach, Charlie assumed his position behind the plate, and ever so close to Matt Barnes. The tall hitter stepped carefully into the batter's box, resting his right foot as far back in the chalk outlined area as legally possible and stared out to the mound. Perhaps remembering how carefully Shane had pitched around him in the fifth, he took a blazing first-pitch strike on the inside corner. Charlie called for the same pitch to the outside part of the plate, and the hitter was ready, taking the fastball the opposite way, but just outside the first base line for strike two.

Charlie glanced at the dugout, and the coach indicated another fastball above the belt and a little out of the strike zone. Barnes had stepped out of the batter's box, continuing to stare at Shane, his competitive mind performing a myriad of mental gymnastics to try to prepare him for what Shane might throw him on 0 - 2. The home crowd was on its feet, cheering their young pitcher and collectively trying to conjure strike three. Neither Charlie nor Shane seemed to notice the noise but stayed intently focused on their present shared, and enormous, task. The ball hit the catcher's mitt at just above 92 miles per hour equidistant from the right and left sides of the plate, and in an area above the belt that could, at times, be called a strike ... but not today. And Barnes' bat never moved. Charlie winced at the umpire's call and threw the ball back to Shane. While there was no argument that the pitch could have gone either way, it was way too close to take with two strikes. Barnes had gotten lucky on the call. Barnes knew it, too ... which made Charlie think that the hitter would be a bit more aggressive on the next pitch. He called for another fastball slightly out of the zone away from the hitter, and low. This time, the hitter flinched, but again let the ball pass for ball two.

Damn! thought Charlie, *This guy's got ice water in his veins.* Glancing again to the coach to confirm what he already expected, Charlie put down a single finger to his pitcher and set the glove up squarely in the middle of the plate. The crowd was not as noisy as earlier, and Shane knew exactly what both his coach and his catcher were expecting from him. He was to go man to man with an extremely talented hitter and try to throw his best fastball by him. With the count at 2 - 2, the pitcher still holds a slight edge over the hitter that disappears on a 3 - 2 count. Pitcher, catcher, coach, Monarch players, and fans all wanted this to be the deciding pitch.

Shane's windup was slow and deliberate, his leg kick high and determined, and he threw his entire body behind the left arm that delivered a fastball that at least one radar gun in the stands recorded at 95 mph. The tightly spinning baseball's flight was straight and true, but before reaching the leather of the catcher's mitt was greeted by a well-swung, 34-ounce bat. The speed of the swing and the whip of the bat brought gasps from both visitor and home fans ... but the baseball flew straight back to the screen, foul ball ... and still 2 - 2.

Pitcher, catcher, and coach exhaled deeply together. To the casual fan, a foul ball is just a foul ball, but baseball coaches and players know that a foul ball going straight back to the screen was struck only a few millimeters short of going a long ways forward. Matt Barnes was right on Shane's best fastball then, and had already homered on one earlier in the day. Things were indeed getting interesting. The crowd noise had died to a respectful, low hum, and Charlie looked over to the coach for a suggestion. With no hesitation, the coach called for another fastball, this one again in the same place as the third pitch of the series that the batter had taken.

OK, thought Charlie. *Probably a good call. Barnes should have swung on that one at 0-2 but didn't. He got lucky, and he knows it. With two strikes and the game on the line, he has to protect. He was just under a fastball down the middle ... take him up the ladder a little, and we may get him to swing under.*

Charlie put down the sign, and Shane delivered the same pitch as the previous one except for 6 inches higher. Barnes' shoulder and body reacted, but his hands kept the bat back. The umpire called, *"Ball three!"*

Amazing! thought Charlie, *This guy has guts ... and he has an excellent eye for strikes!* Charlie looked over to the coach, who gave him a signal Charlie had never seen before. Charlie twirled his fingers indicating the need for the coach to resend the signal. At this point, Coach Blevins yelled out to Charlie loud enough for most in the stands and all on the opposing bench to hear, "I've got no solution for this guy, Charlie. You and Shane decide what to do. Win or lose, I back you all the way."

Thanks, Coach ... NOT, Charlie thought, as he trotted to the mound to speak to Shane.

"Charlie," said Shane, "I don't know what you can tell me that I don't already know. Matt Barnes is a beast ... and he has my number. He has been right on every fastball I've thrown him all day and has also proven that he's willing to take the walk."

"You're right," said Charlie. "That's why on this pitch, we're gonna throw him the change-up."

"Charlie," said Shane, "I appreciate that you've worked with me on a change-up this season, and next year it will be one of my three best pitches, but I've only thrown it at practice. I have never thrown it in a game this year!"

"I know that ... and Matt Barnes probably knows that, too," said Charlie, "Fact is, you haven't needed to throw it in a game this year. Now you do. You've been throwing it great in practice. I think this is the perfect time to take it off the shelf. What have we got to lose? If he swings at it, he's toast. If he lets it pass, it's a ball, and the game is tied. We've fed him a steady diet of fastballs this whole game, and you've shown him that, despite his home run earlier, you're not afraid of him. He's expecting a fastball ... hell, everyone in this stadium is expecting a fastball. Let's show him who has guts!"

"OK," said Shane (not sounding like it was OK).

As Charlie passed the batter on his way to his position, he winked and said, "Get your seatbelt on."

Matt smiled back and said, "Bring it!"

Shane progressed through his same wind-up and same delivery, releasing a baseball at the same location from the mound area as his 90-plus mph fastball ... except this one traveled at only 82 mph. The hitter's eyes widened as they saw the ball coming, and his body reacted to smash a 92-mph fastball either out of the stadium or to a spot on the field that nobody could reach. Something wasn't right, though. The split second between the time the ball left the pitcher's hand and the time it should have arrived at his swinging bat ... was taking longer. His mind screamed at his body, "Stop ... change-up .... *stop* ..." but it was too late. The shoulders, arms, and hands had already exploded with too much energy to be retracted. The bat dipped a bit to try to adjust, but it didn't touch the dying ball, which bounced harmlessly into the waiting catcher's mitt. Strike three; ballgame *over.*

In an incredible show of sportsmanship, the batter looked back at the catcher and said, "Great call ... but I'm going to remember that pitch next year."

Charlie replied, "Thanks, Matt, but I'm a senior and my baseball days will be over in a week. I'm going to remember that pitch for the rest of my life!"

In the stands, the Lefton College fans celebrated the win as well. Tim, Jennifer, Case, and Julia had watched the game together. They were seated next to Jud's parents and Jill. Claude had found a seat close to the third-base dugout. When the game concluded, Jill watched the interaction between Charlie's parents and Shane's parents with interest. It fascinated her that the two couples had become such good friends over the course of the relatively short college baseball season. She had spent quite a bit of time with Shane's parents over the past four months, and her relationship with them was easy, effortless, and seamless. They were genuinely nice people and it would be natural for them to become friends with the parents of other ballplayers on the team. To Jill, though, there seem to be an aura of something stronger than simple friendship when these adults were together, and it was as charming as it was curious to her.

"What a game Shane pitched!" said Jennifer to Case and Julia. "What was that last pitch he threw?"

An exuberant Case answered, "That was a change-up! I haven't seen him throw that pitch all year and when he threw it in high school, it didn't look like that one. I think your son may have had something to do with the improvement of that pitch."

"Don't you mean *our* son?" Jennifer said quietly so that only Case could hear.

Case stopped and looked at Jennifer, then glanced to see where Julia and Tim might be. They were engaged in a lively conversation with the Longs, and Case answered Jennifer's question: "Jennifer, there are so many times this season when I just wanted to yell out, 'They're brothers! Aren't they amazing?' ... and then I feel guilty for having that kind of pride. Charlie is the man he is totally because of you and Tim, not me. I haven't earned the right to be so proud yet."

"That's going to change soon, Case, and certainly you have the right to be proud. I am, too! I also know how you feel about wanting to let everyone around us know about the relationship. What they have accomplished together as teammates is amazing. If folks knew they were also brothers, it would be some sort of epic legend!"

"It would be," said Case, "In fact, it already is. The story just hasn't been told yet. Do you have any concerns about what their reaction might be when we talk to them next week?"

"Yes, I do have some," said Jennifer. "I think all parents want to be known and remembered as heroes to their children. Having to reveal serious flaws is a bit daunting."

"I understand," said Case, "but I think we have handled the situation well ... especially Tim and Julia. Life doesn't give us the opportunity to go back and fix mistakes, and it doesn't give us a script to follow for how to make repairs once mistakes are made. I think these two boys are going to be fine with the news."

"You're probably right and, in the meantime, I have *so* enjoyed watching them this year. What a season!"

245

Julia and Tim had now rejoined Case and Jennifer. Tim said, "Case, I thought you said Shane didn't have a very good change-up! I haven't seen anyone throw a better one than that last pitch this year."

Case laughed, "Believe me, he didn't learn that pitch in high school, and it took as much guts to call for it as it did to throw it. Charlie gets as much credit for that one as Shane does. I wonder what Barnes said to Charlie after the pitch."

Claude had worked his way up the stadium steps to the parents' group and said, "Well, folks, I'm looking forward to seeing this same group again next week in Wisconsin. Jennifer, have you already booked us rooms?"

Jennifer blushed and asked, "Dad, what makes you think I'd have already done that?"

"Am I right or wrong?"

"You're right," Jennifer admitted reluctantly, "but I just wanted to make sure we got someplace close to the stadium. The rooms are only reserved so far; I didn't have to make a payment yet."

All in the group laughed, and Julia said, "Always prepared. I think I see where Charlie gets that from!"

The Division III National Championships were held in Appleton, Wisconsin, a seven-hour bus ride from Lefton. While many of the teams participating in the tournament would fly in from their locations to Appleton International Airport, Coach Blevins chose to use the team bus. He would break the long ride into two legs, with an overnight stop outside of Chicago, on the way up to Appleton. He'd have the bus drive straight back from Appleton to Lefton after the tournament. Even with an extra night of accommodations for the team, taking the bus would save the College a lot of money over air transportation. It would also be much easier to transfer the team's equipment by motor coach than it would be on a small commuter airline. The tournament would start on Thursday, May 25, and end on either May 27 or May 28, Memorial Day. With the overnight stop around Chicago, the team would arrive in Appleton by noon on the 25th, in plenty of time for the first game scheduled at the Fox Cities Stadium for 8:00 PM.

Coach Blevins spoke to the team, now gathered in the lobby of the Doubletree Suites. "We've made some history, men," he said. "This is the first time in the history of the College that Lefton has ever had an athletic team in a Division III National Championship. I am confident that this group will represent the College well. I'm also certain that, by the time we leave here, we will have put the College on the map for many who have never heard of us before. I hope that you will ensure that all here in Appleton will remember you for your character as much as your athletic abilities."

He continued, "There are no easy teams in this tournament, but due to our outstanding showing in the Mid-East Regionals, we earned another number two seed. We'll play Southern Maine on Thursday evening. The

Huskies have been here before. In fact, they have won this tournament twice in the past 20 years. We're not going to look past the first game yet, but if we keep winning, we'll likely see Marietta College, which has won three national championships, and Cal Lutheran, the team that won this tournament last year. The message here is that we have to bring our A-game every day. Shane, you've got the start tonight against the Huskies. The bus leaves at 4:30 for Fox Cities Stadium."

Shane took the mound a little before 8:00 PM and the first game of the Division III National Championship Tournament was underway. Because of their higher seed, Lefton College was the home team. The Monarchs faced the Southern Maine Huskies' senior right-hander, Kap Durling. After Shane retired the side in order in the first using only nine pitches, the Monarchs went to work right away in their half of the inning. Danny Colovito caught the Huskies completely by surprise when he dragged a bunt on the first pitch of the game for a base hit. Phillips followed with a hit and run single on the third pitch of the game, through the right side of the infield. With runners on first and third and nobody out, Jack drove a ball deep to centerfield which was caught but drove in Colovito for the game's first run. Pudge walked on seven pitches, and Charlie took an inside pitch to his butt, loading the bases for Jud. The senior right fielder took the count full before hitting a ball deep to the right-field corner, and nearly out of the stadium. The right fielder made a leaping catch at the wall for the out, but Phillips scored from third base on the tag and Pudge went to third. Shane helped his own cause, driving in Pudge with a base hit up the middle before Billings made the last out of the inning, forcing Charlie at third on a ground ball to the third baseman.

The Monarchs were up 3 - 0 after an inning and had forced the Huskies' starting pitcher to throw almost 50 pitches to record three outs. Shane allowed a double off the right-field wall to the Huskies cleanup hitter. He then retired the next three hitters on a pair of pop flies to the infield and a strikeout. In the bottom of the second inning, Junie Moore did the same thing Danny Colovito had done in the first inning, dropping a bunt toward first base on Durling's first pitch of the inning. The first baseman moved in to field the ball and threw to the second baseman running to cover first base. The second baseman was late to get to the base, however, and Moore was safe. Colovito again bunted, this time for a sacrifice, moving Junie to second with one out. Phillips delivered another base hit, this one to shallow center. Junie never slowed up coming around third, and the play at the plate was close. Junie slid under the tag for another run. Jack flied out to left, and Pudge struck out, but the Monarchs went to the top of the third with a 4-0 lead. Facing the bottom of the Huskies' order, Shane was nearly perfect allowing an infield hit followed by a double play and a strikeout.

The Monarchs went out in order in the third, as did the Huskies in the top of the fourth. At the bottom of the fourth, Shane walked on six pitches, and D'Ante sacrificed him to second. When Durling walked the Monarchs' number nine hitter, his coach called on the bullpen. The senior's pitch count was already over 90 pitches, and South Maine's coach could not afford for the game to get further out of hand. The Huskies infielders, remembering that Colovito had twice laid down exceptional bunts, moved in at the corners. Their reliever, a junior left-hander named Miley, made sure that Danny could not reach the first pitch, throwing it well outside. His next pitch was inside, and Danny shortened his bat as if he were about to bunt. He pulled the bat back to take ball two. Danny had no intention of bunting in this at-bat however and, now, with the count in his favor and half the infield still pulled in, he was looking for a pitch he could drive. The next pitch from Miley, an inside fastball, worked just fine, as Danny drove a hard ground ball between the shortstop and the third baseman for a base hit. Not wanting to risk Shane getting hurt in a collision at the plate, the third base coach held Shane at third. With the bases loaded and only one out, Phillips drove a 2 - 1 pitch to deep right-center field. Shane tagged and easily scored after the right fielder made a good catch. Junie Moore, one of the fastest runners on the team, made the turn at third base after his tag and quickly looked to see where the ball from right field was coming. The second baseman cut the ball off to keep Colovito from advancing to second on the long fly ball. He dropped the ball in front of him as he made the transfer from glove to throwing hand, which was all that the opportunistic and speedy Moore needed to dart home. The throw from the second baseman was both late and off target, allowing Moore to score. Jack grounded sharply to first for the last out, but the Monarchs were now up by a comfortable 6 - 0 lead.

Shane retired the Huskies' hitters in order in the fifth and had an easy sixth inning, allowing a hit but no runs. After Jud hit a solo home run in the bottom of the sixth, Coach Blevins motioned for Stine to get loose in the bullpen. After Shane grounded out in his at-bat, Coach Blevins caught up to him on the dugout steps. "Shane," he said. "Get a jacket on. You're finished for the day. You've got a two-hit shutout going, and you've only thrown around 60 pitches, but we have a seven-run lead. I want to save your arm a bit in case we need it later in the week."

"No problem, Coach," the freshman replied.

Josh Stine was a sophomore, and the Monarchs' number five starter, but he was also a lefty, like Shane. The Huskies hitters had done little against his lefty starter and, while Josh didn't have Shane's velocity, he did have a seven-run lead to work with. That proved to be all he needed. He allowed three runs over the final three innings, and Lefton College won their first game by a score of 8 - 3.

Cal Lutheran had easily defeated Marietta College in their first game, 10 - 2, and the Athletics were starting their number two pitcher, Jim Larson, against Lefton College. Blevins countered with his Junior College transfer, Jack Ryan. It turned out to be an exciting game for the fans, as both pitchers went into the sixth inning with no-hitters. Lefton College broke through in the top of the sixth after Phillips walked with one out, and an out later, Pudge homered to center field.

Up 2 - 0, Jack retired the side in order in the seventh but struggled a bit in the eighth. After walking two hitters, he benefited from a third to second to first double play started by Phillips. He walked a third hitter before getting a fly ball out to end the inning. His pitch count, despite the walks in the eighth, was just over 80. Not liking what he'd seen in the eighth from Ryan however, Blevins had Ten Ton warm-up to pitch the last inning.

Ten Ton got two quick outs to start the bottom of the ninth with a ground ball to second and a strikeout. He walked the number two hitter on six pitches and misplayed a ball hit back to the mound by the number three hitter. This was just the break the Athletics needed to get their cleanup hitter to the plate. He homered on a 2 - 2 pitch to give Cal Lutheran a 3 - 2 walk-off win. Ten Ton was devastated, and the first person he sought out after the game was Jack.

"Jack," he said, offering his hand, "I'm sorry, man. I blew it!"

"Ten Ton," said Jack. "You walked one guy... I walked three in the eighth. You didn't blow anything. You just got unlucky. How many games have you lost in relief this year?"

"That's the first one, Jack," said Ten Ton.

"That's what I thought," said Jack. "Like the coach says, this game is history. We're going to need you again before this tournament is over. Keep your head up!"

Coach Blevins had come over to the area where Jack and Ten Ton were talking and heard the last part of the conversation. As he listened to Jack's instructions to Ten Ton, he realized that he had nothing to add... and was proud of his big first baseman/pitcher.

Back at the hotel, Coach Blevins was addressing the team in the lobby. He was upbeat. "Good game, guys!" he said. "No... Great game! You guys just took the team that won this tournament last year all the way into the ninth-inning and, except for a little bad luck, would have beat them. I think we're going to see them again tomorrow night, but first, we have to take care of Trinity College tomorrow afternoon. Jake, you've got the ball. The game is at 2 o'clock, and we'll leave here around 10:30. We'll have box lunches in the locker room before the game."

In the next day's game against Trinity College, Jake Grimsley pitched one of his best games of the year, and perhaps his four-year collegiate career, going nine complete in a 6 - 3 win. The game wasn't nearly as close as the score indicated. Trinity seemed to be out of pitching, and the Monarchs jumped out early for a 4 - 0 lead. The team was ahead 6 - 0 going into the ninth. Jake was obviously tiring and allowed three runs, but Blevins wanted to save as much pitching as possible for the next game and, hopefully, the next two games. Jake was already over 100 pitches going into the ninth and would not be available for the rest of the tournament under any circumstances. He gutted out a long ninth-inning for his team, finishing the game with an all-time high pitch count of 125 in his last collegiate game.

His coach was ecstatic with his senior pitcher's performance and used it to help ignite his team for the rematch that evening with Cal Lutheran. "Jake just pitched us into a chance at the Championship Game," said Blevins. "It's one of the gutsiest pitching performances I've seen all year ... and just what I would expect from Jake. Folks, that was Jake's last collegiate game ... and the only way you guys can make the memory of that game any better for him is to make sure his complete-game win was part of a National Championship! Sam Casey hasn't pitched an inning this week, so he's fresh. I don't know who Cal Lutheran will start, but it won't be either of their two best guys. I like our chances."

If the Lefton College team was the underdog against the returning champions from the previous year, they didn't look like it in the first inning. As the designated visiting team, Lefton College hit first and scored two runs on the Athletics pitcher, sophomore Les Compton. Colovito led off with a single and went to third on another hit-and-run single from Phillips. Jack flied out, driving Danny home on the sacrifice. Pudge flied out before Charlie cracked a double off the wall in right, scoring Phillips all the way from first. Jud grounded out on a 3 - 2 count to end the inning, but the Monarchs were up 2 - 0.

The lanky Casey kept the Athletics hitters off-balance for the first five innings with a variety of off-speed pitches and a sneaky fastball that, this year, sometimes reached 90 mph. In the seventh, the Athletics broke out with two runs on three hits. The big blow that inning was from the cleanup hitter, who hit a towering two-run home run reminiscent of the one he hit off Ten Ton the day before.

In the top of the seventh, the Monarchs responded with two runs of their own on four hits, including a solo home run from Jack Ryan. Casey retired the side in order in the seventh and, in the top of the eighth, Cal Lutheran sent in a relief pitcher for Compton. After Charlie flied out to deep center, Jud Long sent a home run over the left field fence. Billings and Moore grounded out to end the inning, but the Monarchs now had a 5 - 2 lead in the bottom of the eighth. Young Sam Casey retired the first two hitters before some bad luck left him with runners at second and third with two outs. The number seven hitter in the Athletics lineup chopped a dribbler in front of the plate which neither Charlie nor Sam could get to in time to get the out. Then, the number eight hitter hit a ground-rule double that bounced into the left-field stands. With two outs, men on second and third, and the number nine hitter at the plate, Blevins decided Casey should pitch to him versus loading the bases with an intentional walk. Cal Lutheran responded by sending a pinch-hitter to the plate for their shortstop. Casey got ahead of the left-handed hitter, 1 - 2, when the hitter swung weakly at a ball on the outside of the plate. The result was a bloop pop fly that fell between third base and left field. The ball hit the foul line pushing up a small cloud of lime dust, before skittering to the wall in front of the bleachers. Billings recovered the ball quickly, but with the runners moving on the pitch with two outs, two runs scored easily. Charlie visited the mound.

"Sam," he said, "that was just a little bad luck, but we're still a run up. How does the arm feel?"

"Good, Charlie," said Sam. "I've gotten the leadoff hitter three times today with curveballs. I think I can get him again."

"Okay," said Charlie. "Let's do it."

Sam struck the next hitter out on four pitches, finishing his day with 107 pitches, and holding a slim 5 - 4 lead.

"Good game, Sam," said Blevins. When the pitcher got to the bench. "Get a jacket on. Ten Ton will pitch the ninth." The Monarchs could not add to their lead in their half of the inning, and Ten Ton took the ball to the mound in the bottom of the ninth. The senior right-hander had put yesterday's game out of his mind until he saw the hitter who was waiting to hit on the dugout steps. The third hitter in this inning would be the Athletics' cleanup hitter, who had homered off Ten Ton a day earlier to win the game.

Charlie came out to the mound before the first hitter stepped in against Ten Ton. "How's the arm, big man?"

"Good Charlie, good," said Ten Ton.

"Okay," Charlie said, "no funny stuff, just hard strikes. We've got the meat of their order... and we're better than they are ... You've also got more motivation!"

Ten Ton glanced at Charlie, then smiled, "Yes sir, I do."

The number two hitter grounded to Junie on a 2 - 2 count for out number one. The number three hitter struck out on a 1 - 2 pitch that seemed to have a little extra juice. When the cleanup hitter stepped to the plate and looked toward the mound, he saw a mean-looking giant quietly staring back at him. Charlie put the glove toward the inside middle of the plate, and Ten Ton sent a 95 mile-per-hour fastball just under the chin of the hitter. The hitter moved his body away from the pitch but kept his feet firmly planted. He stepped out of the box briefly, and when he stepped back in, he had just a bit of a sneer on his lips. Ten Ton unleashed a 1 - 0 fastball squarely to the center of the plate which the hitter took for a strike. Ten Ton's next fastball was toward the outside corner of the plate, and the hitter fouled it toward the bleachers in right field.

"Get ready, big boy...here it comes!" muttered Ten Ton.

The 96 mile-per-hour fastball seemed to pick up speed as it got closer to the plate, darting just slightly from side to side. The hitter swung and missed it completely, looking back at the catcher after the swing to ensure that it had actually been a baseball, and not a golf ball, that had been thrown.

"*Strike three. Game!*" yelled the umpire, and the Monarchs would play again tomorrow.

Game time for the Memorial Day Championship Game was set for 2:00 PM and coach Blevins was again addressing his players in the hotel lobby. "Men," he said, "win or lose tomorrow, I couldn't be prouder of how you played this week ... and this year. You have proven to everyone that you deserve to be here. Tomorrow, our goals will be simple. We will attempt to win innings ... or even outs ... one at a time. We'll use whatever we have for as long as we can ...until the last out of the game. Josh will start, but everyone else on the bench who has ever pitched is available, except Sam and Jake. Shane, Jack, Ten Ton ... you all have some pitches left in you, if we need them."

Sophomore, Josh Stine, started for the Monarchs against George Lukens for Cal Lutheran. If fans were expecting a slugfest as the two teams started their number four and number five pitchers, they were soon disappointed. Both Stine and Lukens looked like first-round draft choices for the first three innings. The first hit of the game came in the top of the fourth when Phillips singled with two outs. Jack drove him in with a double to the fence before Charlie struck out on a 3 - 2 pitch. Stine struggled a little in the fourth, walking two and allowing a base hit which scored a run. Junie Moore saved Stine from further damage with a double play to end the inning.

The Monarchs could do nothing in the fifth and Stine escaped a lengthy bottom of the fifth with the game still tied at 1 - 1. Stine was scheduled to lead-off the sixth, and Blevins stopped him at the bench. "Good game, Josh," he said, "but I'm going to try to manufacture a run this inning. If everything works out, you could be the winning pitcher." Blevins was smiling at Josh. "Luis, get a bat. You're hitting for Josh. Jack, get warmed up. You're pitching the sixth."

Before leaving the dugout, Luis was receiving instructions from Coach Blevins. "Luis, I know that you can hit a pitched ball just about anywhere it's thrown but, on this at-bat, I want you to take the first pitch. Don't swing. On the second pitch, I want you to swing as hard as you have ever swung a bat in your life... but I want you to miss the ball. Do you understand?"

"Yes, Coach," he said. "Take the first pitch, swing for the fences on the next pitch, but miss. Should I hit the third pitch?" "

"Yes, Luis, hit the third pitch. The count will either be 1 - 1 or 0 - 2, but it doesn't matter. Also, hit left-handed," ended the coach.

After the warm-ups, Luis stepped into the batter's box from the left side. Cal Lutheran had never seen Spedimente but, because of his size, guessed that he might be a drag bunter. They moved the third baseman and the first basemen in to guard against this, and the pitcher delivered his first pitch, an outside fastball, which Luis took for a ball. At 1 – 0, Spedimente took a vicious cut at an inside fastball. Since the hitter was apparently not bunting, the corner infielders moved back a few steps, closer to their normal fielding positions. On the third pitch, Luis slapped a weak roller to the third baseman, who fielded it cleanly near the bag and made a perfect throw to first base. Luis had, however, passed the base for an infield hit.

Danny Colovito stepped into the box after checking the signs from the third-base coach. With the first basemen holding the runner at first, Danny squared to bunt the first pitch from the Athletics pitcher. He pulled the bat back to take ball one, outside. On the second pitch, Danny took a swing, but the swing was meant to be more of a site block and a distraction for the catcher than an attempt to hit the ball... because Luis had taken off for second as soon as the pitcher's motion had committed him to throw the baseball to the plate.

The throw to second was too late to catch Luis and the Monarchs had a man in scoring position with nobody out. Since, with Spedimente's speed, he could score on any base hit, there were no percentages in having him try to steal third. Pitching from the stretch, the pitcher threw another outside fastball that Danny extended the bat to reach, sending the ball just over the second baseman's head. The centerfielder charged the base hit and sent an accurate throw to the plate, but Luis had already slid across the plate on his belly, avoiding the tag. Colovito went to second on the throw, and Lou Phillips stepped to the plate.

Phillips knew that any base hit would score Colovito from second, but he also realized that Jack, Pudge, and Charlie were the next three hitters for the Monarchs, after him. All he wanted to do was get on base without making an out. On the fourth pitch of a careful at-bat, the pitcher accommodated Lou by hitting him on the hitter's left elbow with an inside fastball. While Charlie had led the HCAC the previous year in Hit by Pitch, Phillips had won that honor this year. Always close to the plate anyway, his normal batting stance seemed to leave his left elbow hanging more in the strike zone than out of it. While Lou never moved that elbow toward a pitched ball, he also never moved it away from one, often resulting in a free base.

With runners on first and second and nobody out, Jack lofted a long fly ball to center field. Danny tagged and went to third on the out, and Pudge stepped to the plate. Playing percentage baseball, Cal Luther decided to walk the cleanup hitter to create a force at any base. Charlie stepped to the plate, as the team's number five hitter, with the bases loaded and only one out. Checking the sign from the third-base coach, he took the first pitch for a ball, inside.

On the second pitch, he squared to bunt with Colovito already running full speed toward the plate. "*Squeeze! Squeeze!*" yelled all the infielders, but the pitcher had already thrown the ball. Charlie's bunt was perfectly placed toward the first base side and the first basemen's only play was to first base, where the second basemen was covering. With two outs, Jud flew to left to end the inning, but the Monarchs had manufactured two more runs. They went into the bottom of the sixth up 3 to 1 in the National Championship game.

Coach Blevins felt good about how he was set up for the rest of the game. A two-run lead wasn't enough against a team like Cal Lutheran, but he now had his number one and number two pitchers for any part of the next four innings that he might need them. Jack had already thrown over 90 pitches during the week, but if Jack could get through the bottom of the sixth, Blevins thought Shane could go three innings. Shane had thrown only about 60 pitches three days earlier in the win against Southern Maine.

Jack retired three in a row in the sixth, using only eight pitches. Blevins sent him out again for the seventh. Again, the righty was perfect, getting three consecutive groundouts using only nine pitches. It was apparent to Blevins that the Athletic hitters were a bit overanxious at this point in the game, wanting to erase the two-run deficit.

While the Monarch hitters could do no additional damage, the team maintained a two-run lead going into the bottom of the eighth. Jack was still looking fresh, and Blevins decided not to change anything for the bottom of the eighth inning. Jack rewarded him with another shutout inning, this time allowing one hit. Blevins had Shane warm-up in the Monarchs' half of the ninth and stopped Jack before Jack left the dugout to pitch the ninth. "Jack," said

Blevins, "how does the arm feel? You've thrown around 120 pitches for the week."

"I'm still good, Coach," said the durable Ryan. "These guys are jumping on first and second pitch curveballs or low fastballs. If they keep that up, they are not going to hit any long balls."

"Okay," said Blevins. "Shane is ready if you get in trouble, but I don't see any reason to change what is already working." Jack ran to the mound to pitch the bottom of the ninth inning. Things started poorly for Ryan in the bottom of the ninth, however, when the leadoff hitter doubled off the wall on the third pitch thrown. Charlie asked for time and went to the mound to check on Ryan.

"I'm fine, Charlie," said Ryan. "Just got too much of the plate on that last pitch."

"Okay, Jack," said Charlie. "We're okay. Still got a run to work with. Don't worry about the runner; let's go after the hitter." Charlie glanced at his coach on the way back to his position, giving him a nod to indicate he thought Jack was still good.

Jack worked the next hitter to a full count before finally forcing him to hit a weak ball to Ryan's left, off the mound. Jack got a glove on it, but the ball squirted past him, toward Pudge at second base. By the time Pudge could recover it, the speedy hitter had already crossed the bag, and the runner at second had advanced to third. *Things are getting interesting,* thought Charlie.

Charlie looked toward the bench, where coach Blevins was indicating that he should go to the mound to talk to Ryan. Charlie also noticed that Shane was still warming in the bullpen. When Charlie got to the mound, it was apparent that Jack was upset with himself. "Sorry, Charlie," he said. "I make that play 99 times out of 100. Just not my day, today!"

"Not your day?" laughed Charlie. "Not your day?" he said again. "Jack, you haven't allowed a run to the team that won this tournament last year! Depending on whether they give the last guy a hit or not, you've only allowed one hit in the three innings you've pitched in relief today. I think it is your day. How do you feel?"

"I still feel good, Charlie, but I'm glad Coach has Reynolds warming up."

"You're at about 30 pitches today, and somewhere around 120 for the week I think, so Blevins won't let you go much further. Let's get the next guy." That wasn't to be, however, as Jack was finally wearing down. He walked the next hitter on five pitches, and Blevins called timeout.

"Good game, Jack," said Blevins, as he took the ball from the pitcher. "You and Josh got us to the ninth. Let's see if Shane can close it out." The coach waited for Shane to get to the mound before addressing his pitcher and catcher. "Okay, guys," he started. "We still have two runs to give before they tie. A base hit could win it for them. We've been here before. Just do what you both know how to do," he said, looking directly at Charlie. As the coach departed, Charlie handed Shane the ball.

"We need to get the odds more in our favor, I think. Let's see if we can work the home-to-second play on the third pitch. Pitch from the stretch," Charlie said, and then he held up two arms as if signaling the outfielders. He had three fingers raised on his right hand. To complete the 'deke,' the outfielders moved around a bit as if following Charlie's signaled instructions. None in the infield appeared to take notice of Charlie's gesture, but all knew that the catcher would be throwing to second base on the third pitch from Shane and that the second basemen would then be throwing home. Charlie resumed his place behind the plate, and the hitter never moved his bat for a first-pitch called strike. Taking no chances, Charlie called for the next pitch to be on the hitter's hands ...and high, which the hitter took for a ball. The count was 1 - 1.

On the third pitch, Charlie called for a belt-high fastball to the outside of the plate. He received the ball already rising from his catching position and snapped a laser shot throw to second base. The runner at second, who had strayed much too far from the bag, had been an easy out for Pudge, who made the tag. Before even hearing the umpire's call, the second baseman had straightened and fired the ball to home plate. As soon as the third base coach saw the catcher's throw to second, he yelled for his runner to go. The Athletics burley first baseman was now barreling toward the plate, where Charlie was waiting. Pudge's throw was on the money and delivered in plenty of time to complete the double play, but the runner had other ideas. With Charlie blocking the plate, the runner's only hope was to separate Charlie from the baseball in a collision.

Dust flew, and bodies rolled around home plate on the play. The umpire said nothing until Charlie's glove hand came out of the pile with a baseball clearly lodged in the glove's webbing. *"You're out!"* yelled the umpire, and the third base coach kicked the dust around his coaching box. Coach Blevins started out of the dugout to check on his catcher, but Charlie motioned him back with his glove hand.

"I'm okay," he yelled to Blevins, and the coach retreated to his spot on the dugout steps. Charlie then trudged to the mound, still carrying the ball in his catcher's mitt. In the stands, Claude whispered to his daughter, "Something's wrong. I think he's hurt."

"Why do you say that, Dad?" Jennifer asked, anxiously.

"He never carries the ball in his glove hand," said Claude. "From the time he played in T-ball, he's known that a baseball is only a weapon when it's in the throwing hand, not in the glove. He's always made it a habit of transferring the ball from his glove to his throwing hand as soon as possible, and leave it there ... even if he's just walking to the dugout or out to the mound."

"Should you tell Coach Blevins?" asked Jennifer.

"Not a chance!" said Claude.

When Charlie got close enough to the mound, Shane greeted him. "Good call, Charlie. You okay?"

"No," answered Charlie, "... and Shane," he warned darkly, "don't you *dare* look toward the dugout in the next moment or two, no matter what I say! I'm pretty sure the thumb on my right hand is broken."

"Crap!" said Shane. "We need to get Roger in here now, then!"

"That isn't happening, Shane," said Charlie. "I can throw back to you with four fingers well enough ... but let's get rid of this hitter on the next couple of pitches. Nothing low that I have to scoop ... and nothing fancy. Challenge him with your best fastballs. One more thing, Shane ... forget about the runner on first. Pitch from a full windup."

As Charlie walked back to his position behind the plate, he kept his right hand in a fist at his side. Claude said to Jennifer and Tim in a low voice, "It's his right hand."

"Oh, Dad, are you sure we shouldn't say something to Coach Blevins?" said Jennifer. "If he's hurt his hand, he could make it worse by staying in the game."

Claude stared at his daughter, and sternly told her, "No, Honey! I don't think we should do anything. Number one, my guess is that Stu has noticed how Charlie is carrying his hand the same as I have. Number two, Charlie knows what he's doing. He's not going to do anything that would hurt the team right now, and he's earned the right to make his own decision on this."

Jennifer crossed her arms, glared at her father, and was wise enough to say nothing more. The family all watched with anxious excitement as Charlie resumed his position behind the plate. Charlie put the catcher's mitt at the level of the hitter's thigh, and directly in the center of the plate, without even giving a sign. Shane stepped onto the rubber with both feet, the ball held in his mitt in front of him, and his body facing the batter. As soon as his left foot came back off the pitching rubber in his pitching motion, the runner at first base took off. Neither catcher nor pitcher glanced at him as a 94 mile-per-hour fastball whistled into Charlie's mitt, untouched by the 34-ounce bat that had swung at it.

"*Strike two!*" yelled the umpire.

Charlie tossed the ball limply back to Shane, who had made a few steps off the mound and toward the plate, to catch it. As Charlie regained his catching position, placing his right fist behind his back, the observant umpire softly asked him, "You okay, Son? Is your right-hand hurt?"

"No, sir," he lied. "My right hand is fine, but the left one hurts a little from that last fastball." The umpire smiled beneath his mask, and Charlie's comment wasn't lost on the hitter, who dug into his position in the batter's box.

Coach Blevins had noticed the way Charlie was protecting his right hand in a fist. "Might have sprained his wrist in the collision, or maybe his hand got spiked," he thought. He trusted his Team Captain, though, and if Charlie didn't want to come out of the game, Blevins wasn't going to do it. When his catcher and pitcher had let the baserunner advance on purpose, it didn't bother the coach. "Good," he said to himself. "Full focus on the hitter. That runner means nothing if we can get the hitter out."

As Shane again stepped into his full windup, the runner on second took off for third. It was wasted energy, however, because somewhere in his travels between second and third base, Shane had delivered another 94 mile-per-hour fastball to the waiting catcher's mitt. As the pitch passed the batter, it had been barely grazed by the top part of a swinging bat. Charlie had gripped the foul tip in his glove as if it were a grenade with the pin still in. The umpire signaled foul tip, caught, and yelled, "*Strike three! Ballgame!*"

Jubilant Monarch players began to rush the center of the diamond, and Shane had raced to a position in front of Charlie. "Stop! Stop!" he was yelling. "Charlie's hurt … be careful!"

The players immediately obeyed Shane's warning and were now directing their attention to Charlie. "I'm okay, guys," he said. "Just be careful of the right hand. I might have hurt my thumb a little. Doesn't matter … we're National Champions!"

The team celebrated with high fives and hugs, as parents and fans started making their way onto the field. Coach Blevins had worked his way through the crowd to where Charlie was standing. "Let me see it, Charlie."

Charlie opened his fist, and any who were looking could easily see that Charlie's thumb was not in the normal position. "Ouch!" said Blevins. "Why didn't you let me know?" he questioned.

"Because you'd have taken me out of the game," answered Charlie

"Yes," agreed Blevins, "… and you'd have watched the rest of it with me on the bench with an ice pack on your right hand!"

"Exactly!" replied Charlie, "... and well, Coach ... the view from the dugout isn't quite as good as the one from out here."

Blevins laughed, and said, "Good point, but now we've got to get that thumb taken care of. Don't even bother changing. Have one of the guys bring your stuff to Trinity Mercy Hospital. That's where you and I are going right now."

They met Case, Julia, Jennifer, Tim, and Claude as they made their way from the diamond, and Blevins told Charlie's family his plan. "We can get him to the hospital," said Jennifer. "Why don't you stay here with the team?"

"Okay," agreed Blevins. "Guess that's a better plan. We don't usually have so many parents around after away games for this kind of thing."

"This 'away' game was a little special," said Tim.

"Yes, it was," agreed Blevins and turning to Charlie, said "Great game, Charlie! Great season! I'll never forget you, son!"

"Thanks, Coach," said Charlie, but before he could leave the field with his family, someone else wanted to speak to him. The Athletics' first baseman was waiting patiently for Charlie to finish talking to his coach.

"Hey, Catch!" he said. "You OK? My coach said you might have gotten hurt in the collision."

"Yeah. I'm OK. Thanks," said Charlie. "I might have hurt my thumb. I'm heading to the hospital to check it out."

"Jeez, Man. I'm sorry! I was hoping that I might make you drop the ball, but I wasn't trying to hurt you."

"No problem," said Charlie. "You did exactly what you were supposed to do, and I did what I was supposed to do. That's the way the game should be played. Thanks for checking on me, though!"

"OK, Catch. Good game! Congratulations. You guys deserved to win ... and I hope your thumb is all right!"

The team's accommodations were paid through another evening since Blevins had figured, win or lose, nobody would feel like the seven-hour drive back to Lefton after the game. Players and their parents, girlfriends, and fans had garnered a banquet room at the Ribs & Things restaurant, just a few blocks away from the hotel. All were enjoying food, beverage, and enthusiastic companionship when Charlie and his parents walked into the room. All stood, and the applause was deafening. Jennifer started crying and grabbed Tim's arm. Charlie's right hand was now protected by a cast that extended from his thumb to his elbow. He listened to the applause, smiling, and hugged his mom. Shane started chanting, "*Speech! Speech! Speech!*" and the rest of the team, including Coach Blevins, had joined the chant.

Charlie seemed a bit embarrassed at first but surprised his parents with his ability to speak to a crowd so extemporaneously. "Thank you, guys, and Coach Blevins, and fans," he began. "This was a special day, and a special season ... and every single person in this room played an important part in it ... from the parents and grandparents who have supported us since T-ball ... to the fans who watched us in freezing temperatures and on rainy days ... to the coaches who have worked with us regularly to refine our skills ... and to the teammates who, on the field, and on the bench helped each other through both the good innings and the bad innings. I'm still pretty young, but I can't imagine there will be too many days in my life as memorable as this one. My granddad would call this 'a great day for baseball.'"

All in the room now looked around for Claude, who was, surprisingly, absent. Coach Blevins came over to Jennifer and asked her where her dad was. She wiped a tissue across her eyes and said, "Dad is still at Mercy Trinity."

"Oh, no!" said Blevins. "What's wrong with Claude?" he asked in genuine alarm.

Tim answered for Jennifer, while Julia and Case joined the small group around them, "While the doctors were working on Charlie's thumb, Claude started looking pale. One of the nurses noticed this, and she got him to sit down. She checked his blood pressure and then immediately had him lie down on another bed in the room. After a physician checked him, they rolled him to the cardiac wing of the hospital."

"Heart attack?" asked Blevins.

"They aren't sure yet, but they don't think so," said Jennifer. "Before we left the hospital, a nice doctor met with us and told us that they would like to keep Claude overnight. The doctor thought Claude might have just had an aberrant muscle spasm in the esophagus that had restricted blood flow slightly to his head. By the time we left his room, dad seemed fine, and was arguing with the nurses to let him go." She continued, "Charlie was upset, as you can imagine. We're going to stop by the hospital to check on him again this evening after we leave here."

"Will you call me after you've seen him this evening?" asked Coach Blevins. "This is my cell phone number, and it doesn't matter how late you call," he said as he handed Jennifer a small card.

"Certainly, Coach," said Jennifer. "Thank you for your concern."

Julia and Case appeared concerned as well, and Case said to the Drakes, "Under the circumstances, let's postpone the chat we were going to have with the boys to a different time. I don't know if Claude was going to be included in that meeting or not, but I don't think anything is going to change if we delay our talk for a bit."

Jennifer replied, "Thanks. I think that's a good idea. Dad already knows everything. I told him right after you and I talked in March, Case, and you should have seen him smile!" Jennifer then put the tissue quickly to her eyes again. "I didn't know how he might take my story after so many years, but he was both understanding and happy. He also thought that, whenever we did talk with the boys, it should just be the parents ... and the brothers present."

Julia hugged Jennifer, and whispered, "Please, keep us posted on your dad, and let us know if there is anything we can help with. Charlie could stay with Shane tonight if that would make things easier."

"No, but thank you. I think after we visit Claude, Charlie will probably want to stay in the suite with us."

Charlie was surrounded by a large group of people, including Shane and several of the other ballplayers. Jill was in this group, along with Jud and her parents, John and Janine. Case and Julia had brought Jill to Wisconsin with them on Wednesday evening. The Longs had driven up from Remington, Indiana, on Thursday in time to see the first game. As players and fans mingled, a tall, white-haired, gentleman approached Charlie. Many had noticed the man in the stands during all the Monarch games, but nobody recognized him as a relative to any of the players. When he got near enough to Charlie, he stuck out his hand, announcing that his name was Skip Greeney. When the man realized that Charlie wasn't in a position to be able to shake hands with his cast on, the man apologized quickly.

"Sorry, Charlie," said Greeney. "Guess you won't be shaking hands ... or catching ... for a little while ... which changes the original purpose of my visit this week to the

Division III Championships. I scout for several major league organizations, as well as for a couple summertime wooden bat leagues. I had planned to recruit you to play in the Cape Cod Wooden Bat League this summer," continued Greeney, "... but that's not going to work now, with this injury."

"Wow! Thank you, Mr. Greeney. But isn't that league mostly for college sophomores and juniors who might still have a chance to play in the pros?" asked Charlie

"Yes," replied Greeney. "That is usually the case, but now and then, we find a senior who has been 'flying under the radar,' so to speak, who we think is deserving of some additional notice. You have gotten the attention of a couple of scouts, and the Cape Cod League was going to give you an invitation."

"Well, thanks," said Charlie, holding up his damaged right hand, "but obviously, I don't think that's going to work out this year."

"No." said Greeney. "It won't, but I also scout for the Florida Instructional League, which plays games in September and October. I made a call a while ago after I learned of your injury, and the FIL would also like to extend you an invitation. As you are probably aware, many current minor league players play in this league, and relatively few invitations are extended to unsigned amateurs. There is no cost to you, other than your room and board."

Charlie looked at his mom and Tim, then to Case for a moment, and nodded. "Mr. Greeney, I'm sincerely flattered by both your visit here and your offer. I'm sorry to have to decline. You see, I graduate from Lefton College next week, and I already have plans for what I'm doing after that. I'm sorry that you wasted a visit here but, as much as I love baseball, I think my playing days are probably over."

Mr. Greeney smiled, and said, "No problem at all, and judging by what I've seen today, you are going to be a success at whatever you attempt. My trip certainly wasn't a waste, because I have seen a lot of talent this week. In fact, we have already picked up at least one player for the Cape Cod League, and he's from your team. Jack Ryan will be joining us in Massachusetts right after classes are finished this year."

"That's great, Mr. Greeney!" he said. "Way to go, Jack! You deserve it! Jack was smiling as he received back slaps and congratulations from the other players around him.

When Charlie was finally able to get over to his family's table, Jennifer said, "That was a beautiful speech, Charlie. I had no idea you were so eloquent!"

"Thanks, Mom," he replied. "I might have another surprise for you as well." Case and Julia had joined Jennifer and Tim, while Charlie continued. "Looks like I've been accepted to Virginia Tech's master's degree program in the School of Environmental Science and Engineering. I'll have to take a few undergraduate courses this summer, but the masters program should only take me eighteen months to complete if I go full time."

"My goodness!" exclaimed Jennifer, looking at Tim. "That *is* a surprise! When did all this happen?"

Charlie blushed a bit, again glancing at Case for just an instant, "I wasn't sure I would be accepted, Mom, and I only found out that I was a few days ago. We've all been sort of busy with other stuff this week."

"Wow! Well, that's true ... I guess ... but I didn't realize you were even thinking about anything like this," stuttered Jennifer. "We're going to have to apply for some loans ... and make some arrangements."

Case interrupted Jennifer, saying, "Jennifer, I'm sorry for the surprise. I'm probably most responsible, and things have happened sort of fast. The fact is, I have offered Charlie a job in my company. That job is only contingent upon his completing a masters program in Environmental Sciences. I'm footing the bill for tuition and any expenses for this degree."

"I see," replied Jennifer, just a bit coldly. "Well, Charlie, you're an adult now. If you think this is what you want, it sounds like a wonderful opportunity."

"Thanks, Mom," he said. "I think it is what I want to do, and it's the reason I took those Physics courses this semester."

When Charlie rejoined his friends and was out of earshot of the family, Jennifer cornered Case and Julia. "Thank you for this unbelievable opportunity for Charlie, but you don't owe either him or me anything. I appreciate where you are coming from, but we don't need your charity!"

Julia looked hurt by what Jennifer said. Case was calm. "Believe it or not, Jennifer," he said, "... my offer to Charlie has nothing to do with what I now know about our relationship. I started thinking about this in Michigan while we were on the ski trip. Charlie is one of the most impressive young men I've ever met, and while we were in Michigan, it became apparent that he has an interest in how things work. I have a company that specializes in creating things that make the world work better and more efficiently. One part of that company, BRIC, manages the consulting in that field and the other part of the company, BRET, manages operations and building infrastructure in that field. My partner in Texas, Shipley Beck, is 15 years older than me, and he has been talking about retiring for several years now. Unless I want to abandon the BRET side of the business, I have to find someone to run it soon.

Charlie is perfect. Paying for his degree isn't a gift to you, it's an investment for me!"

Jennifer's countenance softened as she listened to Case's explanation, and she looked at both Case and Julia. "I'm sorry for my reaction, Case ... and Julia. These last few weeks have been a bit stressful for me, as you can imagine."

Julia reacted quickly, and crossed the space between herself and Jennifer, giving Jennifer a full and tight embrace. "Jennifer," she said, "I can't even begin to put myself in your shoes, but I understand your reaction, and I respect it. I hope you understand that Case and I want to *add* to your family relationship, not detract from it. We *are* all in new territory, now. We need to be sensitive to some very complex feelings and dynamics."

Jennifer didn't attempt to release herself from Julia's embrace, and after a moment stepped back, smiling. "Thank you, Julia ... and Case. We *are* on sort of untrod ground, aren't we, and I appreciate your thoughts and concerns. Since it might be awkward, and perhaps late, to attempt the conversation we had planned to have with the boys this evening, what would you think about next week when Charlie graduates?"

Case responded, "That sounds good to me. We had already planned to come to the graduation."

Tim said, "I agree. If you two come in a day early, we could plan a nice family dinner on the evening before the ceremony. I'm sure Charlie will have a party to attend on the evening of graduation, and he will want Shane to go along."

Sounds like a plan," said Case. "And, by the way ... there is a party on the night of graduation. Charlie already invited Shane and Jillian to come as his guests."

"Great, then," said Jennifer. "We'll plan on that."

After Jennifer, Tim, and Charlie left the restaurant, they stopped at Mercy Trinity to check on Claude. It was after regular visiting hours, but the nurse had allowed Jennifer to go into her father's room. When she had gone, the nurse told Tim and Charlie that Claude was doing fine and that he would most likely be released the next morning. It had only been a few minutes before Jennifer returned to the nurse's station.

Noting the nurse's name tag, Jennifer said, "Maria, my dad seems to be doing great, and I don't want to impose on your hospitality. I sincerely appreciate that you allowed me to visit my dad after hours, but would it be possible for my son, Charlie, to just peek into his room for a moment? His college baseball team just won a National Championship today, and his grandfather is one of my son's biggest fans."

Maria looked at her watch then, smiling, said, "Sounds like a short visit from his grandson would be good for him, not bad. Just try not to be too long."

"Thank you ... thank you!" said Jennifer. Then, Charlie disappeared into his grandfather's room. When Charlie entered the room, Claude was sitting up and laughing with two nurses. The nurses left when they saw Charlie, and he and his grandfather were now alone.

"Charlie!" exclaimed the excited Claude. "What a day! I'm sorry to have put a dent in it! This has been one of the greatest days of my life, and maybe I just got too excited about it!"

"Granddad," said Charlie, "...don't worry about that! I'm just glad to see you looking like this tonight. You scared me while I was getting the cast on my arm earlier."

"I know I did, Charlie," said Claude. "You and Tim and your mom ... and probably a bunch of other folks as well. I feel terrible about that, but I think I'm gonna be fine! Doctors tell me it was probably just some kind of muscle spasm in my throat that affected the blood going to my head. They are gonna' watch me tonight, and I'll probably go home with you all tomorrow."

"That's a relief, Granddad! I just hope that's all it was," said Charlie.

"I know, Charlie, and I guess we'll see," said Claude. "But Son, you gotta realize, I'm almost 70 ... and I'm roundin' third, so to speak. Somethin's gonna eventually throw me out of this game sooner or later. I'm just glad I was in it long enough to see this day! Just wish Floe could have seen it, too."

After thinking for a moment, Charlie answered, "This may sound a little weird, Granddad, but I think she did see everything. When I broke my thumb out there, for some reason, the first thing I thought of was grandma. I could almost see her holding her mouth and worrying. In my mind, I told her I was OK. Sometimes her memory ... seems a little bigger than just a memory. I think a part of her still lives in here," he said, tapping his heart.

Claude gazed at his grandson for several seconds before responding. When he did answer, his words were slow and thoughtful. "I don't think that's weird at all, Charlie. In fact, it makes me think about some things myself." Claude looked out the window near his hospital bed for several minutes, as Charlie sat with him ... in silence. Then, as if coming out of a daze, he said, "Charlie, I think you might be onto something. Floe probably was there today ... she was just sittin' in a different part of the stadium." Claude then sat up straighter in the hospital bed and reached for his grandson's hand, "Charlie, you're at a wonderful time in life where your dreams outnumber your memories. Eventually, if you're as lucky as I have been, you'll reach an age when your memories outnumber your dreams. Despite what folks may tell you, that later age isn't a bad part of life ... especially if most the memories you've made were pleasant ones. You, your grandmother and your mother have given me more than my rightful share of good memories ... and you added another one today. I'm a happy and well fulfilled man, Charlie. No matter when my last out occurs now, I want you to remember that! Do you understand me, Son?"

Charlie smiled, and said, "Yes, Granddad. I think so." As Charlie stood, he told his grandfather that he needed to go. "It's after visiting hours, and the nurse was nice enough to let us visit anyway. She told us to make our visit quick. She also told us she thought you'd be OK to leave tomorrow. We'll see you then."

"See you then, Charlie. Congratulations again on a great day and a great season ... and thanks again for giving me this great memory!"

"Thanks, Granddad. See you tomorrow!"

Jennifer and Tim had invited Case and Julia, with Shane, to attend a special family dinner, at their house on the evening before the graduation. The purpose for the dinner was to, at last, let the boys in on the history of their families that they did not yet know.

After dinner, Tim, Jennifer, Case, and Julia were sitting in the den with Charlie and Shane. Jennifer started by saying, "This has been one of the most exciting years of my life ... full of heroics, fun, and surprises. Case, Julia, Tim and I have one more surprise for the two of you before the day ends," she said, looking at the two boys who were seated next to each other. She continued, "We, meaning your parents, have enjoyed getting to know each other over the course of this baseball season, and we made a group decision a couple of months ago that tonight would be a good time to let you two in on some other things."

Jennifer paused for a moment, catching a big breath and, for the last time, collecting her thoughts. She then looked at Charlie, and said, "Charlie, I told you a long time ago that your biological father had gone off to war and had not returned home. That was true. He did leave Indiana as an army officer, and he was badly hurt in Saudi Arabia. He wasn't killed, though. He just didn't return to Indiana ... at least not right away. He was sent to a hospital in Texas, where he recovered from his wounds. He and I had a very brief romance before he left from Indiana, and by the time I knew I was pregnant, he was in a foreign country. When I tracked him down in Texas, he was too weak to be able to talk to anyone on the phone."

"And when your mom was finally able to reach him at his new residence in Texas," broke in Julia, "the lady who answered the phone wasn't forthcoming in allowing her to talk to your dad. That was me, Charlie, and Case is your father." Jennifer was stunned that Julia had intercepted the dialogue but allowed her to finish. "I am so sorry, Charlie. I didn't know why your mom was trying to reach Case, and I didn't give her enough time to leave her name or telephone number. Until a couple of months ago, Case had no idea he had another son, besides Shane."

Charlie looked confused as he looked, first to his mom, and then to Case. He opened his mouth to speak, but no words came out. Shane sat silently next to Charlie, his mind also working overtime. Case broke the silence. "I know this is a shock, Charlie ... and Shane, but Charlie, don't blame your mom. She did everything she could think of to reach me, and when she realized that I was already living with someone else, she chose not to further complicate my life. She was a brave and very caring young woman."

Finally, Charlie seemed ready to talk. "I'm not angry ... or disappointed ... with my mother, Case. I couldn't have asked for a better life. I'm a little shocked ... but my first reaction is ... that I think I'm glad to find out that I'm also related to you and Julia ... and ... and to Shane ... I guess?"

Shane broke in, "Wait a second!" he said, "Does this mean that Charlie and I are brothers?"

"Well," said Jennifer, "half-brothers, but yes, you're brothers. Is that okay?"

"Okay? Okay!?" stammered Shane. "From the first day I arrived on campus at Lefton, Charlie has treated me like I was his little brother! I just thought he was my mentor ... my catcher ... my friend .... but he actually *is* my brother! That isn't just OK ... that's *great!*"

Jennifer could no longer hold back the tears, and Tim was dabbing his eyes as well. Julia had given up all pretenses of a calm composure and was holding Case's arm tightly. Case said, "We feel the same way, Shane!"

Charlie gave his little brother his left knuckles, and the two exchanged fist bumps, smiling. "This *has* been quite a day," he said.

"More like quite a year!" said Jennifer.

"Am I allowed to tell people?" asked Charlie.

"It isn't a secret anymore," said Jennifer, "but so far, the only folks who know about this are in this room, as well as your granddad."

Case replied, "We're not going to take an ad out in the paper, Charlie, but I don't think any of us have thoughts of keeping it a secret. We've got nothing to hide, and lots to celebrate."

When some of the excitement of the recent announcements had died down, Charlie and Shane rose to leave. They had promised Jud and Jillian, who were staying at the Comfort Inn with their parents, that they would pick them up and take them to the Village Inn after the family dinner at Charlie's house. Jud was also graduating the following day, and his family had driven down to Lefton earlier. As the two boys were going out the door, Case stopped them and gave Shane the keys to his Suburban. "Take my car, Shane," he said, "It will be more comfortable than Charlie's for the four of you. Your mom and I won't be going anyplace else tonight where we can't walk."

Jill's family had two rooms at the Comfort Inn just west of the campus, and Jill had gotten the call from Shane minutes earlier. She told Jud that Charlie and Shane were on their way to pick them up. Shane, driving his father's Suburban, found Jud and Jill sitting at a picnic table in front of their room. He jumped out of the car before Jud and Jill could get into the car and gave Jill an enthusiastic hug.

"Wow," said Jill. "I like that kind of welcome!"

"Hey Jud," said Shane. Charlie had also gotten out of the car and was shaking Jud's hand.

"We've got some news for you," said Shane.

"Great!" said Jill. "Can it wait until we get to the Village Inn or do you want to tell us right now?"

Shane looked at Charlie, and Charlie answered Jill's question. "I think we'd rather tell you here where it's a little more private. Let's sit at the picnic table."

The four sat down at the table and Charlie started, "Shane and I just learned something today that eventually everyone will know. For a while, though, we both would like to keep the information sort of quiet. Jud, you and I have a graduation ceremony tomorrow, and we want everyone's focus to be on that event, not something else. Okay?"

"Sure, Charlie." said Jud, "Is this something bad?"

"Not at all," answered Shane. "I can't wait to tell everyone, but I respect Charlie's opinion on this, and I think he's right."

"Wow!" said Jill. "I'm anxious to hear the news, and I think both of us are honored that you would share it with us. You can trust us to keep it to ourselves."

"Absolutely!" agreed Jud.

"Thanks," said Charlie. Then, over the next fifteen minutes, he related the incredible story that ended with the announcement, "Shane and I are brothers!"

"Oh, my God!" exclaimed Jill, as she burst into tears and rushed to Charlie's side to give him a hug. "Oh, my God!" she exclaimed again, appearing to have difficulty getting her breath. She changed partners, and gave Shane an equally powerful hug, still crying.

Jud gave Charlie a warm hug and waited his turn for Shane, saying to Charlie, "I think this is amazing, Charlie. I'm happy for both of you."

"Thanks, Jud," he said. "Jill, are you okay?"

Jill pulled her head away from Shane's chest and said through her tears and sniffles, "Yes, Charlie, I'm fine. I'm just ... just ... happy ... and overwhelmed by the news, I guess. I'm sorry I'm so emotional ... this just feels like some sort of miracle to me!"

Charlie said, "I think Shane and I feel the same, Jill. It's a little hard to process. I feel like I just got a new baby brother ... and he's already 19 years old!"

Shane and Jud laughed, and Jill said, "Well, I feel like I just got another brother as well! I've made no secret to anyone that it is my plan to eventually become a part of Shane's family, and Shane's family just got even better!"

Jud was looking a little surprised by this proclamation of his sister's and said to Shane, "Sorry, Shane ... I guess you're probably used to Jill just speaking her mind. She doesn't hold much back."

"Nope," said Shane, "and that's just one of the things I like about her!"

"In this case, I hope her plan works out," said Jud.

"Thanks, Jud," said Charlie. "I'd have to say that I feel the same way. Who's gonna make sure that Shane doesn't screw up Jill's plan after we're gone though, Jud?"

"Leave that to me," said Jill. "I think I can handle that one."

"That's a safe bet!" said Shane.

The four friends continued to revel in the news for a few more minutes until Jill said, "Charlie, this may be a little forward of me, but do you think your parents would mind us coming back to your place, rather than going to the Village Inn?"

"No," said Charlie. "They'd probably love that. Shane's parents are still there. What are you thinking?"

"I'm thinking," said Jill, "that I would rather celebrate this news with family versus strangers at the Village Inn. I'm also thinking that Shane and I, on this occasion, might like to have a beer … which wouldn't be possible at the Village Inn. You and Jud could pick some up on our way back to your house if it is okay with your parents."

"I'm sure it won't be a problem, but I'll call mom to make sure." said Charlie.

After the briefest of conversations with Tim on his cell phone, Charlie reported back to his friends. "They're ecstatic that we want to hang out with them tonight, and they told me to not make any stops. They have plenty of beer and can't wait to see us."

If there existed a generation gap between the Lefton College students and the four older adults, it wasn't apparent that evening at the Drake's home. There was laughter and tears, smiles, and hugs. There were also stories, and funny confessions … and there was lots of love.

After everyone had finally left the house, and Charlie had gone to bed, Jennifer hugged her husband. "Thank you, Tim, for helping me through this. It has been a long six months, but I can't imagine a scenario that could have ended better."

"Good people generally find good solutions," said Tim. "And all the people that were in this house tonight are good people."

Charlie's graduation, held at the college's Fine Arts Theater, was a great affair attended by all his own family and most of Shane's. Many of Charlie's teammates who weren't seniors were also in the crowd. Charlie had succeeded in achieving the Accounting degree as well as the minor in Physics. He had also graduated *cum laude*.

The commencement address was delivered by none other than Coach Stewart D. Blevins. As Charlie listened to the coach's relatively short remarks, he realized how fortunate he had been to have had such a close relationship with the man. Blevins' most important function at the College was not coaching baseball. Indeed, his influence on the campus extended far beyond the chalked boundaries of a diamond. He coached lives, and his address to the graduating seniors made this apparent. While he reflected on the important accomplishments of the College's baseball team during the past season, he minimized the role that he had personally played in these accomplishments. He gave the credit to a group of unselfish athletes who were able to combine their diverse individual talents to create a rather magnificent result, as a team. Using the NCAA Championship as an example, Blevins communicated to the seniors that each of them also had the power to accomplish similar results in life. His message was as motivating to those in the audience as it was to those wearing caps and gowns. He concluded his remarks, saying:

"As graduates of Lefton College, you are well prepared for what awaits you outside of the perimeters of this school. The lessons you have learned in the classrooms, on the athletic fields, in your dormitories, and on this campus will serve you well for the rest of your lives.

Your education is not finished, however; it is just getting started. We at Lefton have only provided you a strong foundation for what you add. Outside of these doors you will find a world full of challenges ... and opportunities. It is a world that urgently needs your bright minds and youthful energy. Continue to develop all the unique skills you have in your personal baskets, join good teams, and accomplish great things. I hope, as you reflect back on this day, you will not remember it as the end of an era, but as the start of one."

As the new college graduates circulated among themselves after the program, Charlie saw a strikingly beautiful young woman heading toward him, her graduation gown flowing and her mortarboard cap held in one hand. Remembering the straightforward conversation he had with her just three weeks before, Charlie felt a bit awkward as Linda Hawkins stopped in front of him.

"Well, Charlie Hamilton," said Linda, "I must say you don't look quite as good in that robe as you do in a baseball uniform, but I like your arm ornament!"

"Now, Linda, I'm a little hurt," said Charlie with fake disappointment. "I was just going to say how nice you looked in a gown."

"Thanks, Charlie. I'm glad you think so," said Linda, giving a cute curtsey. "Listen, I've been thinking about the talk we had a few weeks ago. I want you to know that I sincerely appreciated both your directness and your honesty."

"Well, thank you, Linda. You and Doug are both such good friends that I didn't want to be the cause of anything bad between you two."

"I know that, Charlie. Doug is lucky to have a friend like you and I feel lucky that, through Doug, I have been able to be friends with you as well. Like you, Doug is a wonderful person … but we broke off our engagement last week."

"Oh no!" said Charlie. "I hope that had nothing to do with me."

"It had everything to do with you, Charlie, but you are completely without fault. Choosing a partner for life is one of the most important decisions a couple can make. Under the circumstances of this past semester, it would not have been fair to Doug to continue our wedding plans."

"I'm sorry, Linda. I really am. Maybe in a different place, or at a different time, things could've been different for us."

"That's what you said when we talked before," said Linda, "and I believe you meant it. If that's the case, then there might be a different place and time in our future."

Charlie, looking a little confused, said, "What do you mean?"

I think I heard that you're going to be attending Virginia Tech in September for a master's degree," said Linda.

"That's true," said Charlie. "How did you know? I only found out myself about a week and a half ago."

"Charlie," said Linda very directly, "Jill and I are pretty good friends."

"Oh yeah, right. Jill was at the championship game last week when I found out I'd been accepted."

"Yes, she was," said Linda. "Well, as it turns out, it looks like I'll be starting an MBA program in September as well, at Virginia Tech's Pamplin College of Business."

"Wow!" exclaimed Charlie. "When did that happen? I thought you were going to the University of South Carolina for a masters."

"I was," said Linda, "but then I found out that Virginia Tech offered some things that South Carolina didn't. I applied last week to Virginia Tech. Charlie, my GMATs are off the charts, so I'm pretty sure I'm going to be accepted."

"You did this for me?" asked Charlie.

"Not at all, Charlie. I did it for me. I can get a master's degree from a lot of places but, if I go to Virginia Tech, someone else has a chance to keep their options open about me." At that, she gave Charlie a friendly kiss on the cheek and a light hug saying, "See you in Blacksburg in a couple months." Then, she turned and left... leaving Charlie speechless. As he looked around, Charlie saw Jill with her arm around her big brother. She was looking at Charlie and had obviously witnessed the recent communication between Charlie and Linda. When she saw Charlie look in her direction, she covered the smile on her face with her free hand.

Charlie smiled back and shook his head, remembering the final lines of Coach Blevins' commencement address. The next era of his life had apparently started ... and it looked like it was going to be mighty interesting.

Later that evening, Charlie's family and Shane's family and Janine and John Long as well sat around several tables toward the rear of Lefton Township's local Village Inn. Many other families of graduating seniors were in the little restaurant, and Charlie's group was continuing to enjoy each other's company for dinner that evening. Julia and Case had arrived the previous evening and had stayed at Claude's home. They would stay another evening with Claude before returning to Indianapolis the following morning.

Charlie and Jud had a party to attend that evening, and both rose to leave the table with Jill and Shane after dinner. After giving hugs to the members of their families, and receiving the various warnings to be careful, they started for the door. Coach Blevins, who had been dining in an adjoining room, caught up to the boys before they got to the door.

"Hey Coach," said Charlie, "I didn't see you here ... but your address to the seniors today was terrific. I knew you could coach; I didn't know you were such a polished speaker!"

"Oh, thank you, Charlie. It was an honor to be asked to make the commencement address," he said. "Charlie," he continued, "I'm going to miss you on the team. You were the best Team Captain we ever had, and one of the finest young men I have ever had the pleasure of coaching. I think you have made an outstanding decision relative to attending graduate school, and I would predict great things in your future. Good luck, son!" he finished, grabbing Charlie's left hand to shake.

"Thank you, Coach," said Charlie. "I've learned a lot at this college, and much of it not in a classroom. I appreciate all you've done for me. I hope you'll keep me posted on how the team does next year."

The coach winked at Shane, and said, "I have an idea your brother will be taking care of that. Take care of yourself, Charlie." Then he went out the door.

Charlie asked Shane, "Did you tell him?"

Shane said, "Nope."

Charlie, still thinking, said, "Maybe granddad did."

Claude had followed the boys to the door when they left and had seen the exchange between the boys and Coach Blevins. He had heard Charlie's last remark, and said, "Nope. Not me either."

Charlie hadn't seen Claude behind them, and said, "Sorry, Granddad, I didn't see you there. That's strange," he continued, "because I haven't said anything to anybody other than Jud and Jillian yet and, as far as I know, only our immediate family is aware of our relationship."

"Coach Blevins is a smart old goat," said Claude. "He's also pretty observant. My guess is, he's known since you were a freshman, and way before Case ever knew," Claude said, smiling. The boys shook their heads and laughed with Claude as all proceeded out the door.

Back at the table, Case had ordered another round of beer, over Julia's objections. "I'm sorry, Honey. I just don't want this evening to end. Jennifer and Tim don't seem to mind, and we can walk to Claude's home from here."

"OK, OK," smiled Julia. "I'm fine as long as we're not holding Jennifer and Tim up from anything."

"Nothing at all," said Tim. "In fact, we were thinking of walking with you to Claude's house after we finished here anyway. Jennifer wants to check to make sure her dad has coffee and things you will need for breakfast in the morning."

"Claude is well stocked," said Case. "... and has been the perfect host. It was so nice of him to invite us to stay at his house."

"I think he enjoyed the company," said Jennifer. At that moment, someone had fired up the jukebox in the corner of the restaurant. The distinct sound of the old soul group, The Tams, could be heard ... singing something about... 'being young ... being foolish ... and being happy.' Case glanced at Jennifer and said, "Can you still dance?"

"Don't know," she said. "Haven't tried in over 20 years."

"Come on," he said, grabbing her hand before she could resist. Tim and Julia smiled as they watched their partners advance to a small open area in front of the counter and begin to Shag. Awkward for only a few steps, both dancers soon fell into an easy rhythm and captured the eyes of all in the room.

As Julia watched, she sighed, and said, "Adorable!"

Tim, hearing her, said, "She sure is!"

Julia smiled, and said to Tim, "I was talking about him!"

Tim laughed, and said, "Oh ... well ... yes, he is ... but he's just not my type." Julia pushed Tim playfully on the shoulder and laughed with him. When the dancing couple returned to the table, Julia said, "You two looked great!"

Tim agreed, "You sure did. I didn't know you could dance like that, Jennifer!"

Jennifer smiled and said, "I didn't know I could still dance like that either. It was fun! Thank you, Case."

"The pleasure was mine, Ma'am," Case replied with a dramatic bow.

Tim said, "This gives me an idea of what I need to do."

"What's that?" asked Julia.

"I need to learn to dance!" said Tim.

All laughed at Tim's comment, and Julia said, smiling coyly at Jennifer and Case, "Well, it gives me an idea of what I need to do, too."

"Do you need to learn to dance?" asked Tim.

"No, I need to get this fella' out of here. Seems like I've heard what happened the last time these two danced like that!"

Jennifer caught a breath quickly and glanced at Julia to judge the intent of her statement. Julia's eyes were twinkling, and she was still smiling at Jennifer. Jennifer put her hand to her mouth and couldn't suppress the laugh. Case also laughed, which started both Tim and Julia laughing. When the curious waitress came to the table, innocently asking what had been so funny, Case handed her a $20 bill and said, "Life, honey ... just life!"

As Jennifer waited for Dr. Wells to return, she thought back to how long the old physician had been tending to her family. Wells was almost 80 years old and now only worked two days per week, but he had been the only doctor that either she or Charlie had ever seen professionally in their entire lives. When she had called a day earlier, the nurse indicated Dr. Wells wouldn't be in until the following week. Wells had called her later that day at her office. He had checked his messages and had seen Jennifer's request for an appointment. He told her he'd meet her at his office the following morning.

Jennifer had been extremely ill on three successive mornings after waking up, which included nausea and dizziness. Though she had no cold symptoms, she was afraid she might have an ear infection that was causing the dizziness. When Dr. Wells returned to the examination room with a folder of papers, he said, "Nothing serious. You're going to recover."

"Good," said Jennifer. "It has just been so strange … that I was concerned. What is it?" she asked.

"I've seen it before," said the old doctor." Fact is, I've seen this very condition in you before, but that was a few years back now. I think the last time you had this condition, you named it 'Charlie.'"

Jennifer stared at Wells, her brain trying to process what he had just told her. "Dr. Wells, you aren't hinting that … that…" she stopped.

"I'm not hinting at anything, Jennifer. I'm telling you that you're pregnant. Other than that, you are perfectly healthy. We will, of course, take the appropriate precautions mandated for pregnancy in females over 40, but I would anticipate no complications. You are only 41; you're in good shape, and you're in excellent health."

Jennifer sat in amazement. "Dr. Wells, Tim and I have tried for years to have a baby. It just didn't work, and we finally gave up."

"You apparently didn't give up everything," he said smiling. "Sometimes it's just about timing."

"Or about dancing," she said quietly.

"I'm sorry, I didn't hear you," said Wells.

"Oh, nothing, Dr. Wells. Thank you. I guess I need to talk to some of the male members of my family," she said. "I have a feeling I'm going to have some surprises for them."

"Probably not as stressful as the last time?" winked Dr. Wells.

"No, Doctor. This time will be fun, I think."

The Hazelden Country Club was located just outside of Remington, Indiana, about an hour and a half north of Indianapolis, off Interstate 65. Situated on a private golf course, the banquet hall was adjacent to the club's large restaurant. The crowd of approximately one hundred and fifty guests mingled pleasantly within the elegantly decorated room. A live band was playing music at one end of the room, and several bars were set up at different locations along the walls.

The remnants of a gourmet dinner were being cleaned from the large tables and guests had begun visiting friends, old and new, in different parts of the room. The sounds of laughter blended with the music completing the perfect ambiance for the already beautiful setting.

Charlie and Shane looked good in their tuxedos, and they were talking with their old teammate, Jud, near one of the bars. Linda was holding Floey and laughing about something with Julia, who was seated next to Jennifer and Jill at one of the large banquet tables. At the adjacent table, Tim, Case, Claude, and John Long, Jill's father, were discussing the Chicago Cubs' chances for making the playoffs this season. Janine Long was showing Billie Jo the picture album that Jud had given her depicting the Long family in their younger years.

As the band began to play their next song, Jennifer recognized the old beach standard, *May I*, and wondered how a band from Chicago could possibly know anything about Beach Music. When she saw Jill grab Shane's hand to lead him to the dance floor, she had a good idea who had helped John and Janine Long plan this part of the wedding festivities.

Jennifer watched Shane and Jillian dance. They moved effortlessly together on the floor and most in the room seemed to be watching them. Neither of them was showy ... they were just *good*. Two years prior, at Charlie and Linda's wedding, several had been surprised by Shane and Jill's level of expertise on the dance floor. Shane had graduated from Lefton six months before that and, when Charlie saw his younger brother dancing with Jill, he had come over to his mom. "Looks like you might have been tutoring Shane at more than just accounting," he said.

Jennifer remembered laughing and admitting to Charlie that she and Jillian and Shane had spent some time working on their dance moves in the Drake's den in Lefton Township. Jennifer had helped Shane during his sophomore year with his first accounting courses and, after Floey had been born, Shane and Jillian had become regular babysitters for Tim and Jennifer. Tim was living up to his commitment to learn to dance, and he and Jennifer went to a local dance club almost every Thursday evening. Often when they returned home, they found Floey fast asleep in her crib with Shane and Jillian dancing very quietly in the den. The younger couple was always anxious to have Tim and Jennifer show them what they had learned at the dance club before they returned to their dorms on campus.

Jennifer smiled at the memory as she continued to watch the attractive young couple on the dance floor. Her life had taken some unusual twists and turns, and that dance seemed to be a consistent thread woven into its fabric. Some of her earliest, and most fond, memories were of her and her grandmother dancing to those funny looking old records of Floe's that had the big hole in the middle. Then there was the dancing adventure with Case, which had led to Charlie. Over two decades later, a reintroduction to the dance seemed to have been a contributing factor to Floey. Then a random encounter with the dance by her father two years ago at Charlie's wedding had affected

Claude's life as well. Shane and Jillian were not just good partners on the dance floor; they had proven to be unselfish, caring and loyal partners throughout their four years at Lefton College. As of today, they were married, and Jennifer smiled at her premonition that Case and Julia would soon be grandparents.

Charlie rejoined Linda, who was also watching Shane and Jillian from another part of the room. When she grabbed Charlie's hand to join the younger couple on the dance floor, Charlie gently pulled back. "I'm not ready to compete with that yet, Linda," he said.

"Oh, Charlie," she answered. "You're not competing … and besides that, you're getting pretty good."

"Thanks, Dear," he said, "but I'm not in their league yet. Heck, I'm not even in Granddad's league anymore," he laughed.

Linda laughed as well and said, "That's true, Charlie, but that's only because I'm not as good an instructor as either your grandma or my grandma!"

Claude and Billie Jo Hawkins had met at Charlie and Linda's wedding. The reception had been held at a banquet room in the Marriott Hotel in North Myrtle Beach. Billie Jo was Linda's grandmother and the widowed mother of Linda's father, Joe Hawkins. Joe and his wife, Patty, had staged a huge three-day party around the wedding, providing a memorable weekend for all in attendance, on many levels. Linda's gamble to attend Virginia Tech had paid off. It had only taken her about a half a semester to prove to Charlie that she had more to offer him than just a friendship. They married after both had finished their degree programs, and now one of her best friends from Lefton College was her new sister-in-law.

Billie Jo was an integral part of every social event staged during the weekend and, when she discovered that

Charlie's grandfather was also widowed, she set her sights on him. Claude had shyly tried to turn her down to dance at the reception, but she had told him, in no uncertain terms, that 'no' was not an option. She grabbed his hand and dragged him to the dance floor.

Many in the room that evening who were familiar with the vivacious Billie Jo weren't surprised by her aggressiveness. Most in the room, however, were surprised that Claude, once on the dance floor, was not uncomfortable there. To the delight of Billie Jo, Claude knew the basic steps to the Shag and, while he was conservative in his moves, his feet were usually in the right place.

Jennifer wasn't surprised. Her mother, Floe, wasn't the type who would have enjoyed dancing alone... and she figured that Claude had been smart enough to make sure Floe's partner was always him. When the wedding weekend ended, and Jennifer's family were loading up the van to return to Indiana, Claude had arrived at the car with no suitcase. "Honey," she remembered him saying. "It's so nice and warm down here, I've decided to stay for a few more days. Jesse will watch the clinic." Billie Jo had walked up next to him, and Claude continued, "I'll be back by the end of the week ... probably."

"Well ... that's fine, Dad," Jennifer had told him. "Do you want me to extend the room here for you?"

"He won't need that," offered Billie Jo. "He's got a place to stay," she said smiling, and with not an ounce of guilt.

Claude said, "Billie Jo, here, said she'd get me to the airport when I'm ready to go. If you could pick me up on the other side, that would be great. I'll let you know when."

Jennifer and Tim had smiled at Claude and told him, "Have fun, Dad."

Billie Jo answered for him, "Oh, he will!"

Claude had all the men laughing, and he seemed to be enjoying the attention. He was a natural-born storyteller, and some of his stories were also true. "Granddad," said Charlie. "I remember you telling me after the championship game that you thought you were 'comin' round third', metaphorically, in life. I didn't like that particular analogy at the time ... for obvious reasons, because, at age 70, you didn't seem that old to me. What happened? You're not acting like the 'game' is going to end so soon anymore. Does that have something to do with Billie Jo?" he playfully needled his granddad.

"Well, Charlie, you make a good point," he answered, "but a funny thing happened around the time you got married. I think I <u>was</u> comin' round third heading for home at the time. I didn't realize then, though, that I had really been a run behind in the game ... ever since your grandma died. Anyway, when I scored down in Myrtle Beach, the game wasn't over ... I had tied it! I've been in extra innings ever since!"

Again, all the men laughed, and Jennifer, noting the laughter, came over to the group. "What's so funny over here?" she asked.

Claude gave Charlie a subtle shake of his head and a warning look, saying to Jennifer, "Oh nothing, Sweetheart. We were just talking baseball and telling lies," he laughed.

Jennifer looked suspiciously at the men in the group, who had all averted their eyes to avoid hers, and said, "Judging by the inability of anyone to look me in the eyes, I

300

have a feeling that those stories might have been of a bawdy nature."

"No, Mom," said Charlie, attempting to save his granddad, "Granddad was just saying about how difficult it is to score by stealing home!" All at the table again laughed; Jennifer smiled and turned away, not believing Charlie's explanation for an instant ... but also not caring. Her son's relationship with his granddad had provided her with some of her happiest moments in life and, just briefly, she wondered how many more Claude and Charlie could possibly have left together. The thought passed quickly, and she resolved to simply enjoy each one that she could.

After Jennifer left the table, several of the others who had been sitting with Claude also got up, leaving Charlie and Claude alone. Claude looked to Charlie and said, "Charlie, that conversation we had at the hospital a few years back sort of changed my life in some ways. You remember what we talked about?"

Charlie thought and asked, "Besides the reference to 'rounding third'?"

"Yes... besides that."

"I think I remember talking a little bit about grandma, didn't we?" asked Charlie.

"Yes, we did, Charlie," said Claude. "You told me how you thought Floe was more than just a memory... that she was sort of still alive in your heart."

"I remember that, now, Granddad. I still believe that, although I couldn't explain it any better today than I could back then."

"You explained it very well, in my opinion," said Claude. "You said things that I had never thought about before. Ya' see, I'd spent some part of just about every day since your grandma died still thinking about her ... remembering her. And when I did, it made me sad ... because I couldn't talk to her ... I couldn't be with her anymore. I missed her so much. Then, after you told me about how you believed that she was still living in your heart, it dawned on me that you were right! She wasn't just a memory ... some part of her was still there in my heart and my mind. Of course, she wasn't going to just desert me! After that, the memories and thoughts of her didn't make me sad anymore ... they made me happy. While I couldn't see her or touch her, those thoughts and feelings were just her way of letting me know she was still there."

"Is she still there even after Billie Jo has come into your life?" asked Charlie, curiously.

"More than ever, Charlie," said Claude. "At your wedding, when I met Billie Jo, I didn't want to dance with her when she asked me. Dancing was something your grandma loved, and I didn't feel right dancing with somebody else. When I started to turn Billie Jo down, though, something in my mind told me to get my fat butt off the chair and go dance!"

"Grandma!" said Charlie.

"I can't say that for a fact," said Claude, "but it was a powerful thought! And, when I started dancing with Billie Jo, I had the distinct feeling that I was dancing with two women."

Charlie laughed and said, "That might not be something you should share with Billie Jo."

"Not planning to, Charlie," he said. "This whole story is strictly between the two of us. My guess is, though, that when Billie Jo is dancing with me, there's another man on the floor with her, too. And, you know what? It doesn't matter! I think all four of us are having fun!"

The bride and groom had come to Claude's table, and Billie Jo was with them. Claude said to Shane, "You and Jillian look great together anywhere, but especially on a dance floor! Seems like I might have seen a couple of your dance moves before," he said, winking at Jill.

"Ha!" she said. "You probably have, Mr. Hamilton, since Jennifer and Tim are the ones who taught us how to Shag."

"And I danced a lot with the woman who taught Jennifer," said Claude, smiling.

"Well," said Billie Jo smiling at Claude, "If that's the same woman who also taught you, I owe her big time!"

Claude hugged Billie Jo and said, "You have more than paid her back over the past three years, I think."

Case returned to Claude's table after the others left and sat down with the older man. "Claude," he said. "I can't remember a time that I've been happier in my life. Today, seeing Jill and Shane getting married... and being at this reception with you and Jennifer and Tim and Charlie and ... well, it's a little overwhelming!"

"I hear you, Case," said Claude. "It is pretty special ... especially considering what we've all had to do to get here. My advice, from an old man, is to just enjoy it. Don't try to figure it out. Just enjoy it for what it is."

"Believe me," Case said, "I am ... we are. Julia is just as excited about the family part of our lives as I am."

"We've all been pretty lucky I'd say," offered Claude, "or, maybe ... blessed!"

"Agree!" said Case. "Did I hear from Charlie that you are thinking of coaching a T-ball team next summer?"

"Ha!" answered Claude. "Yeah... you probably did hear that. Stu Blevins retired last year as the coach for Lefton College, but he's still the Commissioner of the Lefton Township Little League. He thinks we ought to coach a T-ball team together next year."

"Are you going to do it?" asked Case.

"Probably will," said Claude. "Stu and I have been friends for a long time, and we both still love the game. I told him that my only condition would be that, as Commissioner of the league, he change the rules relative to genders allowed to play. If he allows the leagues to be co-ed, I'll coach a team with him."

"Do you think he will?" asked Case.

"Oh yeah... he will," said Claude. "Ya see, I have a granddaughter that has some pretty good genes. She's only three, but I already see some potential! Blevins coached her grandfather, her brother, and her uncle. He's got some skin in this game too!"

Case laughed and said, "Claude... I need to drive down to Lefton to see some of those games!"

When Charlie and Linda returned to the table after visiting with Claude and Billie Jo, Case said, "Linda, your grandmother appears to be enjoying Charlie's grandfather!"

"Oh, she is," replied Linda, smiling, "but I think Claude is enjoying her company as well!"

"That may be the understatement of the evening," laughed Charlie. "They are fun to watch."

"So are your little brother and Jill," said Case. "I had no idea Shane could dance like that. Am I seeing things or does Jill just make him look that good?"

"Probably a little of both," said Charlie. "Jill makes everyone she's with look pretty good."

Jill had finished medical school in June and had been lucky enough to get an internship at Indianapolis General Hospital. She hoped to also complete a residency at the hospital and one day have her own private practice as a Pediatric M.D. Charlie and Linda had moved from Texas to Indianapolis in the spring and the two couples did things socially together almost every weekend.

Shane had passed the state CPA exam after graduating from Lefton College and had joined his father's firm in Indianapolis. After a year in the company, his father had named him the Chief Financial Officer. Charlie, in the meantime, had been in El Paso, Texas, since obtaining his master's degree at Virginia Tech, learning the BRET side of the business from Case's longtime partner, Shipley Beck. Shipley quickly became as fond of Charlie and Linda as he had been of Case and Julia years earlier. Before the end of Charlie's first year in Texas, Shipley made Charlie an unusual offer.

"Charlie," said Beck, "your father and I have owned this business for over 20 years, and I wasn't a young man when we started it. I'd like to sell my share of it to you, now."

"Shipley," replied an astonished Charlie, "I'm not sure what to say! I am flattered of course and need to talk to Case about this ... but maybe, more importantly, you need to know that Linda and I haven't had any time to build any savings yet. I don't have the money to buy this company."

"Of course, you don't, Charlie," answered Shipley, "that's why I'm willing to finance the purchase. You don't have to come up with any initial money."

"Well ... thank you," replied the still unsure Charlie. "What do you think the company is worth?"

"Don't have a clue," said Beck, "and it doesn't matter. The only thing that matters is what I want for my seventy percent share. It is subject to negotiation, but I'd like one dollar."

"What do you mean, Shipley?" exclaimed Charlie. "You can't just give your company away!"

"Charlie," Beck said, "I can do anything I want, but that's beside the point. I don't have a family to pass this business to. I'm closer to your family than anybody else in this world. Case and I have made a lot of money in the past 20-plus years, and a good bit of my share is still in a bank. I'm almost 75 years old and financially comfortable. There is nothing I would enjoy more than to see you and your little brother take BRET and BRIC to a whole new level!"

"Does Case know about this?" asked Charlie.

"Yes, he does, and he's as stubborn as you," said Beck, "but he told me I could talk to you. The other thing you need to consider is moving BRET to Indianapolis to join it with BRIC. Seems you and your brother are pretty tight and the two of you might do better working out of the same place versus working remotely. Our contractors are located all over the country, so there isn't anything that would require our division to stay in El Paso."

Charlie discussed the offer with Case, and the two decided to take it, under the condition that thirty percent of the income from both BRET and BRIC would still accrue to Shipley for as long as Shipley lived. Beck had reluctantly agreed but had set up another financial vehicle for the funds that neither Case nor Charlie knew about. All the money accruing from BRET and BRIC earned by Beck was being funneled into a trust fund set up for the future education of Charlie's kids, Shane's kids, and their kid's kids ... for as long as the trust funds lasted. It would be another 18 to 20 years before anyone in Case's family would find out about this trust fund. Charlie moved the offices for BRET into the building in Indianapolis occupied by BRIC. His personal office was now three feet from his younger brother's space in the same building.

Shane's baseball career at Lefton College had been the stuff of legend. After making the last pitch of the NCAA Championship Game to his older brother as a freshman, Shane led the HCAC for the next three years in most of the important pitching categories. The team had won the HCAC during all those years and made it back to the NCAA National Championships in Shane's senior year. The team lost the championship game to their old rival, Ohio Wesleyan. Shane was recruited by several major league teams and drafted in the 19th round by the Chicago Cubs. The major league club's negotiation with Shane went nowhere, however, as Shane seemed set on joining his father's business in Indianapolis. For Shane, the thought of playing rookie league baseball in Little Rock, Arkansas, had less appeal than joining his brother, Charlie, in running BRET and BRIC.

The doors to the banquet hall opened and a giant of a man dressed as a police officer stepped into the room. When the people seated at the tables closest to the door recognized the new guest, they immediately stood and began to applaud. Table by table the wave continued, until all in the room were on their feet and applauding.

Ten Ton seemed embarrassed by the attention but, at his size, he couldn't hide. He began shaking hands with old college friends, until he got to the bride and groom's table. After shaking Shane's hand politely, he lifted Jill two feet into the air, before setting her gently down on the floor. His enormous hug hid her from the rest of the room for several seconds, before Charlie greeted his old friend and teammate, "Ten Ton! I guess we can start the party now that you're here! We've been waiting for you."

"Charlie, my man," said Ten Ton, giving Charlie a hug that was nearly as warm as the one he had just given Jill, "Sorry I'm late, but I drove here straight from the airport without even changing from the ceremony this morning."

Denton Jones had, that morning, been awarded the Medal of Honor for Public Safety Officers by the President of the United States. The White House ceremony had been televised by CNN and many of the guests at the wedding reception had watched it earlier. Captain Denton Jones, Commander of the Central Business District, Cincinnati Police Department, had, several months prior, become a national hero when he, single-handedly, saved the lives of six young hostages being held at gunpoint in a police force – gang confrontation. Captain Jones had done this by entering the building being held by the gang members, unarmed, and convincing them to release their hostages. Neither the hostages nor any gang members had been hurt in the incident; the gang members were subsequently arrested. As it turned out, several of the gang members had participated in summer programs sponsored by Denton in their youth.

After college, Denton had returned to Cincinnati as a police officer. He continued to work with 'at risk' inner city children, managing the city's Children In Trauma Intervention program. Gaining respect from both his community and his law enforcement peers, he had recently been promoted, and was now the youngest District

Commander in the history of the Cincinnati Police Department.

It took little convincing from Charlie and Jud for Shane, Jill and Ten Ton to recreate the dance that had started Jillian's and Shane's relationship. To the sounds coming from Charlie's iPhone held up to the microphone, the three performed *The Judge*, to the delight of all in attendance. When the dance concluded, Jessica Long, Jill's cousin and one of the bridesmaids, found her way to Jill's table. Jessica was two years older than Jill, but the two girls had been best friends throughout grade school and high school. Jessica had graduated from Indiana University and, more recently, from Duke Law school. "So, Jill," said Jessica, "Why have you never mentioned Denton to me?"

"Probably," answered Jill, "because I liked Ten Ton too much. You have a reputation for being tough on men!" Jill said, laughing.

"Ha," said Jessica, "That's probably true, but that one looks big enough to take care of himself. My business takes me down to Cincinnati quite a bit. I might have to introduce myself to Denton."

"Oh," said Jill, "I didn't know that. I thought your firm was based in Indianapolis. When did Cincinnati get into the picture?"

"About twenty minutes ago, when that man walked through the door," answered Jessica. The evening went all too fast for both Denton and Jessica, and it hadn't ended at the reception. Their colorful and romantic story continued well beyond the limits imposed by the pages in this book.

A photographer was trying to get the family organized for a picture at the reception, and it was apparent that she was having difficulty identifying who was in the family and who wasn't. Jill's side seemed relatively easy, but Shane kept pointing out new people in the crowd that needed to be in the picture as part of his family. Jud was helping Shane in this effort. Jennifer smiled as she looked at the finally assembled group. Besides herself, the group included Claude and Billie Jo, Tim, Floey, Charlie, and Linda, as well as Case, Julia, Shane and Jill. While the boundary lines encompassing this unique family were a little blurred in some areas, this, indeed, was *her* family. There had been much joy and some pain in putting it together over the years, but she thanked whatever Divine Providence was responsible. It was a great family, and she squeezed little Floey, saying, "You are one lucky little girl!"